Breached

Breached

A Jewel Cruise Line Adventure

Christine R. Whitlock

To the late Rev. Mark Galo, student pastor,
who made an eternal impact on my family.

And to my father, the late SGM David Robertson,
my favorite Vietnam veteran.

Through many dangers, toils, and snares,
I have already come;
'Tis grace hath brought me safe thus far,
And grace will lead me home.

"Amazing Grace"

Prologue

August 1968
Saigon, Vietnam

"Look out, Magnet! Retreat!"

"What is it?"

"We've got punji stakes straight ahead. And I hear snakes hissing. Bamboo vipers must be tethered somewhere. It's a trap. Go back!"

Magnet, a nickname that implied he was attracted to bullets, began crawling backwards as quickly as he could. The Củ Chi tunnels were dark and cramped, and neither man was able to use his flashlight traveling in reverse.

"Move faster! I hear Charlie coming our way."

"I'm moving. There's a side pocket fifty yards back. I'll divert, and you keep going. We'll trap him between us."

Magnet touched the sides of the tunnel with his shoulders until he felt an opening on the left side. He backed in and remained still. Sweat was streaming into his eyes, causing them to sting. The tunnel was entirely black, so the sweat did not affect his vision, or lack of vision. His eyes would have to sting. They would always have to sting.

Being the smallest of his peers was a curse as a teenager in high school, and it continued to be a plague as a teenager in the Army. The smallest in the platoon was designated as the troop's tunnel rat, without question. Magnet hated the job but conducted his business with honor and zeal. The tunnels in Vietnam were vast and dangerous, but a man could survive by keeping his wits.

"I hear you, Tex. Keep going back."

Magnet could hear his First Calvary comrade shuffle past him to the right. Once Tex passed, he could smell the enemy getting closer. Could there be more than one man? Am I sitting duck? Magnet instinctively touched the two grenades hooked to his belt. He carried frags. Smoke grenades were of little use on this assignment. If the mission went south, he would deploy both. Anyone in the tunnel within ten feet of them would be killed, including himself.

Two Viet Cong soldiers approached Magnet's hideaway. Their voices exposed that they were teenagers as well. Magnet waited. And he prayed. He had begun doubting that God could hear him in the tunnels. They were too isolated. Too dark. And too evil. But he promised his Granny Ray that he would pray whenever he was in danger. And a promise was a promise.

The soldiers crawled right past Magnet's crude hideout. He was sure they could hear his heart beating like the bass drum in his hometown's Thanksgiving parade. Any louder, and his heart might explode out of his chest. But the boys were talking amongst themselves and continued traveling past him. They didn't know that he and Tex were in this vein. Otherwise, they would have released poison gas, or worse, behind them. Magnet's mission was to capture these soldiers, so he waited for Tex to seal the exit. Then he would move.

As the voices became fainter, Magnet listened for his partner's cry of "contact" to indicate that they were engaged in the seizure. But he could only hear the VC boys talking. No word from Tex. After what seemed like an eternity, Magnet left his refuge and followed the sounds. The opening was less than one hundred yards away. Soon the soldiers would come above ground and discover his troop's temporary defensive position. He couldn't let that happen.

Magnet crawled as far as he could and then slithered on his belly when the tunnel became narrow. Something was wrong. Where was Tex? Just as the tunnel began to widen again, the bottom fell. He had hit a trap door and was falling.

"Ahhh . . . !"

PART ONE

High Seas

Be alert and of sober mind. Your enemy the devil prowls around like a
roaring lion looking for someone to devour.

1 Peter 5:8

CHAPTER ONE

Wednesday, June 10

"Quiet! Quiet! We have a lot of information to share." Joe's efforts to speak over the excited seniors were nearly futile. The recent high school graduates were feverishly talking over their youth pastor's announcements, even over his weak attempt at whistling. Tonight was the final meeting before the much-anticipated senior cruise. Joe had just finished a series on spiritual warfare with a discussion on attitude and how a bad attitude could quench the Holy Spirit. He even used packing peanuts as a visual demonstration.

The seniors, who had been invited to a once-in-a-lifetime trip aboard Jewel Cruise Line's newest adventure ship, *Buccaneer Bounty*, remained after the lesson to receive their final instructions. The ship's captain, Jenny Lu, had been working with the youth group since she and her son, Zach, joined Holy Cross Church three years earlier. They moved to Miami after Jenny had been promoted to staff captain of *Golden Fortune*, Bounty's sister ship. Previously, they lived in Charleston, South Carolina, where Jenny served on a smaller cruise ship.

Jenny's husband, Brian, died suddenly on his fortieth birthday. No one expected the avid runner to drop dead of a brain aneurism at such a young age. He woke in the middle of the night, screaming with head pain, and died as Jenny was calling 911. She never got to say goodbye to him. He never got to open his presents.

With no family in Charleston, Jenny's also-widowed mother, Joy, moved from California to South Carolina to help care for Zach.

They struggled to raise the energetic thirteen-year-old boy together. Thankfully, their church family stepped up and helped with home repairs and some of the carpooling. The move to Miami two years after Brian's death was an unexpected blessing. The increase in pay helped immensely. Plus, their new condo required no upkeep, and Zach could ride his bike to school. Joy, or Lao Lao as Zach called her in her native Chinese, was around to help when Jenny was out to sea and enjoyed the solitude when Zach accompanied his mother on the ship during school breaks. Jenny sailed ten weeks on and ten weeks off, so she was fully home half of the year. Much to Jenny's displeasure, Zach was planning to attend The University of Florida in the fall. She had never been a fan of the Gators. When he moved to Gainesville, Joy's care would no longer be needed. She and Jenny were still discussing the grandmother's plans for this new season in her life.

To celebrate her promotion to captain last fall, Jenny arranged for the active graduating seniors in the church to join the inaugural sailing of Bounty at a significant discount. The teens had worked all year to raise the funds needed to pay their minimal balances. At last count, twenty-six youth members would sail with the group, plus Pastor Joe's family. Each student was required to bring one adult as a chaperone, even though most of them had already turned eighteen. Jewel did not want any bad publicity on the highly anticipated voyage. So all the teens would be "officially" supervised by adults.

The first sailing of Jewel's mega-ships exclusively included members of the media, travel agents, and special guests. The line comped the fares of the special guests as a goodwill gesture to the community. As always, one hundred cabins were donated by Jewel

Cruise Line to local foster families. This year, fifty military veterans were also offered free trips on the inaugural sailing.

The key selling point of Jewel's ships was the lure of hidden treasure. Each week, a chest filled with $50,000 of gold coins was hidden, usually on one of the private islands, for guests to find. Passengers were given clues to the whereabouts of the treasure throughout the trip. The media coverage of dozens of winners fueled the success of the two previous adventure ships, *Golden Fortune* and *Plunder*.

To quiet the energetic youth, Jenny walked to the front of the room without an invitation. Known for commanding the ships in high-heeled stilettos, she drew attention from everyone around like a two-carat diamond in a mud puddle. Tonight, her sleek black hair was pulled up in a loose knot, and she wore a Miami Hurricanes T-shirt with cotton shorts. Instead of her trademark heels, she wore Havaianas flip-flops.

"Okay! Okay!" Jenny started. "I know you all are excited. But we must go over the rules. A few things have changed since our last meeting." The room quieted. "Joe, are we still meeting here at the church on Sunday?" Jenny waved an arm toward the youth pastor once the crowd quieted.

"Yes, we are, Captain," Joe began, giving Jenny a thank-you nod. "Our check-in time is noon, so let's meet in the overflow parking lot at 10:30. That will give us plenty of time to get to the cruise terminal. Remember, church will be in session, so don't block any entrances. And be respectful of the worshipers. We have four volunteers driving the vans to get us there. Are there any questions about when and where we meet?"

Seeing no hands raised, Joe continued. "You are allowed to bring as much luggage as you can carry. My suggestion is one suitcase and one backpack. Jenny, would you remind us of what we should pack for the week?"

"Sure." Jenny smiled at the large group. "You will need plenty of swimsuits, of course. Bring magnetic hooks if you have them. Those will stick to the metal walls and are great for hanging wet clothes. Be sure to remind your parents to pack any medicine you will need for the week. I forgot to mention last time that you will need lots of sunscreen, but I'm sure you've already thought of that. The sun in the Bahamas is often stronger than in Miami." Before she could finish, a hand shot up.

"How many fancy outfits do we need?" Lena Mallard asked.

"You girls are excited about the formal nights, aren't you?" Jenny joked. "There will be two 'fancy nights.' We are eating as a group on the first one, and the second one is optional. There will be a teen prom the night of the first formal dinner. The rest of the evenings are up to you. Wear something nice if you want to eat in the dining room on the other nights. Otherwise, you can hit the buffet in casual clothes."

"Can we eat at both?" Joe's son Jonah asked. A few of the boys nodded in anticipation.

"Yep. You can eat all you want. There is even late-night pizza." Jonah high-fived Josh. Jenny continued with her suggested list of items to pack and turned the attention back to the pastor. "Carry on, Pastor Joe."

"Thank you, Ms. Jenny. I've already packed my fancy tuxedo for formal night." Most of the group laughed at his comment. "Now, you should have the app downloaded on your phones. That is how we will communicate with each other and is very important. Once we are on the ship, we can add fun activities and shows to our individual calendars. There will be three events you are required to attend. Otherwise, you are on your own. You already have a copy of the cabin assignments, so you can find everyone easily. Mandatory check-in is at eleven each night. You must contact your chaperone at eleven p.m. every day." Joe continued with the van assignments and expected expenses. Finally, he asked for questions from the group.

"If we are legally adults, then why do we have to check in?" Naturally, the question came from Ronnie Ledbetter. He was determined to push the limits with everything he did. Joe knew that his home situation was to blame for his bad attitude, but he did not accept that as an excuse for disrespect.

"You are all receiving a serious discount for this trip because you are members of the Holy Cross Church youth group," Joe answered. "I am responsible for your behavior and well-being. Mr. Morgan has agreed to be your chaperone, so I expect you to treat him with respect. If not, you are welcome to book a cruise on your own." With that sharp answer, Ronnie quieted. "Any more questions?"

"What if we get seasick?" Petite Macy Dial stood while asking her question.

"Ms. Pam will be our on-call nurse for the week. She will be bringing plenty of Dramamine. You can reach her through the app if you need anything. And you can always ask one of the adults in our group for help. Anything else?"

The group was quiet before Lena Mallard's dad was asked to pray for the group. Joe noticed Ronnie roll his eyes but ignored him. The group would be traveling to another country. Any number of problems could arise. Mr. Mallard prayed for his daughter and the other travelers to be alert and kind. At Holy Cross Church, eighteen was a pivotal year. Many knew that church attendance dropped drastically after that age. Engaging the youth after graduation was critical to the church and their parents, and this trip was one activity designed to keep them connected.

Marissa March sat through the meeting with the parents in the back of the room, hoping to be "unseen." As usual, her husband preferred to not go to the church "after hours." Gene agreed to attend the Sunday morning services, but that was usually all the time he would commit. Marissa was still nervous about taking her son Josh on a cruise ship for a week. She had seen *Love Boat* reruns. The adventures seemed fun but much too glamorous for her lifestyle. Last week, she found two sparkly dresses at Goodwill and bought a new bathing suit for the trip just in case. Otherwise, she planned to stay in her room and read books the entire week.

Since the cabins were assigned by gender, Marissa would share hers with Ryan's mother, Bettina, and their sons would share a neighboring room. Bettina looked like a CoverGirl model every day of the year. Her carefully highlighted brunette hair was never out of place. Marissa wished she could stay in a cabin on her own but understood the financial restrictions. She and Josh would never be able to go on such a fancy vacation without the cruise line's generous offer.

Besides the new dresses, Marissa also bought a fake pearl necklace, two used suitcases, and lots of sunscreen. Josh got his dark complexion from his father but could still burn in the sun. Especially the sun on a tropical island. And especially when surrounded by distracting friends.

"I guess this is it, roomie." Bettina smiled as she sat beside Marissa at one of the tall tables. "I'm excited that we will be spending a lot of time together."

Marissa did not like the sound of that. "I guess so. It will be fun."

"I'm looking forward to it. I haven't been on a cruise in three years. We took the kids to Cozumel and Roatan when Ben graduated. Both boys learned to surf on the Flow-Rider. And I swam with dolphins. It was so much fun."

"That does sound like a lot of fun," Marissa lied. "I would love to swim with dolphins." Another lie.

"Well, get lots of sleep. I'm sure we will be up late dancing and eating greasy pizza with thousands of our new friends." Bettina walked off, but Marissa remained seated. Maybe this trip was a mistake. She did not want thousands of new friends. She would never get into the ocean with a dolphin. And she did not dance in front of strangers. Maybe Josh would understand if they had to cancel. She could take him to the Miami Seaquarium and let him meet one of those dolphins. But Marissa knew she could not cancel. Josh would be heartbroken. This was his chance to be "one of the guys." When they returned, he would begin working with his father while most of his friends went off to college. Josh didn't complain about his lot in life. Marissa had a feeling that he was relieved to not be attending college. But he would miss his friends regardless. The upcoming week would be a unique chance to make lasting memories and live carefree.

"Can I go to Zipper's with Jonah?" Josh asked excitedly. "Pastor Joe said he'll bring me home afterwards."

Marissa had no problem with Josh going for burgers on Wednesday nights. But the weekly trips were cutting into the family budget. She dug out eight one-dollar bills and handed them to her son. "Have fun. And be sure to thank his parents."

As she was leaving the room, Marissa noticed a table of moms giggling and sharing pictures on their phones. Each was wearing a cute top and name-brand sandals. Maybe she should go back to Goodwill and find some nicer outfits. Gene was probably unhappy with what she had spent on the "free" trip, but a week of plain tops would be embarrassing. Marissa decided that she needed to save money and vowed to spend even more time alone in her cabin. At times like these, she wished she had a best friend. Tracy Meyer, her high-school bestie, hadn't spoken to her since the "prom incident," and her own sister hadn't made contact since Christmas.

Marissa's sister Dinah lived in Cocoa Beach and had invited the family to stay over numerous times. But visiting the successful investment banker at her 4000-square-foot beach house was never going to happen. Gene considered Dinah snooty, and Marissa had felt inferior to her since they were teenagers. Dinah was ambitious and fell on the popularity A-list in high school. Marissa and Tracy weren't even on the C-list. They wouldn't have known where to find the lists if someone had asked for them.

Despite her chronic lack of popularity, Marissa enjoyed her high school days. Her family attended church sporadically, but Marissa was allowed to attend summer camps and occasional youth events. She met Gene at an Amy Grant concert sponsored by one of the local churches. They talked on the phone every day after that night and quickly became an item. Marissa got the last-minute idea of having Gene escort her to the prom, thus bailing on Tracy two days before the event. And her best friend still hasn't forgiven her for it.

"Marissa!" Toni Mallard called out from the mom huddle. "Can I get your number? We're forming a GroupMe so we can keep in touch during the week. I think I can make it work on the ship, and we want to make sure we know what everyone's wearing to dinner and where we'll hang out each night." Marissa wasn't sure what a GroupMe was, and she certainly did not want to hang out with the others, but eight sets of eyes were staring at her. So she quietly recited her phone number. "Does Josh have a phone yet?"

"No, he uses his dad's when he needs one. You can reach him through me on the ship." Marissa thought she noticed snickers but didn't care. A third phone in the family was too expensive and not really necessary. Josh would be working with Gene every day and could borrow his if he had to go somewhere. "Thank you for the GroupMe. I need to get home. See you on Sunday."

"Tootles!" Toni sounded slightly rude with her comment. And it drew a few laughs. But Marissa once again did not care. Other women didn't like her. And she didn't like them. She had her family and her job to keep her busy. When her mother died twenty years ago, Marissa declared Jesus to be her best friend. And He had not let her down yet. He was a better listener than Gene and less demanding than Josh. Marissa was just fine without the girl drama.

"Ready, Freddie?" Pastor Joe asked as he turned out the lights.

"I'm ready." Josh felt the dollar bills folded in his pocket. Pretty soon, he would have his own money. And he would order milkshakes like the others instead of water. Working at the store with his dad might be fun. But getting regular paychecks would be awesome. He couldn't wait.

Before leaving, Josh went to say goodbye to his mother. Out of nowhere, Ronnie walked up and punched him in his arm. "Clean up on aisle four!" The youngest of the infamous Ledbetter brothers just laughed. Josh would not let him see how much the sudden hit hurt. And what did "clean up on aisle four" even mean?

"Very funny," Josh replied. "See you on Sunday." He walked away and noticed that Ronnie sat down at the table. He deserved to have Mr. Morgan as a chaperone. He was a bully and always had been. Jonah walked up, and Josh followed him out of the room. Ronnie watched them as they left.

On the ride to Zipper's, Jonah's younger sister began crying for no reason. She was seven and often super-sensitive.

"What is it now, Evie?" Elle, Jonah's mom, asked.

"I didn't know we could get sick on the boat," Evie whimpered. "What if I throw up? Can I stay with Nanny and Pop Pop instead?"

"No, sweetie. You will be just fine. This is the biggest adventure our family has ever taken. I don't want you to miss it. And I really don't think any of us will get sick."

Her father chimed in. "Plus, we need your help finding the treasure. What if the clues are about soccer? You're the only one in our family who could answer them."

Evie smiled. "I know you're just saying that to make me stop crying. But I probably will be good at treasure hunting." For the rest of the drive, the discussion centered around the hidden gold coins and their possible location. Jonah was convinced that the treasure would be hidden on the ship for its first sailing. Joe speculated that it could be hidden at the top of a palm tree. And Elle hoped there wouldn't be much late-night searching. She would need her sleep to recover from the long days of supervising teenagers.

Josh listened to the banter and nodded appropriately. He wasn't as confident about finding the big prize as the others. Those types of things happened to other people. Not to him. And not to his friends.

At Zipper's, Josh and Jonah ordered super smash burgers with large fries and rushed to a large, high-top table in the back. Soon, five other guys from the youth group joined them. A handful of parents and two younger sisters sat at smaller tables near the front of the restaurant.

"What's up with Ronnie?" Hunter Bernard asked. "You'd think he would be grateful that he is even going on this trip. I still can't believe his dad is letting him go."

"Yeah," Zach Lu agreed. "He always has a bad attitude. Do you really think he got into Florida State? I think he's lying. We'll probably never see him again after this trip."

Josh felt sorry for Ronnie. One time, he saw Ronnie's brothers shove him out of their car on the road behind the high school. Josh and his mom had happened to be driving by and offered him a ride home. Ronnie refused, but Josh could tell that he was upset. He wondered if all older brothers were like that.

"You know he has a rough home life," Josh added.

Zach scooped a French fry in his chocolate shake. "You always say that. I don't see it as an excuse to be a creep."

"Enough about Ronnie," Ryan interrupted. "What are we wearing for the big formal night? I have a tuxedo that my mom bought for vacations, but I wore it to prom. I want to wear something else for the dinner. We should coordinate."

Jonah looked up. "I thought we were skipping the fancy dinner."

"No way your parents will let you skip," Zach declared. "It's required. I say we do something funny or memorable."

"It's too late to buy something," Josh added, relieved. "What can we wear that we already have?"

Hunter spoke up. "How about Hawaiian shirts?"

"With ties!" Zach added. "That would technically be dressy." The seven boys agreed that they would wear dress pants with Hawaiian shirts and neck ties. They also agreed they wouldn't tell the other boys and would surprise the group by walking in together.

Zach leaned in while finishing off his milkshake. "Can you keep a secret?" Josh knew where this was going and didn't like it.

Jonah didn't like it either. "C'mon, Josh. I don't want to hear this. If I don't know, I don't have to tell my dad."

Josh agreed and picked up his food tray. Jonah followed. "See you Sunday." The others said goodbye and huddled together to hear what Zach had planned. No doubt, he was planning to sneak around with Macy when their parents weren't looking. He would probably sneak alcohol onto the ship too. Ronnie might have a bad attitude, but Zach was a fraud.

Back home, Josh's parents were watching funny videos on YouTube. Josh grabbed a bottle of water out of the refrigerator and joined them. No one said anything until his father abruptly paused the pranks and spoke. "I sure will miss you two, but I want you to promise me that you will have fun. This is a once-in-a-lifetime trip."

Surprisingly, Josh's mother didn't reply. So Josh reassured his father. "Of course, Dad. I can't wait."

"Only four days to go," Gene noted.

Josh perked up. "And don't worry about us. I will keep an eye on Mom. She'll be fine."

Marissa chuckled. "I'm supposed to be keeping an eye on you, right?"

"Either way," Gene said while pointing the remote at each of them, "I want you both to be safe. But have lots of fun while you're at it. The March family doesn't sail the seven seas very often."

"I promise, Dad. And I'll be ready to start work at the store as soon as I get back."

Gene leaned forward. "That's good, because your schedule was posted this morning. I can't tell you how proud I was seeing your name up there." Both parents smiled. "They've got you on afternoons. And your days off will be Sundays and Thursdays. This is getting real."

It was getting real. Josh hadn't thought much about his schedule. But now it was written in permanent ink, or something like that. His life as an adult would begin in ten days, whether he liked it or not.

CHAPTER TWO

Sunday, June 14
Embarkation Day

Joe walked into the kitchen to an unusual Sunday morning at home. Normally, he was at the church early on Sundays, and the rest of the family arrived in time for the 9:30 service. This morning, since he was home, he had plans to surprise his family with a ship-inspired breakfast. The image in his mind was glorious. Now all he had to do was create the soon-to-be-famous breakfast boats in full-color reality.

The foundation of his surprise needed to be something in the shape of a ship. Then he would fill it with eggs, cheese, and sausage. Before presenting each dish to his family, he would add a toothpick decorated with a tiny flag crafted out of painter's tape. What could go wrong?

A realistic hull was critical. Joe scoured the cabinets for something close to a boat in shape. He was about to grab some wheat bread when he noticed a package of hot dog buns. Perfect! They would probably be stale when they returned from the trip, so Elle wouldn't mind him using the buns for his breakfast masterpiece.

Joe took six hot dog buns and placed them on a baking sheet. He opened each and pressed the insides to create hollow indentations on each half. The edible ships were going to be better that he originally thought.

Next, Joe scrambled eight eggs and placed some of the hot mixture into each bun shell. The eggs leaked out of the ends, but Joe was able to scoop them back into their holders quickly. Joe then cooked sausage crumbles in the pan. The sausage was greasier than he expected, so he used paper towels to absorb as much oil as possible. Of course, the grease was extremely hot, so he had to quickly use tongs to hold the paper towels.

As he was about to sprinkle the cooked sausage onto the eggs, he noticed that his bun shells had become wet and pliable. The eggs forced the buns into a flat, doughy mess. That won't do. I'm making ships, not rafts.

Joe decided to roll small pieces of aluminum foil into tubes and place a foil tube on each side of the buns to support the boat shape. Perfect! He then added the sausage, which rolled off the eggs and onto the pan. Not ready to give up on the surprise, Joe molded the creations into taco shapes and used more foil tubes to keep them upright. To finish the creations, he sprinkled shredded cheddar cheese on top of each taco boat.

To keep the breakfast yachts warm, Joe placed them in the oven and set the broiler on low. Let's brown the cheese just a little. He then formed small pieces of blue painter's tape into mini rectangles and wrapped them around six toothpicks to form tiny flags. He briefly thought to write S. S. Waller on each but didn't want to go overboard. Ha! Pun intended.

As Joe was pouring himself some orange juice, which would also go bad before they returned, the hallway smoke detector sounded. He rushed to silence it and noticed as he turned around that smoke was billowing out of the oven. The ear-piercing shriek of the detector would not stop despite Joe pushing every button on it. Smoke now began filling the room.

Elle rushed into the kitchen and was followed by Jonah and Evie. "Fire! Fire! Get out, kids."

"Where do we meet?" Evie yelled. "The mailbox? I forgot."

"I don't remember either," Elle bellowed in a panic. "Let's get to the mailbox. Joe, call nine one one."

His family ran outside in their pajamas, and Joe finally quieted the shrill siren. He turned off the oven, opened a window, and joined the others outside.

"Where's your phone?" Elle asked from the end of the driveway.

"Don't worry," a dazed Joe answered. "There isn't a fire. I was just cooking breakfast. Surprise!"

Elle and the kids looked at him in amusement and began walking toward the house. "What? You were cooking?"

"Yeah. Apparently, not very well."

Elle shook her head and continued walking. "I can't wait to see this. C'mon. Let's get more of the windows open. Jonah, get that fan out of your room and bring it to the kitchen. We need to clear out the smoke before we leave."

The family followed Elle's orders, and the kitchen was cleared of most of the smoke in a matter of minutes. Joe took the blackened breakfast yachts out of the oven. "Anyone hungry?"

"Gross," Jonah said. "What were you making? Charcoal toast?"

"There's metal in them!" Evie announced, causing the entire family to break into laughter.

"We've got enough milk for cereal," Elle announced. "Let's eat and get dressed. Today's gonna be a big day."

When the kids and Elle poured their cereal, Joe added his flag masterpieces to the bowls before they added the milk. "There! Enjoy your S. S. Cap'n Crunch."

Josh felt like he hadn't slept a wink. Today was the day! Not only would he leave Florida for the second time in his life, but he would leave the country for the first. When Ms. Jenny first mentioned the possibility of a senior cruise to the Bahamas, Josh knew the chances were slim for him to go. But the cruise line was footing most of the bill, so his parents couldn't deny him this chance.

The idea of getting out of Miami and listening to the ocean was more than Josh could imagine. He didn't remember living in Orlando as a baby. Even if he did, it was a big city just like his hometown. But leaving for the islands was way better than visiting Orlando. Josh really wanted to see a tropical rain forest and some lush vegetation on a beach. The private islands on their upcoming trip weren't exactly Tahiti. But they were close. And they weren't his same old neighborhood.

Josh didn't mind his destiny to work with his dad at Shelf Stockers grocery store. His father had worked at a store in Orlando at his age and moved to Miami to head up the meat department when he turned thirty. Strangely, Josh wasn't allowed to work at the store while he was in high school, even though his dad declared his position as the "best job in the world." His parents wanted him to enjoy his childhood before he began the decades-long journey of a wage earner. Even more strange was the fact that Josh did not mind starting at the store when he returned. An entry-level position as a cashier would let him meet different people throughout the day without much pressure. He saw the stress his friends had been under as they took AP courses and applied to colleges. Josh's goals were to have enough money to live on his own, get a dog, and be happy. And not necessarily in that order.

The only awkward part of the next year would be church life. Most seniors at Holy Cross either moved onto the college ministry or attended new churches near their college campuses. To be honest, most stopped attending church as soon as they participated in the annual Senior Celebration in May. But Josh wanted none of that. He wanted to move into an adult Sunday school class. Unfortunately, all the young adult classes were for couples. So Josh would hang out with the youth for the summer and blend in with the college students in the fall. His best friends would be off at college, but a few of his classmates would still be in the Miami area.

As he was trying to zip his suitcase on his bed, his dad walked in. "Your mom thinks that she is chaperoning you. But you are really the chaperone. You know that, bud. Right?"

No. Josh did not know that. But he went along with his father. "Yes, sir."

"I'm asking you to look after her. Make sure she doesn't get lost. And help her make friends. I know this is your big senior trip, but please don't abandon your mom. She doesn't do well with these types of things."

Josh was surprised that his dad knew that much about his mom. He was usually quiet during dinner and asleep in his recliner shortly afterward. Perhaps he was a better listener than Josh had assumed. "I'll stick by her, Dad. We can't go far on the ship anyways. And our cabins are next door to each other."

"Thanks." His dad helped with the sticky zipper. "She's a great woman. But she has never seen herself that way." He lifted the luggage off the bed and onto the floor. "I hope you have a lot of fun this week. Do I need to give you the speech?"

Josh was not sure which 'speech' his dad meant, but he was sure that he did not want to hear any of them. "No, sir. I will behave."

"Ha! I know you will. Just be careful with all those bikinis walking around on the pool deck. Those can get you in trouble."

And with that one nugget of wisdom, Gene March walked off to help his wife with her luggage. Josh smiled to himself. The "speech" wasn't so bad. And he had no intention of getting in trouble with the bikinis. Pastor Joe had preached enough on Wednesday nights about biblical dating. "No purple!" he'd insisted, meaning that the pink girls and the blue boys should remain physically separated until they were married. Not mixing into purple. All shades of purple were off Josh's mind right now. Maybe he would think about a girlfriend once he got an apartment and a dog. But not any time soon. And certainly not this summer.

Marissa zipped up her suitcase just as Gene walked into their room to help her carry it to the car. She knew she had overpacked but wasn't sure what to expect. Clothes were not the issue. Entertainment in the cabin was. So she packed the three books she had checked out of the library and a Sudoku book her boss had given her at Christmas. Plus, some old playing cards.

Marissa loved working as a records clerk at Dr. Schell's office. Gary Schell was one of the most popular pediatricians in Coral Gables. Known affectionately as Doc, he treated his office staff exceptionally well. The office area and examining rooms were decorated as children's science labs, and the waiting room was arranged as a spaceship's flight deck. Marissa had a nice office with a window and did not have to make small talk with anyone all day. She enjoyed looking at the beakers and flasks painted on the walls. Gene often suggested that she find a position that paid better. But a change would never happen. She did not want to relinquish her perfect setup.

"I'm gonna miss you, Maisy." Gene began dragging the suitcase down the hall.

"I will miss you too. We'll be back next Sunday. That won't be long. And it will be Father's Day, so we'll go to lunch at Beefy's if you want."

"Sounds good. But the house will be quiet without you."

Marissa thought that Gene's comment was a little odd, since neither she nor Josh spoke nearly as much as he did. "I'll text you when I can. And Josh said he'll help me send emails when we are out to sea." Out to sea? Was she about to sail on the ocean in a cruise ship? Butterflies began to hatch in Marissa's stomach. "And there's chili and pot pie in the fridge. Plus, plenty of sandwich stuff."

Gene stopped in the hall. "Thank you, but enough about me. You go have a good time. You deserve it. I won't starve. And I'm gonna work on that leak in the hall bathroom sink." He laughed to himself. "There's enough work around this house to keep me busy for a month. I'll be fine."

"I know," Marissa said softly. "But we've never been apart this long. Your trip to Tampa for the store was only six days."

"It will go by quickly. Be sure to take lots of pictures. Especially the tropical islands. They are supposed to be like those we've seen in movies." Before Marissa could reply, Gene yelled for Josh to hurry. They needed to "load up and get a move on" so they wouldn't be late.

Marissa became more nervous as they drove to the church, and she briefly considered backing out when she saw the four vans in the parking lot. Dozens of people were standing near them in groups as fathers and sons were loading luggage. Josh was clearly excited, and Marissa couldn't imagine disappointing him by quitting. This week would be the unofficial end of his childhood. His lifelong memories with his friends would be worth her week of unease. Thousands of people overcame their fear of the sea every year. She could do it also. But the sea would be easier to overcome than her other fear. Her anxiety about socializing would be a little more difficult to defeat, especially with a supermodel as her roommate.

As Gene and Josh were unloading the suitcases, Marissa walked toward Bettina. Her cabinmate was wearing a coordinated linen short suit with expensive-looking sandals. Marissa immediately regretted wearing a Schell Pediatrics T-shirt.

"Hey, roomie! Are you as excited as I am?" Bettina turned toward Marissa and flashed a perfectly capped smile.

"Yes," Marissa replied. "I could hardly sleep."

"Same here. Toni and I were just going over today's schedule on the app. What do you think about going to the ice-skating show after dinner? It's set up like an oldies TV show. Sounds like a hoot."

Marissa had planned to rush back to her room after dinner. But an ice-skating show did sound exciting. "That sounds fun. I'll see if I'm up for it after we eat." Bettina seemed satisfied with the answer and walked toward a group of boys that included her son, Ryan, and Josh.

Gene startled Marissa as he walked up behind her. "I think you're all set. Your suitcases are in the back of the third van. Make Josh help you get yours out."

"Thank you." Marissa appreciated that Gene recognized the possible difficulty she might have unloading the heavy luggage.

"Do you have enough money?"

Marissa looked at her husband. "I think so. I don't think we have to spend money on anything."

"Well, do you have enough to by a souvenir? Or a fancy coffee?"

"Yes," Marissa replied with a smile. "I have enough."

"Great." Gene put his arm around his wife and led her toward Josh and the other boys. "Just don't fall off the boat like those people did on the first one." He was laughing, but Marissa didn't think his warning was funny. If it could happen to a travel agent, it could happen to her. Or even worse, to Josh.

"We'll be careful. I promise." Satisfied with her answer, Gene then put his arm around Josh. Marissa could not hear what he was saying, but she figured that he was giving their son the same advice he had given her, especially when he took out his wallet and handed Josh several bills.

"Ahoy, mateys!" Pastor Joe walked to the parking lot wearing an eye patch and a pirate's hat. He was pulling an extra-large suitcase that had a sombrero attached to the handle. As the excited crowd began laughing, Elle announced that the get-up was entirely Joe's idea. "Who's ready to sail the mighty seas?"

"We are!" the crowd rang out.

"I have a few announcements. Then we will say our goodbyes and load up. Please board your assigned van and your assigned van only." Joe had led dozens of youth trips in his sixteen years of pastoring. But he had never taken a group on a cruise. He had flown to different countries and had even taken a train to New York City with middle and high school students, but traveling on a megaship would be a new challenge. He had asked his father to pray throughout the week for the safety of everyone involved. His father, in turn, had asked his Sunday school class to pray as well.

Joe stood on a nearby milk crate and gave the final instructions. "When we arrive at the terminal, go ahead and enter the building with your chaperones. We cannot stand around and wait on the group. Porters will take your suitcases. Do not give them your backpacks. Have your passports ready. When you clear the security checkpoint, walk to the left and wait for the rest of the group."

Lauren Lu—no relation to Jenny and Zach—raised her hand. "Yes, Lauren?"

"What is a terminal?" The group chuckled, and Lauren's mom, Pam, whispered the answer in her ear.

Joe continued. "When everyone has cleared security, we will take a group photo. Then we will all board the ship together. Do. Not. Go. Nuts!" A collective groan spread through the students. Joe was known for regularly warning them to "not go nuts."

"The first person to go nuts will walk the plank," Joe said in his best pirate accent. "Now. . ." As Joe was about to give the next directive, a clunker truck clearly missing a muffler drove up. Ronnie jumped out quickly, and the truck drove off. The crowd noticed that Ronnie was carrying a reusable grocery bag and his school backpack. No one had bothered to ask earlier if he had a proper suitcase, but Ronnie didn't seem to mind. Jim Morgan kindly took the bag, tied the handles together, and put it in the back of the third van. Ronnie quickly fell in with the rest of the students.

"Dinner will be on your own tonight.," Joe resumed. "Check the app for locations and times. We have a group reservation at seven sharp tomorrow night at the Galley dining room. Everyone is expected to be there. It is a formal night, so dress your best. Tomorrow is also the teen prom at ten p.m." Lena and Macy clapped their hands with joy. Joe's phone buzzed. He saw that he had received a message from Fred Katz and then put his phone back in his pocket. "Don't forget to check in with your chaperone every night at eleven. Zach, you are staying in your mom's cabin, but she may be busy 'captaining' the ship, so you are to check in with me every night." Zach saluted with one finger. "Finally, remember to be the light. We are to represent Jesus wherever we go. Shining our light on the ocean is just a different way to be a follower. I expect you to be polite to the staff and the other guests, and I expect you to use your best manners. Look for opportunities to be like Jesus throughout the week. You are adults now. So I am expecting even more from you this week. And still . . ." Joe raised his hands, and the students spoke the famous phrase along with him.

"No purple!"

Joe asked Ty, Hunter Bernard's dad, to say a blessing for the week. As the boys and men removed their hats, Joe sent up a silent prayer for the Holy Spirit to equip him with effective leadership for the week. When Ty finished praying for safety and good judgement, the travelers hugged those staying on land goodbye and boarded the vans.

As the convoy of vehicles was leaving the parking lot, Joe hung out the front passenger window of the first van with the pirate hat on his head and yelled, "Onward, ho!"

Jenny Lu felt at home at the helm of a modern megaship. She had moved up the ranks to captain after years of specialized training and experience. She watched the greats like Luca Barone handle unexpected complications with professionalism and efficiency. From sudden storms to equipment failures to persons falling overboard, the best ship's captains followed procedures and made their passengers' well-being a priority. Jenny prided herself on carefully monitoring every aspect of the ship while carefully obeying all the line's policies and procedures.

Today was Jenny's first day as captain of a cruise ship. She was responsible for everything that happened on *Buccaneer Bounty*, including the passengers and crew. She had most recently served as staff captain on Golden Fortune, the first ship of Jewel Cruise Line. As a sister ship of Fortune and third in the line behind *Plunder*, Bounty was identical in structure and design. All three of the ships held nine decks for passengers and three decks for crew members and behind-the-scenes facilities. Jenny had visited every venue and personnel team in the past few days. She oversaw the system tests, and she gave a cheerful speech at the ship's christening. Jenny was not involved in the sea trials but had led a test run from Miami to Jewel's private location, Treasure Island, three weeks ago. In addition to their usual duties, Jewel Cruise Line's captains also oversaw the widely popular treasure hunt. They were ultimately responsible for the purser's selection and distribution of clues but rarely knew where the treasure was hidden. At the end of each week, they spoke at a press conference celebrating the treasure hunters who found the gold.

Assisting Jenny in her duties at the bridge were Staff Captain Aksel Borg and the first, second, and third officers. An environmental officer and deck cadet were also assigned to the command deck. And the cruise director kept in close contact with everyone.

Overlooking the commands, Jenny took a bran muffin from the breakfast display and walked toward her coffee. The deck crew usually ate at the ship's buffet in the mornings, but a heavier breakfast was served directly on the bridge on embarkation days. When Jenny finished the muffin, she checked in with each member of the crew. All was in order. Four of the department heads appeared shortly after her inspection and reported that there were no immediate issues. Jenny was thrilled to hear that the hotel director, head doctor, chief engineer, and cruise director had nothing of concern to report.

"Well, there is one tiny thing," Shawna Thames, the cruise director, chimed in.

"Let's hear it," Jenny replied with a sigh.

"The Wi-Fi on the ship is glitchy."

"What do you mean by glitchy?"

The staff captain and hotel director overheard the conversation and walked toward the women. Shawna answered with a smile. "It seems that the crew routers are working, but the passenger ones are losing connectivity. I think it has something to do with a satellite."

Paul Taylor-Ramos, the hotel director, became alarmed. "Why wasn't I told of this? We advertised free Wi-Fi for the maiden voyage so the reporters and travel agents could send their glowing reports while still onboard. I should have been told if it wasn't working."

Shawna shrugged her shoulders. "I don't know. I just heard this from some of my team."

Jenny excused Paul to investigate the networking situation and alerted Lee Alexander, the chief engineer, of a possible situation. She then walked back to Shawna. "Are you ready to greet our first guests?"

"Yes, ma'am. I'm excited." Shawna twirled around. "Let's get Aksel." The women found the staff captain and made their way to the elevator bank. It was a practice at Jewel Cruise Line for the captain, staff captain, and cruise director to meet every guest at embarkation. Jenny had participated in the custom as staff captain while serving on *Golden Fortune*. Today would be her first meet-and-greet as a full-fledged captain. To Jenny, meeting the passengers was the best part of her job. She especially loved the multigenerational vacationers. Grandparents sharing a week with their energetic grandchildren. Newlyweds beginning their married lives at sea. High school seniors traveling with their parents on graduation trips. Each making lasting memories and family traditions together.

Joe rode in the first van so he could control his group as they arrived and direct them into the terminal. On the way, he typed a quick reply to Dean Katz reminding him that he would be sailing today and would have his decision soon. The unsolicited job offer was appealing. Nice salary and benefits. An office overlooking a duck pond. And a flexible schedule. Teaching religion classes full-time at a large community college was a dream job. Right? No unspoken expectations to grow the youth group. No serious teen issues to navigate. Better pay. Regular hours. And peers. Over time, Joe had tried to link with several youth pastors in neighboring churches, but none were willing to even have lunch with him. The head pastor and children's minister at Holy Cross were wonderful colleagues. But they had their own concerns and different job stresses.

Joe hadn't told Elle about the job offer, and he felt guilty about that. She was his best friend, who shared everything with him. But he wanted to confirm with God that the move was the right thing. If he were honest with himself, he didn't feel at peace about the job. But he didn't feel a peace about not taking the job either. Elle would help him figure out the direction God wanted him to go.

Joe had sought the proverbial "wise counsel" a week ago when Dean Katz had offered the job unexpectedly. The Social Sciences program had seen a recent growth, and the dean received permission to hire four additional faculty members for the upcoming academic year. Classes began in the middle of August, so Joe needed to respond to the offer soon. Very soon. He would need to give his church enough time to place an interim youth pastor before middle and high school classes began in the fall.

Right after Dean Katz's surprising offer, Joe called his father. Retired Staff Sargeant Mark Waller was the wisest man he knew. He had the skill of peppering any situation with a biblical perspective. He had been an encourager and comforter for most of his seventy-one years. When Joe's mother left the earth five years ago after a long battle with breast cancer, Mark openly thanked God for healing his precious wife, Ria. He reminded his family that Jesus had conquered death on the cross and that Ria had surrendered her life to Him daily. She was probably making her famous beef tips for the saints already that day.

Joe recalled his father's advice. Pray for wisdom and trust God's plan. So Joe had prayed. But a clear answer hadn't materialized. He knew not to rush God. But the decision required a rush. That must mean that it was meant to be.

Joe would tell Elle about the offer when they had some time alone this week. And sooner would be better than later. She would support him no matter the decision. She always did. She would also agree that they could use the extra money. Her preschool teaching job helped, but their kids were getting older and more expensive. Thankfully, Jonah had received enough aid to pay nearly all his tuition and fees at Florida International University. He would live at home the first year of college. If his freshman year went well, he would move into an apartment after securing a part-time job and like-minded roommates. Evie would be starting dance lessons in September, and they were not cheap. Plus, the transmission on Joe's truck was skipping third gear. The upcoming cruise was the first week-long vacation their family had taken since his mother passed away.

Money was nice, but Joe knew that was not God's priority. Joe's work at Holy Cross Church was affecting young lives, and he understood that. Yet a teaching position would enable him to affect even more lives, but at a bit of a distance. *Where should I go, Lord?*

Before Joe could sense a clear answer, the van turned toward the cruise terminal, and the massive pirate ship came into view. A chorus of oohs and aahs came from the teenagers in the back.

"It looks real!" Alejandro squealed.

"I'm gonna get sick," Macy joked.

Joe stood and faced the back of the van. "No one's getting sick on my watch. Remember to stick with your chaperones until we are on the ship. After you clear security, meet our group on the left."

"We know. We know," a few students groaned.

Joe looked at Elle. Without saying a word, she told him how proud she was of his leadership and his divine calling. He smiled back, and she instantly knew how much she meant to him. They had been "speaking without words," as Joe called it, for twenty-one years.

Elle and Joe were assigned as lab partners in an introductory chemistry class during the fall of their sophomore year at the University of Miami. And according to Joe, they had the "right chemistry" from the beginning. Elle made the first move by inviting Joe to her sister's wedding in Homestead. She desperately needed a date to keep the older family members from single-shaming her. Joe reluctantly agreed to miss four hours of college football to watch two strangers get married. What he did not expect was to get along so well with her family. Her parents treated him like a long-lost son, and her brother and sister were hilarious. Joe had such a good time that he completely forgot to check on the Hurricane score until he dropped Elle off at her dorm. He called her as soon as he got home, and they talked for nearly two hours. The rest is history. . . or chemistry, as Joe joked.

Joe and Elle were married the summer after they graduated and immediately moved to Graceville for Joe to attend seminary at the Baptist College of Florida. Elle worked at the school's library to pay for their small apartment. The early days were amazing and fun, and God surprised the couple with a son three years later. Money was tight, but student loans and occasional help from their parents kept the young family afloat.

After graduation, Joe began work as a youth pastor for a small church near Deerfield Beach. There were six regular students, with five related to church staff. Joe emphasized the process over the outcomes and refused to add flashy gimmicks like neighboring churches were doing. He shared Jesus and the Bible with the students and related to them personally. Within two years, the group grew to over twenty regular attendees. When Holy Cross Church had an opening for youth pastor, the head pastor reached out to Joe, who asked God for guidance and accepted the job two days later.

Van number one stopped at the Jewel terminal with the others close behind. When the doors opened, the sound of confusion entered the vehicle. Students and parents filed out, while Joe helped unload the luggage. The entire port scene was organized chaos. Porters were placing suitcases into large rolling bins, and families were standing in a cue that zigged and zagged eight times. The Port of Miami was not owned by the cruise lines, and it ran like a well-oiled ant farm. Hundreds of people were rushing to get people and property onto the modern-day pirate ship. This type of madness concerned Joe. He threw up a quick prayer that the fifty-three people in his care would make it onto the ship safely.

"Where's my other bag?"

"Is there a bathroom?"

"Which way do we go?"

The questions pelted Joe at once. But years of experience had prepared him as he directed his charges toward the cue line. Answers spilled out quickly.

"Thank you for doing this, Dad." Today, Jonah knew the right thing to say in the middle of the chaos.

As Marissa stepped out of the van, Josh rushed to retrieve their luggage from the back. She had never seen so many people rushing in different directions. Leaving a concert venue had a similar chaotic vibe. But when people left a concert, they headed toward their vehicles scattered about. Today, everyone was aiming for the same point: the entrance of the megaship.

On the way to the port, Marissa had studied the layout of the ship. Josh helped her install the cruise line's app last night. The design of the program was user-friendly and fairly easy to navigate. The ship, on the other hand, did not seem user-friendly at all.

Josh and Marissa were staying in neighboring cabins with balconies on Deck Ten. From the list that Joe distributed, Marissa could see that most of their group was also staying on Deck Ten. The rest were on Deck Nine. According to the deck plans, those floors held mostly cabins.

The lowest deck regular passengers could visit was Deck Five, which held more cabins, a few restaurants, and the medical complex.

Marissa hoped to get a few pictures of the examining rooms at the medical center to show her friends at work. At the back of this deck was the lower half of the Galley dining room. Marissa could not envision the two-story restaurant but assumed it would be glamorous. She would be eating with the group there tomorrow and was slightly eager to see the décor.

The top level of the dining room was on Deck Six. Marissa noted smaller restaurants past that with a huge dance hall in the center of the floor. Toward the front of the ship was the lower level of the Swashbuckler Theater. According to the daily schedule, two shows were held in the massive auditorium. *Charlie Tuna* was about a frisky puppy who lived on a pirate ship, and *Mad Money* was about the ruthless pursuit of wealth by people around the world. Marissa put both shows on her virtual calendar.

Deck Seven held the upper level of the theater and a massive mall area named Shipwreck Boulevard. This hub was connected to the theater by four separate garden paths that looked like ideal locations to read a book if Marissa needed to escape her cabin—or her roommate.

A modern ice-skating rink was on Deck Eight above the dining room. Marissa had the *Frozen Flashback* show also marked on her calendar. She really didn't want to join the others for the show, but decided that the dazzling production would be worth the hour of awkward socializing with the other moms. The rest of Deck Eight housed a soda shop, game room, pizza restaurant, and more cabins.

Decks Nine, Ten, and Eleven held a variety of cabins. Marissa noticed a gym, a spa, and a walking track on Deck Eleven. She planned to ask Josh to show her the track sometime today. If it felt safe, she would attempt to walk for thirty minutes each morning. Jannet at work warned her about the dangers of unlimited food for a week. They joked about packing stretchy pants for the last day, but Marissa vowed to exercise a little each day to avoid wearing them.

The rest of the ship looked to house the "fun" areas. Deck Twelve hosted the main buffet for the entire ship. Marissa marveled at its name, Blackbeard's Fortress. Thankfully, it was open all day. The ship did not list a Deck Thirteen, which Marissa assumed was for superstitious reasons. The top and final deck was Deck Fourteen, which held the massive resort-style pool. On one end of the pool area was a kiddie splash zone, and on the other was a movie arena complete with comfortable chairs and a popcorn machine. Marissa tried to prioritize the venues but ultimately decided that she wanted to visit all of them.

"Mom, let's go." Marissa hadn't noticed Josh standing nearby with their luggage. She took her suitcase and began pulling it in line behind him. He was practically skipping to the end of the entry line. Marissa checked to ensure that they had all their bags and took out their passports. Before the que, they passed their suitcases to baggage handlers.

Marissa saw the "cool cluster" of moms chatting ahead in the line. They were giggling and not paying attention to their children. She heard Joe, already inside the terminal, ordering his young charges to "not go nuts." Ironically, Pastor Joe was the only one going nuts. Marissa smiled at that image and gave Josh a pat on his back.

Once inside the terminal, employees checked Marissa and Josh's paperwork and directed them to the security line. Marissa noticed several people removing their shoes only to be told to put them back on. Removing shoes must only be an airport security thing. A woman with curly brown hair piled high on her head was pulled to the side. Marissa watched as security officers removed a clothes iron from her carry-on bag. The woman seemed unfazed and scurried back to her group. Marissa also noticed the security officers asking Joe to remove his eye patch and sombrero.

Thankfully, Marissa and Josh zoomed through security with no issues. They met the growing Holy Cross group and waited for the last few people to join. Marissa noticed Pastor Joe looking at his phone a few times as he gathered the group. She could tell that something was on his mind, and she hoped there wasn't a problem with the trip. From her fearful perspective, anything in the world could go wrong.

"Is this everyone?" Joe asked loudly. "Elle, please count again." The pastor's wife undertook the nearly impossible task of counting squirming teenagers and their chaperones and eventually announced that they were all there. Joe replaced the eye patch and pirate hat and ordered the group to assemble for the group photo in front of a Jewel photographer. He then ordered them to "board the ship."

The mass of teens and adults traveled the gangway to the ship with a rapid pace. Marissa was surprised that she herself was becoming excited as they got closer to the entry. Josh was walking alongside quietly. Both were overwhelmed with the massive pirate ship before them and excited to explore every part of it.

Josh was amazed at the inside of the ship. The entry gangway ended at Deck Seven and Shipwreck Boulevard, which was alive with excited passengers. A live band was playing pirate music, and officials were greeting every person. Josh recognized Jenny Lu at the head of the line. She gave each of the youth members a hug or a handshake, and she was wearing her captain's uniform and three-inch heels. Josh noticed Zach beaming with pride over his mother and her role on the ship.

"Welcome aboard!" Jenny greeted Josh and Marissa. "This is Staff Captain Aksel and Cruise Director Shawna." Josh shook their hands and was slightly embarrassed that his mother said nothing to the crew members. They simply moved on with the rest of the group toward the elevators.

"Should we go to our cabins?" Josh asked his mother.

"I'm not sure. What are the others doing?"

Josh looked around. "I don't think anyone knows what to do."

Elle walked up to several of the group. "Now is a good time to drop your backpacks at your cabins. Make sure that your key bracelets work. Then you might want to go exploring and have some lunch. The buffet and pizza restaurant are open right now."

Marissa smiled at the pastor's wife. "Thank you."

"Let's go, Mom," Josh announced. "There's room in that elevator." Marissa did not want to squeeze into the overcrowded car but accepted that the elevators would be crowded for the near future, so she followed Josh. Every passenger was making his or her way onto the ship and into a cabin. After pulling her backpack in enough for the doors to close, Marissa stood facing the doors.

Thankfully, the elevator doors opened to Deck Ten first. Josh shot out of the car and pulled Marissa and her backpack out as well. Clearly, Josh was more excited about the upcoming week than his mother had realized.

"What's my cabin number again?" Josh began walking toward the cabins.

"You're in 1023, and I'm in 1025. Looks like the odd rooms are to the right."

"Starboard!" Josh added. "I remember that much."

Marissa giggled. "Lead the way, Captain."

Josh found the cabins easily. They arrived before their cabinmates and took one key bracelet each from the envelopes attached to the doors.

Marissa held up her arm to Josh. "What do these do again?"

"That is your key to your room. You can use it to buy things and check in for dinner and show reservations. It also gets you on and off the ship at the islands," Josh informed.

"Be sure not to lose yours," Marissa warned. "That would be a mess."

Josh helped his mother get her things into her room. She asked for a few minutes to settle in, so he declared that he would be back to get her for lunch in thirty minutes. Then he went into his cabin. Thankfully, both bracelets worked flawlessly.

The cabin was smaller than Josh expected, but it had everything he and Ryan would need. Two beds. A desk. A tiny bathroom. And a full-size window with a balcony and a view of the port. Soon they would be able to watch the ocean sail by from their cabin.

Josh threw his hat and backpack onto the first bed. He secured the key bracelet to his arm and texted Ryan, who replied that he and his mom stopped by Guest Services to check on the Wi-Fi. They would be up soon and wanted to eat lunch with Josh and Marissa.

"Sure thing," Josh wrote. "I already claimed the first bed." Rather than unpack, Josh walked out to the balcony. Dozens of workers were moving luggage and loading the ship with a week's worth of food. He watched for a while, then went back into the cabin to wait for Ryan to arrive.

Marissa was unsure about her cabin. It held everything she needed but was too small for two people. It would have been ideal for her to occupy alone. She didn't want to select a bed that Bettina might want, so she sat on the small couch and waited for her roommate to arrive. As she looked around, her phone buzzed. She was surprised to see that the incoming text message wasn't from Gene but from her friend Jannet.

"Have you boarded yet?"

"Yes. I'm in my cabin now."

In seconds, Jannet responded. "What is it like? Send pictures!"

Marissa hadn't thought to take pictures, so she snapped a few shots of the cabin and the bathroom. Then she sent them to her coworker. She sent them to Gene also and told him that they were safely onboard. As soon as she sent the messages, she heard the lock on her cabin door open.

"Roomie!" Bettina barged in and quickly filled the entire space with her presence. "I'm so excited! Wanna go to lunch with the rest of us? We can unpack afterwards. Our luggage should be delivered soon."

Marissa didn't have a response. She just stood speechless. Bettina rescued her by adding that they could see what the boys wanted to do. As Marissa quietly agreed, Ryan and Josh walked into their cabin.

"This is so cool!" Ryan declared. "We can see the Hard Rock Hotel from our window. And our shower looks like a space capsule." Josh nodded at that comment.

"I hope there's room for my loofahs," Bettina joked. "Are you boys ready to eat? I can't wait to see the buffet."

"Yes, ma'am!" Josh replied. "I'm ready."

The foursome began walking down the passageway toward the elevators, when Macy Dial popped out of her cabin a few doors past theirs.

"A clue! We found a clue!" At Macy's announcement, the four in the hall rushed toward her. Marissa found herself caught up in the excitement before she knew what happened.

"What does it say?" Ryan asked.

"We're not telling. You have to find the clue yourself." With that, Macy began laughing and went back into her cabin. The boys rushed back to theirs. After a few unsuccessful tries at opening door with their key bracelets, they finally entered the room. Their mothers followed.

"There it is!" Josh cried out. "There's a blank envelope on the desk. I can't believe we missed it." He opened the flap and found a card inside. The clue was written in bold letters.

The treasure is close, so do not fear.

Just look for another word that means "pier."

Before anyone could speak, Ryan took out his phone and looked up synonyms for pier.

"Wharf," Ryan started. "Jetty. Landing. Levee. Slip."

"Look for a slip?" Josh asked. "What could that be?"

Bettina stood on her tiptoes. "Let's see if we have the same clue." She tugged on Marissa's elbow and dragged her toward their cabin. They did indeed have the same clue on their desk. "This is so mysterious. Let's work on it at lunch."

"Okay" was all Marissa replied. Bettina placed the clue in her bright-pink fanny pack and put her arm around Marissa. The mothers and sons once again walked toward the elevators, which were still crowded with boarding passengers. They decided to take the stairs up two levels to Deck Twelve. Thankfully, Blackbeard's Fortress wasn't busy yet, so they marched past the greeter toward the food. Bettina pointed to an area to meet after gathering their meals and took off. Marissa didn't know where to start, so she walked around for a bit before grabbing a plate and utensils. She finally opted for meatloaf and mashed potatoes with a healthy grilled vegetable medley.

Marissa was the first to complete her plate, so she chose a four-person table close to a window. When the boys arrived, they were accompanied by two friends, so they sat at a nearby table. That left Marissa alone with Bettina, who had filled her plate with a small piece of fish and fresh fruit. Marissa immediately regretted her substantial lunch and decided to only eat half of everything. Peer pressure was alive and well on *Buccaneer Bounty*.

"Everything looked so yummy," Bettina declared. "I could just eat it all." Marissa inwardly rolled her eyes at that comment. Before the women could discuss the clue, two other moms arrived. Toni and Pam promised to join the women at the "fun table" as soon as they found their food. Marissa wondered if one of them would come back with a small pile of birdseed and silently scolded herself for judging the diet habits of others. Of course, both did come back with low-calorie finds. More fruit and some dressing-less salads. Marissa joked to herself that dessert was now out of the question. If she continued to eat with the others, she may involuntarily lose weight by the end of the week. So much for needing the stretchy pants.

Since the other moms did not bring up the clue, Bettina wisely avoided it. Instead, she droned on and on about her nail polish color and the latest celebrity gossip. Marissa listened patiently and laughed inappropriately when Toni lamented that her nail salon was no longer making emergency house calls. The women lived in a different stratum than Marissa, but she didn't mind. She loved her comfortable life with Gene and Josh. Really loved it.

"Our cabin is sooo cute," Bettina remarked. "Not quite the Ritz, but still usable. How are you pressing your clothes without an iron?"

"Ugh," Pam moaned. "We will have to hang everything up and spritz it with water. I read that you can use a flat iron in a pinch."

"Um . . . no," Toni objected. "Not on my Lela Rose-ware. There must be a better option."

Pam nodded. "Let's ask our attendant when we get back. What was his name?"

"Sunny," Toni answered with a grin. "From India. Have you met him yet?"

"No," Bettina replied. "But he sounds cheery."

"He is," Toni said. "I'll ask him about ironing when we get back to our cabin. There must be a better solution than 'spritzing.' Now, what is our plan for the day?"

The women devised the perfect schedule for day one, while Marissa mentally countered their plans with her own. She would stay in the room when Bettina was out and find a bench on one of those garden paths if necessary. As she was mentally recalling all the books she packed, Bettina was calling her.

"Earth to Marissa. Are you there?"

"Oh. Sorry. This is all a little overwhelming. I'm not sure I can even find my way back to our cabin."

Bettina smiled and put her arm around Marissa. "That is exactly why we will stay glued at the hip all week. Stick with me, roomie. I'll show you a great time on the S.S. Buccaneer Bounty." Marissa would now have to implement plan B: "Unglue My Roomie."

Josh was already having the time of his life, and he had only been on the ship one hour. Spending a week in a cabin without his parents felt like the first step to independence. Of course, his mother would be in the next cabin. But she wouldn't get out much, and she wouldn't follow him around every day. Eating at an all-you-can-eat buffet with his friends was the cherry on top. He didn't see pizza, so he opted for a plate full of chicken tenders. Ryan and Jandro did the same, while Ty created a massive cheeseburger. Josh wondered where Jandro and Ty's fathers were but didn't ask.

"What do you think Zach's gonna do this week," Jandro asked. "He's been hinting that he's planning something big." Josh knew that Zach would be skirting the rules on the cruise, and he didn't want to get caught up in whatever the captain's son had planned.

"I don't know," Ty replied. "But he told me that his bracelet will let him get alcohol. There's a mistake since his mother is the captain, and no one has figured it out. I think he can get it on the islands too."

"He probably brought some in his luggage somehow," Ryan added. "He's been talking about having a party in his mom's cabin when she's on duty one night. My parents would slaughter me if I got busted at a party this week."

"Yeah, mine too," Josh agreed.

"I may try to go," Ty confessed. "My dad goes to sleep early. I'll just text him at eleven, and I'll be fine." Three sets of eyes looked up at Ty. "Don't worry. I'll behave."

Josh had always appreciated that his church friends rarely encouraged him to break rules and never teased him when he didn't. Pastor Joe had created a culture of appropriate behavior, and Josh had never resented it.

"What should we do first?" Ryan asked. "The ship is crazy right now."

"I'd like to go exploring," Josh answered as he swiped a French fry through ketchup. "Maybe we can see everything before we decide."

"Sounds like a plan," Ryan said, as Ty and Jandro nodded in agreement. "And we can look for a wharf or slip or whatever the clue is about."

Ty pointed a finger in the air. "But first, chocolate ice cream." The boys rushed to the dessert counter and returned to the table with enough sugar to drop an elephant.

As the boys were talking at their table, Ronnie and Mr. Morgan walked into the restaurant. They didn't see the boys and walked toward the food.

"Do you think Ronnie has anything sketchy planned?" Ty asked.

"He's probably planning to jump off the ship and swim to Puerto Rico," Jandro joked. "Do you think Zach will tell him about the party?"

Ty shook his head. "I doubt it. Ronnie would probably drink all the alcohol." The boys laughed and stood in unison to rush for seconds of dessert. Josh noticed that his mother was smiling while eating with some of the mothers. She seemed happy. He would make a point to text his father before they sailed. His dad was concerned that she wouldn't be comfortable with the other moms. Thankfully, she looked happy, but she hadn't eaten much of her lunch.

Joe knew that embarkation day would be chaotic, but he had not expected so many issues within the first few hours. And his shirt still smelled like smoke from the charred breakfast boats. The cruise line left paperwork in his cabin to be completed before sail away. Apparently, they wanted basic information on his entire group for media releases. Joe planned to ask Elle for help with the forms, but she was occupied with missing luggage and cabin assignment concerns. Their family, as well as a dozen students and their chaperones, had not received their luggage yet. It was normally delivered within two hours of embarkation, but could arrive as late as seven or eight p.m.

"Any luck?" Joe asked as Elle returned to their cabin.

"No. But I saw a corridor full of luggage down the hall. I'm sure ours is on the way." Elle walked toward the desk. "What are you working on?"

"The line wants the demographics of everyone in our party. They will issue several stories about this cruise since it's the inaugural sailing. I wish they had sent this earlier. But no worries. I'm almost done."

Elle's phone had buzzed three times while Joe was talking. She sat on the bed and opened her phone. "Looks like Lauren is getting nervous about the sailing. Pam says that she has it under control . . . for now."

"Next," Joe asked as he continued to write.

"Kinsleigh and Ava are asking if they can stay in a cabin together and their moms, Sherri and Anita, in another."

"No. I don't think we can move rooms. It's a Coast Guard thing or something."

"Last one. Zach is checking in now." Elle laughed. "He says, 'I'm sure that Mr. Joe is busy, so I'm letting you know that I am fine. I'm in my mom's cabin and will get lunch soon. Let me know if you need any help.'" Elle held the phone to her chest. "What a considerate young man. We should have him over more often. Maybe he and Jonah could go fishing together."

Joe put the pen down. "Yeah. Sounds like a plan. Speaking of Jonah, where is he? And where is Evie?"

"They are next door in my cabin. Evie is waiting on the luggage so she can get us unpacked." As Elle finished talking, Jonah and Evie walked into the cabin through the adjoining door. Elle and Evie would be sleeping in one cabin while Joe and Jonah would sleep in the other. The cruise line had thoughtfully placed them in neighboring cabins with a connecting door.

"We're hungry," Jonah declared. "Can we eat?"

"I don't know," Joe joked. "Can you?"

"Don't joke about food, Daddy," Evie pled. "We're starving."

"I'm sorry. Let's go find the buffet. Just. Don't. Go. Nuts."

Marissa was relieved to see her suitcase in the hallway near her cabin door when they returned after lunch. Thankfully, Josh's was nearby, safe and sound. She pulled hers into the cabin as Bettina held the door open. Honestly, Marissa had to admit that she enjoyed lunch with the girls. It was nice to have people in a similar stage in life to talk with, even if she hadn't gotten enough to eat. Toni shared that her parents were in bad health. And Bettina warned the group about the "gelatin-like meat" at the new Italian restaurant near the church. But Marissa had nothing to contribute. She would never feel comfortable enough to make jokes about her thighs squeaking as she walked or offer summer fashion tips. But listening was fun. At least this once.

"Pick a side of the closet, and I will take the other," Bettina kindly offered.

"Either is fine with me." Marissa smiled, so Bettina chose a side. The women plopped their luggage onto their beds and began unpacking.

"Did you know that Toni and her husband are separated?" Bettina blurted out. Marissa knew that gossiping was wrong, but she felt a need to understand the lives of the other moms. She felt like she truly cared.

"No, I didn't know."

"Lena told Ryan that her dad is living at his parents' house for now. I put two and two together. I don't mean to judge. But I do hope to talk about it with her this week. She must be anxious about the future. Of course, it's possible that she is relieved. Who knows?"

"Thank you for telling me. I will pray for them. Pastor Joe has warned the youth about the spiritual warfare they face every day. I believe that marriages are under a special attack."

Bettina sat on her bed. "I haven't thought about marriages being under attack. I guess Satan can do a lot of damage if he can split up a family."

"Yeah. Even if it's for a few weeks," Marissa added. "We should keep an eye on Lena as well."

"Sounds like a plan, roomie." Bettina continued to unpack. "Since we couldn't bring an iron or a steamer, I brought a spray bottle. We can spritz our clothes with water and hang them like Pam was explaining. That is the best we can do about wrinkles—without paying to have our clothes pressed by the crew. Do you have any pure silk that would be ruined by water?"

Marissa chuckled to herself. "No silk. Thank you for asking." Marissa finished unpacking and stretched out on her bed with one of her books.

"Have you figured out another word for pier?" Bettina asked as she pulled her hair into a high ponytail.

"No. I forgot all about it." Marissa sat up.

"We can ask around. I'm not good at puzzles. Let me know if you think of anything though. We can put our heads together and find the treasure. I'm sure of it."

Marissa appreciated Bettina's optimism but recognized that the odds of them winning were miniscule. "I will keep thinking on it."

"Great! I'm gonna go exploring," Bettina announced as she adjusted her key bracelet. "Sail away is at three o'clock. Want to plan somewhere to meet?"

"No, thank you. I'll just stay here until supper. That's at seven, right?"

Bettina put her hands on her hips. "I will leave you be for now. But you cannot spend the week holed up in this cabin. We're gonna have some fun whether you like it or not." Bettina left the cabin, and Marissa moaned inside. She would have to come up with an excuse to avoid the other women. Gene should be the one taking Josh on his senior trip. But he did not have enough vacation time to take the entire week off work, and the store was already beginning to stock up for the big Fourth of July "meat rush." Unfortunately for Marissa, he needed to be home, not sailing the waters for a week.

Marissa tossed her sandals off and fluffed the pillows behind her. She had a respite for the afternoon. Supper and the ice show would be tolerable. But she would insist on an early bedtime. One day figured out. Six more to go.

CHAPTER FOUR

Jenny was pleased with her first embarkation as a captain. The dreaded task of shaking hands with every passenger was not much of a bother. It went by quickly, and she met thousands of joyful travelers. Now, she and Aksel must work with the local harbor pilot to maneuver the ship out of the port. It was already facing the ocean, so they would only have to engage the side thrusters to move the massive vessel away from the pier and then guide it forward.

As she gave the command to "spin up" the propellors, Jenny heard clapping from the bridge crew. She didn't respond and remained focused on her immediate tasks. Buccaneer Bounty was officially underway on its inaugural journey. Jenny Lu was now a full-time captain on the world's newest adventure cruise ship. One of only three women in the U.S. commanding a vessel like Bounty, Jenny was a pioneer. Right now, thousands of passengers were experiencing the thrill of the ship's sail away at various venues. Jenny blew the ship's thunderous horn and imagined Zach's friends from church, clapping in excitement. Today was a very good day.

As the ship pulled away from the pier, Jenny monitored the elaborate steering system and walked to the other stations to check on their readings. The bridge was the command center of the ship and held advanced GPS and communication technology, as well as radar tracking and weather forecasting tools. Jenny was surprised that she wasn't at all nervous about the sailing. She had trained for years and was fully ready to supervise every aspect of the cruise. She knew that problems would arise regularly. Most likely daily. But she knew that God would help her solve them when they did occur. He always did.

As the ship began its forward crawl, Jenny touched the cross on her necklace. Brian had given it to her on their first wedding anniversary, and she felt close to him whenever she held it. She also remembered that he told her that Jesus was always a whisper away.

Thank you for this opportunity, God. Please help me bring the passengers and crew back to Miami safely.

"We're moving!" Ryan shrieked.

"Are you sure?" Josh asked. "It doesn't feel like we're moving."

"Look at the buildings." Josh looked out at the horizon and was amazed to see that the ship was indeed moving. He and Ryan had gathered with more than a dozen others from their group on the top deck. It seemed that most of the passengers had the same idea. The area was crowded with couples, families, and crew members waving from the ship to crew members working at the port and locals going about their daily lives near the area.

After a few minutes, Bounty passed a parked ship waiting to sail. Travelers on each ship waved to each other. Josh noticed someone on the other ship holding a five-foot cardboard sign of a human hand. The woman was waving it back and forth. He waved to her along with the others.

"I guess this is it," Josh joked. "No turning back now."

"Don't say that!" Lauren squealed. "What if we sink? Right in the middle of the ocean!"

Josh started to joke back to Lauren but realized she was seriously worried. "We'll be fine. Ms. Jenny is in charge. And I'm sure she has checked everything. Nothing is going to happen to any of us." Lauren didn't seem entirely convinced of their safety and remained quiet.

The group watched as the ship inched farther and farther away from land. Josh couldn't believe that he was now sailing on the ocean. He didn't have a phone to take pictures, so he made mental pictures in his mind. This view was worth remembering forever.

When they could no longer see Miami, the group decided to check out the soda shop on Deck Eight. Zach led the way, since he had been on *Golden Fortune* and *Plunder*, Bounty's sister ships, and he knew the layout of the decks better than anyone. They found a table near the juke box and sat down. Everyone but Josh pulled out their phones. He was used to this and chuckled to himself as his friends were frantically telling people back home that they were officially sailing on the ocean.

Zach reminded his friends to put their phones in airplane mode. When he finished adjusting his settings, he quickly asked about the clue. "Anyone figure out what we're supposed to do next? Look for a wharf?"

"What does that even mean?" Ryan asked as he put his phone in his back pocket. "It said the next clue is close."

"What words did we come up with?" Josh asked as the rest of the group put away their phones and huddled around the boys.

Ty put a finger in the air. "Wharf. Jetty. Slip. I don't remember the others."

"I think slip makes the most sense," Ryan declared. "Where would we find a slip?"

"It's dock, you dorks. Could all of you not figure that out?" Ronnie appeared out of nowhere and sneered his comment as he walked past the group.

"He's so rude," Lauren piped. "Ignore him."

The group laughed, but Josh spoke up. "I think he's right. Doesn't the ship have a doctor? A doc?"

"Solid!" Zach replied. "It does. And I know where he lives. Deck Five!" The group giggled and decided to immediately search for the next clue.

The crowd had to take two separate elevators, which were both filled with passengers and their carry-on luggage. Josh was amazed that twelve people and their belongings were able to fit into his car. When they finally arrived on Deck Five, the other half of the group was already looking around the area.

"There's a morgue in there," Zach announced.

"Ewwww!" every girl nearby replied.

"Where's the doctor?" Lauren asked. "Shouldn't he be here?"

Zach spoke to the crowd proudly. "No. He is answering questions in the theater right now. There are several people talking in there, including my mom."

"Let's go to the theater," Ryan suggested.

"We should look here first," Lena added. The group agreed and continued to inspect the area. "It's really cool down here." The group could see that the ship's medical facility had examining rooms flanking a reception area. A nurse welcomed the group and showed them the operating room.

"Is there really a morgue?" Lauren asked with a weak smile.

"Yes, there is. We hope we won't ever have to use it."

Lauren's face turned ashen.

"We're looking for the clue," Josh shared.

The nurse raised her eyebrows. "Well, have fun with that. I don't know anything about the clues."

The group walked around the reception area and did not see anything promising. In the hall, they looked over the walls and door frames.

"Over here!" Macy Dial spoke for the first time. "Look under this sign. It says 'Dr. Cruz' on the top. But I see tiny writing below his name." The others gathered around Macy.

"Read it!" Zach begged.

"Should I tell everyone, Lena? We found it first." Lena shrugged her shoulders. Macy leaned closer to the sign. "Okay. It says, 'Doc hopes that you stay well and dear. If not, get stronger when Monday gets here.'"

"That's easy!" Ryan bellowed. "The gym! Isn't there a gym on this ship?"

"Yep," Zach added. "It's on Deck Eleven. But the clue won't be there until tomorrow."

"Could it possibly be something else?" Josh asked. The group groaned.

"No," Zach moaned. "It's the gym. We can go there after breakfast tomorrow." The group agreed that they were finished clue-hunting for the day. They made plans to meet for breakfast and then rush to the gym afterwards. "Wanna see something cool?"

Zach led the group down the corridor to one of the TorpedoX lifeboat launch sites.

"What is this?" Lauren asked. She was standing close to the site.

"This is one of the torpedo lifeboats that my mom can shoot out of the ship," Zach replied excitedly. "They've already used them twice. Once on the very first cruise of *Golden Fortune*. And once this year on *Plunder*. The people were saved, but I wouldn't take any chances." The group giggled and followed Zach farther down the passageway. They came to the lower level of the Galley dining room.

"Ooo, this is so fancy," Lena declared.

"Yeah, it's nice," Zach said. "We'll eat here tomorrow for formal night. What do you think about hitting the buffet tonight?" Lena's smile dropped, but the group agreed to have a casual dinner on the first night.

"Where next?" Lauren asked as she took one more picture of the launch site.

Marissa was enjoying herself in the cabin. She had read several chapters in a new book about a woman who hoards cats and tennis balls and then dozed off for a few minutes. She had three hours until she would eat dinner with the other moms. That wouldn't be so terrible. And the ice-skating show sounded fun. She'd never seen a live ice show, and certainly not on a cruise ship.

Thoughts of Josh filled Marissa's mind. He was officially a grown-up now. That didn't seem possible. He was so tiny and helpless when he arrived a month earlier than expected. How could the years have passed so quickly? Marissa felt a little guilty that she never encouraged him to apply for college or seek a job in another town. She would have missed him terribly. And she would have worried about his safety nonstop. Marissa knew that Satan was stalking around young people, and she couldn't bear the thought of Josh getting caught up in some sort of evil scheme on a college campus.

The grocery store had been a blessing for Gene. It had provided a happy life for their family and fulfilling work for her husband. Josh never seemed interested in pursuing anything else, so Shelf Stockers was the perfect destination for him . . . for now. Marissa acknowledged that he may become bored or disinterested with their local store or the grocery business entirely. But she would face that hurdle if and when it arrived. For now, he would still be living at home, and he would be part of the family's daily routines. Marissa couldn't ask for anything more.

Someone knocked on the cabin door. Marissa rushed to answer it and was delighted to see it was only Josh.

"Hi, Mom. The guys are going to the top deck, and I wanted to check in."

"Come in. Tell me what you've been doing."

Josh walked in and sat on the small couch. "Not much. We ate lunch and walked around a little. We saw one of those lifeboat torpedoes. Well, not the boat, but where they are shot from the boat."

"That sounds scary."

"It's not. I promise." Josh's eyes got wider. "We saw the doctor's office. You have to see it. I know you'd like to see the other rooms."

Marissa nodded. "I do want to see it all. I am hoping to send pictures to Jannet at work."

"Have you figured out the first clue?" Josh asked quietly.

"You don't have to whisper. No one will hear you. And no, we haven't figured it out."

Josh thought for a few seconds. "Do you want a hint?"

Before Marissa could answer, the cabin door opened, and Bettina walked in. "That was so fun. I hate you missed it, roomie. Toni and I were dancing with the big group by the pool. It was a hoot." She noticed Josh. "Are you having fun, sweetie? Where's Ryan?"

Josh stood to leave. "He and some of the guys are changing into bathing suits. We're going up to the top deck to hang out at the pool."

"Have you made dinner plans?" Bettina asked.

"Yes, ma'am. We're gonna eat at the buffet."

"That's perfect. Your mom and I will see you there. And keep an eye on Ryan. Let me know if he starts acting inappropriately." Josh nodded. "And watch out for Ronnie too. I'm not so sure about his upbringing."

"We will." As Josh was leaving, he whispered to his mother, "Dock." At first, Marissa was puzzled, but then she smiled knowingly.

"Be sure to put on some sunscreen," Marissa warned. "And have fun!"

When Josh left, Bettina turned toward her cabinmate. "We have a few minutes before dinner. Wanna get into some trouble?"

Marissa could only imagine what Bettina was suggesting. "No, thank you. I think I'll work on this book. I'll be ready for dinner at seven though."

"That's probably for the best," Bettina conceded. "I'm getting a little edgy."

"Edgy?"

Bettina sat on her bed. "I get like that when I don't have control of a situation. This whole trip is out of my control. And I don't like it. Plus, I have no idea what Ben and Jason are doing back home. I planned their meals for the week and gave them strict instructions on upkeep of the house. But I know they are watching baseball in their underwear and eating Cheetos for dinner."

Marissa laughed too loudly and quickly regretted it. "I'm sure they are fine. We are fine."

"Wanna play Just a Minute?" Bettina asked abruptly.

"Just a Minute?"

"Yeah, my therapist suggested that I play a 'gabby game' whenever I get edgy. It works."

Marissa sat on her bed with a curious look on her face. She was slowly grasping that Bettina, who looked model-perfect every day of the week, had some sort of anxiety. She may look flawless, but she wasn't. Or was this some big joke that the women were playing on her? Would Bettina report back that plain Jane Marissa fell for their big embarkation-day joke?

But Bettina's hand revealed the truth. The woman was nervous about something. She was wringing her hands and tapping one of her feet. "Sure. How do you play?"

"We take turns throwing out random topics, and the other person has to talk about that for a whole minute." Marissa's stomach dropped. In what universe did she want to casually talk about random topics for an entire minute? The thought gave *her* anxiety.

"I don't know about that," Marissa answered.

"Please. We'll just do a few words. Jason and my mom usually help. But they are back home, so it's got to be you."

The conversation was bordering on absurdity, but Marissa couldn't say no. "Okay. You start."

"Easter eggs!"

Marissa jerked. Then she realized that Bettina was serious. She had to speak about Easter eggs for an entire minute. "Um, I like Easter eggs. They are colorful. We used to hide them in the yard when Josh was young. And I use them to make deviled eggs for Easter dinner."

Bettina was waving her arm in the air to get Marissa to continue. "That's only thirteen seconds."

"That's all I can think of," Marissa said softly.

"Okay. You're new. We'll let that go. What's my topic?"

Looking around the room for ideas, Marissa wondered how long this nonsense would last. "How about magnets?"

"Magnets?" Bettina said in surprise. "Magnets?!" She added ten seconds of dramatic sighing. "I don't know anything about magnets." With that declaration, Bettina started sobbing. "This isn't helping. You're supposed to be asking me about sea creatures or nail polish. Not science."

Inappropriately, Marissa began laughing. She knew she should stop but couldn't. The ridiculousness of her sitting in the middle of the ocean with some woman from church crying about magnets was too much to take. How had this even happened?

Fortunately, Bettina stopped crying and began laughing too. "I'm sorry. Jason knows the right topics for me to discuss. I guess that's sort of cheating. You probably hate me now."

"Oh, no. I'm happy to discover that you are human."

"Really?" Bettina asked. "I don't feel very human."

Marissa moved beside Bettina and began patting her back. "You are the prettiest person I know. And you have been very kind to me. To be honest, I thought you would be too snobbish to even notice me. But you've been the opposite. Thank you."

Bettina's eyes became wide. "I've been thinking the same thing about you. You are so collected and reserved. I've been nervous about being clever enough to even hold a conversation with you." Marissa moved back to her bed with a look of shock. "I'm serious."

"Well, I think we have had some sort of breakthrough," Marissa joked. "I will never look at a magnet the same." Both women fell back laughing. "I would like to get some rest. Maybe read a little more in my book."

"It wouldn't hurt to rest a little. I probably should pace myself for the week. Don't want my battery to get too low. I'm gonna log off for now. Wake me at six-thirty."

"Will do. No problem." Marissa was amazed to watch Bettina lay back on her bed and fall asleep within minutes. She was snoring rather loudly within five minutes. Oh, to be able to fall asleep that quickly. What will the next six days hold? Marissa had no idea what to expect.

Sail away went smoothly, and Jenny was pleased. Very pleased. She had asked each of the department heads to report to her within an hour of departure. It was critically important that everything ran perfectly—especially on the inaugural sailing. Hundreds of media reporters and travel agents were on board, and they would be reporting successes and failures to their constituents. Jenny was determined to have no failures on *Buccaneer Bounty*.

The first to report to the captain was the hotel director, Paul Taylor-Ramos. "The passenger routers are working for now. I have asked Guest Services to inform me immediately if they receive any complaints.”

“That’s good news,” Jenny replied. “Thank you.”

“Now for the bad news,” Paul added. “Actually, I have two issues to report.”

Jenny walked toward the coffee machine. She would need extra caffeine fortification today. “Go on.”

“First, we have already received a handful of complaints from the older veterans on board. Apparently, the thresholds between the cabins and the bathrooms are a little too high for them, and some of the mature passengers are tripping over them.”

“Already?”

“Yes, ma’am. Already.” Paul pulled a coffee cup off the stack and poured himself a dose of liquid reinforcement. “I tried to reach the chief engineer, but he was busy with a water leak in the galley.” Jenny took another sip of her coffee, as did Paul. “I’ll see what he thinks and get back to you. Maybe we can put reflective tape on them for now.”

“If we are already receiving complaints, we need to put out a warning. Please have the press staff print something out for the stewards to place in each cabin. I don’t want anyone to get injured.”

“Sure thing.” Paul saluted and walked away, then quickly returned. “I almost forgot the second issue.”

“Let’s hear it.”

“We have a family from California complaining that their cabin windows don’t open. They have three cabins total and expected ‘ocean view’ to involve open windows. Guest services has explained that the panes are for viewing and were not advertised as movable. But they aren’t happy.”

"That's odd," Jenny replied. "Most travel professionals understand the designs of the cabin categories. Please find out who they are and offer them a breakfast with me toward the end of the week. We are at capacity this week, so moving them to another room is impossible."

"On it!" Paul walked toward the coffee station and refilled his cup before he left the bridge.

Next, the human resources manager, Peggy Davis, walked toward Jenny. "We are fully staffed on board. That was quite a feat."

"Very good work, Peggy," Jenny commended. "So, what's the bad news?"

"Ha! You know this job all too well. Yes, we do have a little bad news. Treasure Island and Cutter Cay are still understaffed. They are fine on the days that *Fortune* and *Plunder* are docked, but are shorthanded on the Bounty days."

"How shorthanded?"

"A little." Peggy twirled some of her red hair with her left hand. "We have enough lifeguards and food service crew on both islands. We need more sanitation and ground crew but can make do for now. The line will continue interviewing for island staff this week and next. My concern is the shark scrubbers. As of today, we have no scrubbers on either of the two islands."

Local teenagers were hired as shark scrubbers to run jet skis near the beaches when ships were in port. The presence of the loud vessels warded off resident reef sharks. Some of the teens liked to show off for visitors, but most were professional and took care to protect the beaches and the visitors.

"What are our options?" Jenny asked.

"I'm hoping to hear that the line has found a few people before Tuesday. But if they haven't, we can put out red flags to advise against swimming in the ocean. Or even double red flags to completely forbid swimming."

"I don't like that sort of publicity," Jenny started. "But we must think of the passengers' safety. The sharks are running this time of year."

"Another thought is to pull one lifeguard and a bathroom attendant from each beach and put them on the jet skis. Just until we can hire a few more people."

Jenny quickly weighed her options. "Let's plan on putting out the double red flags for now. Please report back to me tomorrow afternoon before we make a final decision. I hope the line can find some new employees in the next twenty-four hours. Is that all?"

"Yep," Peggy replied with a smile. "That is all I have to report."

As Peggy was walking away, Cruise Director Shawna Thames walked up. "Would you believe that I have no issues to report?"

Jenny's eyes widened. "No."

"Ha!" Shawna laughed. "We are in good shape for the entertainment. The show talent is thoroughly prepared, and the activities are running smoothly for now. Everything looks good for the week."

"Well, that's nice to hear," Jenny added as she finished her coffee.

"If you have time, I'd love for you to greet the crowd at the ice rink. Show starts at nine o'clock tonight."

Jenny scanned the bridge. "Operations are calm for now. I'll be there. Can't miss the beginning of our very first show."

"Great. I'll meet you backstage at ten minutes to nine and will go out first to introduce you," Shawna said with a smile. "You are much calmer than Captain Barone, you know."

"Don't be so sure about that."

Jenny met briefly with the chief engineer, the purser, and two members of the engine department. Thankfully, none had any major issues to report. The ship was performing perfectly, and the passengers seemed to be enjoying its maiden voyage. According to the purser, the first clue was already sending dozens of treasure hunters to the medical facility.

The final briefing was from Doctor Cruz. "We are well-stocked and ready, Captain."

Jenny sighed. "That's good to hear."

"Please try to keep the ship from rocking too much. We only have a thousand barf bags. The rest should be in Miami when we return."

Jenny laughed. "I will try my best."

"Seriously," the doctor added. "Everything looks great. All but one of the nurses have plenty of seaside experience. The new one is a little shy but will be fine."

"Good to hear. Some of our older passengers are having trouble managing the thresholds to the lavatories. Paul is dealing with it. You may want to check with him to offer advice."

"Will do." Doctor Cruz left promptly. Jenny had a few hours to monitor the ship's progress before her next obligation. She would be eating at the Captain's Table tonight. Each week, random guests were invited to dine with the ship's leader on embarkation days. They would ask plenty of questions and would most certainly want to hear about the passengers who went overboard on *Golden Fortune* when

Jenny was staff captain. Tomorrow she would join the youth group for their formal meal. Jenny quickly texted Zach to see how he was doing. He wrote back immediately. As always, he was "okey dokey."

The luggage finally arrived, and Joe sat watching as Evie unpacked his and Jonah's suitcases. She wasn't exactly a "mother hen," but she did seem to appreciate order and organization. Elle was setting up her cabin, while Joe wondered how God would use Evie's tidy nature for His kingdom in the future.

As he was quietly pondering, his cell phone buzzed, and his cabin phone rang at the same time. Without much thought, he answered the landline phone. Was a plugged-in phone at sea still called a landline?

"Hello?" Joe answered and was surprised that Evie didn't even seem to notice that the phone rang. She kept unpacking.

"Hey, Joe. This is Jenny. I was looking over the dinner assignments and noticed that our kids have been assigned seats at tonight's dinner."

"Oh, Jonah said that they were going to eat at the buffet tonight."

"Yeah. That's what Zach told me. But I think it would be nice for them to eat in the dining room tonight. I'm sure you remember that the line offers an opportunity to be matched with random passengers on the first night."

"I do. Elle, Evie, and I are participating." Evie looked up when she heard her name. She clearly had his "selective hearing" ability.

"Well, the kids are randomly assigned with other teenagers, either children of the media or the foster kids from Miami. I think it would be great for them to meet some other youth at dinner. I apologize for not catching this earlier."

"I agree that it's a great idea," Joe declared. "And no need to apologize. The kids are already having a blast. My Evie is having a lot of fun unpacking our things."

"Ha! She's going to be an accountant one day. You just watch."

"Thanks for the heads-up. I will figure out how to send out a blast chat to everyone and let them know that we'd like them to hit the dining room tonight. Do they just show up?"

"Yep," Jenny answered. "Seven o'clock. The maître d's will show them to their tables. They will have fun. Plus, the galley is preparing their famous lasagna tonight. You don't want to miss that."

"Sounds good! One more question . . ."

"Sure."

"Who's driving the ship while you are talking to me?"

"Very funny. You aren't the first one to ask me that today. Say hi to Elle for me."

"Will do."

When Joe hung up the phone, he watched Evie arranging the four bottles of sunscreen on a shelf in order of size. He marveled at the variety of personalities that God created. He took out his cell phone and confirmed for the tenth time that it was in airplane mode. He noticed a recent email message from Dean Katz: *Just wanted to let you know that all three of your fall classes have filled during early registration. Two have students on the waiting lists.*

Joe chose to not respond to the dean's comments. Was God telling him to teach those classes? They filled quickly. That must be a sign. But they weren't officially his yet. So maybe it wasn't a sign. Joe needed to talk to Elle soon. Perhaps there would be time after dinner. For now, he needed to let his current students know that the dining room awaited their presence tonight.

CHAPTER FIVE

"Did you get the message from my dad?" Jonah asked his friends. Josh watched as the others checked their phones. "He wants us to eat in the dining room tonight. Something about meeting other teens. What do you think?"

"Sounds lame, but I'm in," Zach replied as he was drying off. Six of the boys had been swimming in the large pool and were already thinking about their next meal.

"I'm in too," Hunter added. "Looks like we just have to wear nice shorts and shirts. That's not too bad." Josh nodded with Hunter in agreement.

The group messaged some of the girls, and all agreed to meet at the elevators at 6:45. It appeared that their entire church group would be eating at the upper level of the Galley dining room at 7:00.

Back at their cabin, Josh and Ryan finished unpacking their luggage. Both agreed that living out of suitcase for a week would not be a burden. But unpacking and storing their empty baggage under the beds did add much-needed space to the cabin.

"We've got a few minutes till dinner," Ryan announced as he sat in the desk chair. "What shall we do?"

"I dunno. It's weird not having anything that we have to do." Josh lay back on his bed and tossed a throw pillow repeatedly in the air.

"Yeah. It is weird. No baseball practice. No homework. No chores." Ryan took out his phone. "Let's go through the app and put some stuff in our calendar." Josh liked the idea, so Ryan began listing activities. "Flamingo Bingo?"

"Nope," Josh snickered.

"The prom is tomorrow night. I'll mark that."

"Sounds good."

"Ooh, how about a movie on the top deck? There are action movies playing on Tuesday and Thursday nights."

Josh put his fist in the air. "Book 'em!"

Ryan continued his search. "What about ice skating?"

"Maybe. Put it down just in case."

"Pickleball?"

"No."

"Belly flop contest?"

"No."

"Ballroom dancing?"

"Double no!"

"Ooh, cannon practice on Friday. What could that be?"

Josh sat up. "Cannon practice? Do you think we can fire real cannons?"

"I don't know. The descriptions says we will 'learn how to shoot like a pirate.' Let's check that out." Josh added the cannon practice to their virtual schedule. "Mind if I take a shower first?"

"Nah," Josh replied. "Go ahead. I'm gonna go back out on the balcony till you're done."

Josh walked to the balcony door and lifted the heavy handle to pull it open. Immediately, he heard the ocean rushing by the ship. They were traveling faster than he had realized.

Pulling one of the two chairs to face the railing, Josh sat and stared at the sea. He had never seen that color of blue before. It wasn't turquoise blue like the color on the Miami Dolphins uniforms. It was more like the color of the Buffalo Bills. Josh scanned the horizon for shark fins but saw nothing but waves. An endless sea of waves. Years later, he would still remember the first time he was alone with the ocean. It was a humbling feeling.

"How did you make all of this, God?" Josh asked aloud. For the first time, he felt very small. But he also felt close to God. The vast sea demonstrated how out of control people really are. It was endless. And it had the control.

Watch and pray.

Josh looked around but did not see Ryan. Who could have said that? Was someone speaking to him? He sat still for a while and waited to hear more words. But they did not come.

Watch and pray? What could that mean? Josh decided to keep the message to himself for now. It was probably the wind making a weird noise. But he couldn't deny that being alone with the ocean made him feel somewhat closer to God. It was like the noise from the city and his friends wasn't blocking His messages. He remembered hearing that Jesus took time to get away and pray by Himself. This must be what it was like.

Feeling like he had matured in ten minutes on the balcony, Josh went back into the cabin. He could hear Ryan fumbling around in the bathroom, so he found some shorts and a shirt for dinner and waited for Ryan to finish. He knew deep down inside that the "watch and pray" message was real.

I'm not sure what to pray about, but I will be watching, Lord. Please show me what I need to see.

"Next!" Ryan marched out of the bathroom wearing dinner clothes and shaking his wet hair.

"Right this way, ladies." The maître d escorted Marissa, Bettina, Toni, and Pam to table number 364. He announced that the remaining guests should be arriving soon. Marissa couldn't believe how beautiful the dining room looked. The entire area was crisp and silvery. Battery-operated candles were glowing in frosted glasses at the center of each table. Relaxing jazz music was playing at a pleasant volume. And the aroma of oregano wafted throughout the entire dining area. For a moment, she missed Gene. But she remembered that he wouldn't be very comfortable in this elegant environment. He much preferred a sawdust-on-the-ground steak restaurant. But he would have happily escorted his wife to the Galley dining room just to see her smile, and Marissa appreciated that.

"So how does this work?" Pam was obviously not as impressed with the dining room grandeur as Marissa was. "Do we just sit where they tell us?"

"The cruise line likes to have guests mingle on the first night," Bettina explained. "You can opt out, but most people choose to socialize with new people. I think it's fun."

"Me too," Toni squealed. "We get to meet four new people tonight. Lena told me that Pastor Joe asked them to participate too. She and Macy are hoping to meet some girls their age."

"Ha!" Pam sputtered. "Lauren is hoping to meet a *boy* her age." The women laughed, and for a moment Marissa got a knot in her stomach. Josh would have more freedom this week than he has ever had. She hadn't thought about strange girls seducing him on the ship. Then she smiled to herself. Her imagination was starting to write an episode of *Love Boat* with her son as the lead. Josh had a good head on his shoulders. And he wouldn't jeopardize his future for a girl he met on a senior trip. She and Gene had prayed for his adult life. God's protection wouldn't stop on a modern-day pirate ship.

"Hi!" A high-pitched squeal startled Marissa out of her thoughts. Four women looking surprisingly like her group were led to their table.

"You must be our dates for the night." The Pam look-alike laughed to herself and then snorted in amusement. Bettina looked at Marissa and opened her eyes wide. Marissa couldn't help but smile.

The women found their seats and an awkward silence fell upon the table. Bettina's double spoke first. "Well, I'll state the obvious. We've entered the Twilight Zone. This ship is haunted, and the ghost pirates have secretly gathered us together. It's like a *Scooby Doo* mystery."

"What are you talking about, Gina?" Pam's double asked.

"Look around. We've been cloned."

The eight women were silent for a full ten seconds before all of them began laughing. Then they began talking at once.

"I'm Gina."

"Who are you?"

"This is weird."

Finally, Toni shushed the table and asked for each woman to introduce herself. A tall waiter managed to take their drink orders during the introductions.

"I'll start," Gina announced. "I'm Gina. These are my friends. We are all travel agents from Atlanta. Sam and I work together. We know the others from trade shows."

"Tell them about your daughter," Sam added.

"Yikes! I want these women to like me," Gina said. When no one spoke, she finished the thought. "My daughter Leigh tried to dye her hair on her own last week, and it turned out tomato red—and super frizzy. She looks like Ronald McDonald. The funny part is that she is a chemistry major at Tech. And she couldn't mix the chemicals correctly." Sam laughed harder than appropriate. "Okay. I've told you one embarrassing thing about myself. The rest of you have to fess up."

"I guess I'm next," Sam stopped laughing and spoke. "I am Sam. And my husband, Dean, is being investigated by the FBI for fraud." Bettina spit out the water she was sipping. "Oh, it's okay. He says he's innocent. He just can't leave the country for a while. I'm fine with that. After this cruise, Gina and I are going to Italy for ten days. Dean can watch the dogs while I'm gone."

"I'm Marley," a shy woman said, who looked very much like Marissa. "This is my first cruise. I've flown on planes but haven't sailed yet. I'm a little nervous about it, to be honest. Can that be my embarrassing thing?" The group nodded and looked toward the next woman.

"My name is Alex."

"Hi, twin," Toni said with a huge smile.

"I think I'm gonna like you," Alex returned. "Maybe we are long, lost sisters who were separated at birth. My mom did grow up in the seventies. Anything could have happened."

"Wouldn't that be cool?" Toni asked as she clasped her hands together.

Mimicking her twin, Alex held her hands together too. "It would!"

"I'm sorry," Toni said. "Finish your introduction, sis."

"Sure. I'm Alex, and I lost eighty-five pounds last year. The beet diet. My hair is still falling out, and I have short-term memory problems. But I'm happy. And a funny story is that I keep my *big* picture on the online dating sites. I want the men to be shocked when they see me in person."

Once again, the table grew quiet. Marissa was overwhelmed by the brutal honesty of the new women. She wondered if this must be what it would be like to live in a college dormitory or sorority house. Hormonal oversharing. As she was judging, she felt a conviction to listen to the women. They weren't bragging or criticizing. They were being open and transparent. If Marissa were honest with herself, the introductions were refreshing. Just women being themselves.

Bettina was next. "I'm Bettina. Gina's twin. We are all parents in a church youth group invited to attend this cruise. The captain is one of the parents."

"Get back!" Gina squealed. "You know Jenny Lu?"

"We do," Bettina responded. "She's super nice. We can introduce her sometime."

"Yes!" Sam added. "We want to meet her."

"You're next." Bettina pointed to Marissa.

"No, no," Gina admonished. "You didn't tell us something embarrassing."

"I was hoping that you hadn't noticed. I'm not sure what to share." Bettina stared at the ceiling. "Okay. I had an imaginary friend until my senior year in college." The group stared at Bettina at once. "Her name was Polly, and I talked to her all the time. When I started dating my now-husband, I kept her a secret. Eventually, I stopped talking to her."

"Wow, that's sad," Alex said as she put her arm around Bettina.

"No, it's okay," Bettina shared. "I haven't thought about her for a long time."

Alex removed her arm. "Well, it sounds to me that your husband killed your best friend. I don't like him now." After a second, Alex laughed. The rest of the table joined her.

Marissa was next. And she wanted to crawl under the table. "I'm Marissa. My husband is Gene, and my son is Josh. I don't have much else to say." Marley nodded in solidarity.

"We'll wait," Gina added rudely.

Marissa mentally scanned her life to think of one thing to share but came up blank.

"Did your husband happen to kill your best friend?" Gina asked.

Marissa looked at her lap. "Yes, he did." Gina's eyes widened. "I ditched my best friend to take Gene to the prom, and we haven't spoken since." The table again quieted. Marissa looked at Marley. "And this is my first cruise too." Marley was now smiling all the way to her eyes.

Pam shared that she had a shoe addiction. Over one hundred pairs! And Toni embarrassed herself by announcing that she cannot tell the Kardashian's apart. Marissa thought she might reveal that she and her husband were separated, but understood when she did not.

The waiter arrived to take the women's orders but discovered they hadn't looked at the menus yet. He promised to return in *cinco minutos*.

"The lasagna is always good," Bettina offered.

"I was hoping to find a beet salad but will go with the lasagna instead," Alex announced.

"Good choice," Pam added. "Let's all get the lasagna." Marissa was relieved because she was hungry and did not want to be shamed into eating celery sticks for supper.

The waiter took their orders and encouraged the ladies to order two desserts. Everyone but Alex obliged.

"Cheesecake *and* apple pie," Pam said with a clap of her hands. "My shorts aren't going to fit by Wednesday."

"No kidding," Sam agreed.

Marissa didn't mind the table conversation. She would have preferred to eat alone. But the women were interesting. And the uncanny resemblances couldn't be a mere coincidence. How could four women look so much like four other women? Gina asked the waiter to take a group picture, and Marissa made an effort to ask for a copy to be sent to her phone. She couldn't wait to show Gene their "cruise clones."

After dessert, no one opted for coffee or tea. The Atlanta group had reservations for *Charlie Tuna* that night, while the Miami group was scheduled to attend the *Frozen Flashback* ice-skating show. A decision was made to meet the next morning on the pool deck. Marissa noticed a slight flinch by Marley. The woman did not want to be enveloped by the group either. Marissa guessed that she brought a stack of books too.

As the octet dispersed, Marissa falsely agreed to meet the next day. She made a mental note to come up with a plan to avoid the extended socializing. Of course, she had no legitimate reason to be withdrawn. The others were friendly and inviting. She realized that she was being a snob but had no plans to change. Not this week.

Josh, Ryan, Jonah, and Zach quietly waited to be seated for dinner. Ryan broke the ice. "What if we get to sit with four supermodels?"

"Really, Ryan?" Jonah chuckled. "Supermodels?"

"It could happen." Ryan hoped.

The maître d finally led the boys to their table near the back of the dining room. Josh gaped at fancy table settings and the huge chandelier hanging from the center of the ceiling. He also noticed Ronnie eating with Mr. Morgan near the port side of the ship. They were at a table of military veterans.

"You were right, Ryan," Zach announced. "We *are* eating with supermodels." Josh noticed that four girls were already seated at their table. They smiled quietly as the boys were seated.

"Hi, ladies, ole chaps," Ryan said with a weak British accent. The entire table burst into laughter. "Okay. I'm not from England. We're from Miami. How about you?"

"I'm Lizzy. And I'm from Jacksonville, Florida. This is my sister, Fifi. Our mom is a travel agent. She and my dad are eating at the steak restaurant right now."

"Pleased to make your acquaintance, Lizzy." Ryan made the group laugh again by attempting a British accent. Before the next introduction, a waiter took the drink and food orders. The boys hastily reviewed their menus and ordered.

"I'm Winnie from Alabama. I'm on this trip with my parents. My brother and sister are working this week, so it's just me. My mom is a writer and is starting a travel blog. She went on *Plunder* last year with my sister and caught the cruising bug." Winnie shared that she had just graduated high school and was hoping to become a teacher.

"And I'm Makenzi. I just graduated too. My parents own a travel agency in Tate, Alabama. And my mom has already texted me a million times since I sat down. She thinks I will be kidnapped or fall overboard. And she's just at the table over there."

"It's not so bad," Lizzy said softly.

"What do you mean?" Jonah asked.

"She fell overboard on *Golden Fortune*!" Fifi exclaimed. "It was on the news."

"That was you?" Zach asked, amazed.

"Yeah, and my mom. And some other guy. They got us out pretty quickly, so it wasn't that bad."

"My mom was the staff captain," Zach added. "She told me all about it. Captain Barone was a hero. And your mom saved your lives."

"Your mom is Jenny?" Lizzy asked.

"Yep," Zach said with a twinkle in his eyes. "The famous Jenny Lu."

"I would love to see her."

"That can be arranged." Zach pointed to a long table near the back of the room. "She's right over there. We can say hi when we're done eating." Lizzy and Fifi pretended to shake hands with Zach to confirm the plan.

The boys made their introductions and shared that they were on a senior trip with their church youth group. Josh liked the way that Winnie spoke. She told everyone up front that she wanted to somehow work for God. She didn't want to work for money. The noble concept drew him in.

After some discussion about plans for the upcoming fall, Jonah asked if the girls would be attending the prom the next night. All but Fifi would be. Her name was actually Sofia, and she was only ten.

"I'd love to see you there," Josh said to Winnie.

"Geez, Josh," Zach blurted. "She just met you." Josh wanted to kick Zach under the table but restrained himself. For some reason, he wanted to spend more time with Winnie.

Winnie rolled her eyes and looked at Josh. "That would be nice. Save a few dances for me." For the rest of the night, Josh's mind was on the girl with the crystal-clear soul.

Dinner at the captain's table was never the same week to week. Rather than offer the spots at a hefty price, Jewel Cruise Line chose the diners randomly. So Jenny never knew what to expect. For her first captain's meal, she was dining with newlyweds from Nashville, four Vietnam veterans, and a swarmy YouTube travel reporter. The newlyweds spoke very little throughout the meal. Apparently, they worked for a travel booking site and met one year ago. The wedding was at a working dairy farm, and the twenty-four attendants formed a human pyramid before the couple left the reception. Jenny stopped discussing the ship with them when she realized they were more interested in each other than the workings of a modern-day cruise ship.

The veterans, however, were riveted with her description of the satellite navigation and multifaceted communication system onboard *Bounty*. She promised them a tour of the bridge and explained four times how sensitive the ship's radar system could be.

"Can you really spot a single fish in icy water at night?" retired Sgt. Jack Gallow asked.

"We sure can," Jenny said proudly. "But we usually look for larger objects. Like whales or icebergs." The group laughed and gave their orders to the cheerful waitress.

"I recommend the lasagna," Jenny offered. "It is the best on any ocean." The newlyweds chose the rosemary chicken, but the rest of the guests went with the legendary lasagna.

Jack revisited the radar topic. "I was a tunnel rat in Vietnam."

"So was I," Sgt. Robert Thomas replied. "Củ Chi tunnels."

"Small world," Jack remarked. "I ran in the Vinh Mốc tunnels. We ran important missions, but man were those caves dangerous." Robert smiled and nodded in agreement. "The Củ Chi tunnels ran for thousands of miles and mostly hid the enemy; the Vinh Mốc system farther north was hand dug by the villagers as safe housing during the bombings. Some were built with booby traps like spikes and snakes, and most had concealed entrances."

"Booby traps?" Jenny asked.

Jack leaned forward in his seat. "You bet. They would place camouflaged boxes of scorpions and snakes near the entrances to prevent us from traveling deep within the tunnels." The newlywed wife put a hand over her mouth.

The YouTube reporter became interested in Jack's stories. "They dug the tunnels themselves?"

"Yep," Jack confirmed. "Limestone can be dug like that. They used simple tools to create an elaborate community network. We knew they were sending supplies to the north and dropped thousands of tons of bombs on them. But every single person in the Vinh Mốc tunnel survived the bombs."

Robert spoke up. "The Củ Chi was much bigger than that. Did you know we even built a base over their tunnels and didn't know it? When we got GPR, we could map the tunnels a little better."

"GPR?" the reporter asked.

"Ground penetrating radar," Robert explained. "Basically, electromagnetic radiation that reaches below the surface of the ground."

Jack looked at Jenny. "So, you can see that we old geezers are interested in your modern radar. Ours was very limited sixty years ago."

Jenny's eyes widened. "Of course, I would love to show you our navigation system. And I would love to hear more about the tunnels. I know very little about all of that. How about Wednesday morning? That's a sea day, so I won't be tied up with docking. I can show you our UAV drone. Unmanned ariel vehicle. Our chief engineer is trained to deploy it if we need ariel surveillance."

All four of the veterans nodded with excitement. "Can I come too?" the reporter asked. Reluctantly, Jenny agreed and offered for the newlyweds to visit the bridge as well.

When the food arrived, the travel reporter took pictures of everything.

"Which channel do you work for?" Jenny asked.

"I'm Flying Fred. You can find me on YouTube. I'd love to interview you, doll. My viewers would flip out."

Jenny smiled politely. "We'll see if there is time on Wednesday."

"No worries, J-Lu. I have all day. The lighting will be great up there, and my voice carries farther in a smaller environment, like the ship's bridge."

"I'm not sure that would be a good idea." Jenny regretted her response when she saw Fred's shoulders droop. But she knew that he would want more than a quick interview. His type would expect a complete tour and inside information. It was better for her to nip his request in the bud before he began planning a full production.

When the dessert arrived, talk returned to the war. One of the veterans had served in the Navy and was knocked overboard an aircraft carrier when an oxygen canister exploded. It took two hours for him to be rescued, and he joked that he would never stand near the railing again.

Jenny peppered the soldiers with questions about combat and leadership. She was especially interested in their limited food choices overseas. All agreed that Chiclets gum was a treat in the rations and that they still prefer to drink their water lukewarm. Even the newlyweds listened to Jack's story about training with live tigers. "You learn to survive anything with a hungry tiger staring you down."

As Jenny was finishing her cheesecake, Zach walked up with two girls. "Hi, Mom. Can you talk?"

"Of course, honey. How are you doing?"

"We're having a great time. I wanted you to meet Lizzy and Fifi. They were at our dinner table."

"Oh, my goodness! I remember you!" Jenny stood and hugged Lizzy. "How are you doing, sweetie?"

"I'm good. Fifi and I got adopted, and we live in Jacksonville. Our mom is on the ship too. We're supposed to meet her and our dad at the ice-skating rink. I'm sure she would like to see you."

Jenny grinned. "I will make a point to track her down. I think about you a lot. God worked a miracle that night to keep all of you safe." Fifi gave Jenny a hug and declared that she was going to be a sea captain when she grew up.

"I would love to show you the ropes, young lady." Jenny hugged Zach and made him promise to check in with Pastor Joe at eleven o'clock. Jenny wouldn't be up that late, and she asked Zack to be in their cabin by midnight.

"Aye, aye, Captain!"

After dinner, Jenny returned to the bridge to monitor the ship's progress. So far, the vessel was performing perfectly. They were crawling at six knots to reach Cutter Cay on Tuesday morning. The weather forecast called for clear skies and calm seas for the entire week. Jenny couldn't ask for better conditions for *Bounty's* inaugural sailing. Thankfully, the week should be uneventful and enjoyable for everyone.

Joe escorted Elle and Evie to the dining room. Both girls were apprehensive about dining with strangers, but Joe reassured them that the meal would be fun. They would have a chance to make new friends and were under no obligation to remain friends once the dinner ended. Plus, the teenagers were making new friends, so they could too.

When they arrived at their table, a family of five was already seated. The father stood and shook Joe's hand. "We're the Munsons from Fort Lauderdale. I'm Dave, and this is my wife, Kate. Our girls are Mary, Breezy, and Stevie." Joe immediately wondered if the younger two children were foster children because they did not look at all like the older girl, who resembled their mother.

"Nice to meet you, Dave. I'm Joe. This is Elle. Our daughter is Evie, and we are from Miami. I am the youth pastor at Holy Cross Church, and we have two dozen recently graduated seniors on this trip."

Kate smiled in amazement. "That's awesome! We visited that church when we first moved to South Florida. Dave is a professor of optometry at Nova Southeastern."

This time Elle smiled. "That's awesome! I always thought that being a college professor would be fun."

"Best job in the world," Dave declared. "I've been in college for thirty years."

Joe laughed at the joke and decided that God was sending him reassurance with Dave and Elle's comments. He must want him to take the teaching job. He couldn't wait to tell Elle about the offer and the assurance from God.

The waiter took their orders, and the adults discussed modern-day parenting. Dave and Kate were amazed that Joe was leading a youth group trip on the ship and that the family knew Jenny Lu. Evie and Stevie talked nonstop and asked their parents if they could be "cruise besties." The adults agreed, although they didn't know for sure what the designation entailed.

The adults enjoyed the famous lasagna, while three of the children opted for the treasure chest mac-n-cheese. Breezy had a serious allergy to dairy, so she ate chicken fingers and tater barrels.

"Have you cruised before?" Dave asked.

"Nope," Joe answered. "This is our first time out to sea. And our first time on a real pirate ship." Stevie's eyes widened.

"He's joking," Evie said. "He does that a lot. You'll get used to it."

"Anyhoo," Joe continued, "what about you?"

"We've sailed on some small boats," Kate answered. "But nothing like this. Did you see the full-service spa? I can't believe a place like that is on a ship."

"Or the shopping mall area," Elle added. "Just amazing."

After dessert, the entire group went to see *Charlie Tuna* together. Jenny welcomed the crowd before the show and encouraged everyone to enjoy the other shows throughout the week.

Evie and Stevie sat next to each other and laughed every time the puppy acted silly. At one point, the dog needed help from the audience with barking to alert the captain of the ship. All four of the girls added barks and howls to the audience's attempts. The children begged their parents to go to the soda shop afterwards, and the parents quickly agreed. Joe danced with the four girls to jukebox music and eventually declared that he was "knackered." The mothers made plans to meet at the Parrot Perch in the morning.

"That was fun!" Evie announced as the family returned to Joe's cabin. She and Elle said goodnight and retired to their neighboring room. As Joe waited for Jonah and Zach to check in, he realized that he never spoke with Elle about the teaching position. Not wanting to wake her, he made a promise to himself that he would tell her at breakfast. The time to accept was running out, and he really needed to discuss the offer with his wife.

Before he went to sleep, Joe found the webpage for Faith Community College on his phone. He read the publicity blurbs about the programs and scanned pictures of the campus. Everything about the college was appealing. The eager students. The picturesque landscaping. The modern academics. Joe began imagining himself teaching in front of a classroom but forced himself to flash back to reality.

Don't get ahead of yourself, Joe. You still need to talk with Elle.

At precisely eleven o'clock, Jonah messaged that he and some of the guys were hanging out at the arcade. He would be coming to the cabin soon. A few minutes later, Zach messaged his "okey dokey." After receiving the messages, Joe fell asleep quickly. Everyone was on the ship, safe and accounted for today. Only six more check-ins to go.

CHAPTER SIX

Monday, June 15
Sea Day

Marissa awoke and was confused to see that the room was darker than usual and that she was in a smaller bed. She quickly remembered that she was sailing on *Buccaneer Bounty*. And she was surprised to realize that she had slept amazingly well. Bettina was still asleep, so Marissa grabbed some comfortable clothes from a drawer and rushed to take a shower.

The ice-skating show last night was adorable. The skaters were obviously talented, and Marissa found herself snapping a few photos to show Gene when she got home. Jenny greeted the crowd before the show started, and she looked glamorous and powerful in her uniform and heels.

The other women went to the dance hall after the show, but Marissa excused herself to her cabin. She planned to sit on the balcony and talk with God but didn't have the courage to step out there in the darkness. Instead, she readied for bed and read a few chapters in her book. Jonah sent a message from Josh right at eleven o'clock. Before she fell asleep, Marissa typed an email message to Gene letting him know that she and Josh were alive and well. Remarkably, he wrote back in less than a minute. Hearing from him so quickly made him seem closer and not a hundred miles away. She was homesick but admitted to herself that she was having fun.

Bettina was awake when Marissa left the bathroom. She dressed quickly, and the two were eager to head out for their first breakfast at sea. Marissa envied Bettina's ability to look so gorgeous that quickly.

"We forgot about the clue," Bettina said. "Toni said it has something to do with the medical area."

"I think that's right," Marissa added. "Another word for pier is *dock*. Maybe we can go by the medical facility after breakfast. It's on Deck Five."

"Look at you figuring the ship out. Good job! I say we go by there *before* breakfast."

Marissa agreed, and the women made their way to the medical facility. They searched the area and were about to give up when Marissa noticed writing beneath Dr. Cruz's nameplate.

"It says, 'Doc hopes that you stay well and dear. If not, get stronger when Monday gets here.'"

"The gym!" Bettina announced excitedly. "It must be the gym. Should we go now? Or eat first?"

"That's on Deck Eleven. I guess we could go now before it gets too crowded." The two boarded an elevator and traveled to the gym.

"Where do we start?" Bettina asked as she exited the elevator. "This place is huge."

"Let's walk around and look for anything obvious. That shouldn't take very long."

"Good idea, roomie." Bettina put her arm around Marissa. "I'm having the time of my life right now. God knew that I needed some friends. Jason doesn't talk to me much these days. He's so tied up with work. I needed someone to bond with. Maybe we can have lunch or something when we get back home. Do you like to shop?"

"Not really." Marissa instinctively avoided Bettina's offer of friendship. That was her usual response. But Bettina was a very nice person. Not like Marissa had expected. Had stereotyped. Perhaps it wouldn't hurt to have a friend back home. One who didn't hate her for bringing Gene to the prom. "But I like to eat lunch."

The women scoured the gym. Marissa noticed other people looking all around the equipment and classroom. Once again, the two were about to give up when Marissa noticed something. "Look at that."

"What?" Bettina asked.

"That picture of a flag." Marissa was discretely pointing at a laminated photo of a red flag on a stick. It was triangular, and the stick was standing in sand. "It is a clue?"

Bettina bent her knees awkwardly to catch a glimpse of the picture without drawing attention to herself. Marissa couldn't help but laugh at her feeble acrobatics. "It must be a clue. What else could it be?"

"I don't know."

"Well, I think it's our next clue. There's no other reason for a red flag to be taped to a treadmill." Marissa took out her phone and pretended to drop it on the floor near the marked treadmill. "My phone! I dropped it!" Others in the gym saw the commotion and quickly ignored her. Marissa began laughing at the absurdity of the situation and ran out of the gym before anyone figured out what Bettina was doing.

After a minute, her friend ran through the gym doors. "Got it! I took a picture without anyone else noticing." Marissa didn't have the heart to tell Bettina that behind her a group had gathered around the treadmill.

"You did great. Let's see the picture."

Bettina opened her phone and sighed when she discovered the picture was blurry and halfway covered by her hand. "Well, I'll never be a spy."

Marissa put her arm around Bettina—her new friend—and walked toward the elevator. "It's perfect. The picture is perfect."

The women briefly considered eating breakfast in the formal dining room, but both hoped to see their sons, so they made their way to Blackbeard's Fortress buffet. Thankfully, the area wasn't crowded yet, and they were able to score a table next to a window. Marissa was still amazed at the vastness of the ocean just miles from home.

After gathering French toast and fruit for breakfast, Marissa opted for a fancy hot chocolate to go with it. She was enjoying her cocoa while Bettina was waiting for a freshly made omelet when a man with a handheld camera approached her. He was talking, but not at her.

"Here we have a middle-of-the-road passenger enjoying breakfast." He moved his camera closer to Marissa. "This is the fluffy French toast and assorted fruit. Ma'am, what are you drinking?"

Marissa stared blankly. She wasn't sure what to say.

"I'm gonna go ahead and say that this woman is drinking a specialty coffee, possibly some sort of latte. Notice the salt and pepper shakers. Every table is appointed with one of each." The man was about to move on when Bettina arrived.

"Ooh!" Bettina squealed. "What are you filming?"

The man stopped filming. "Good morning. I am Flying Fred, and I am laying down some footage of early morning sights."

Bettina placed her plate on the table and fluffed her hair. "Which network?"

"I have my own YouTube channel," Fred answered. "Flying Fred's Fantastic Journeys."

Bettina's shoulders sank. "Oh. Thank you, but we have something important to discuss. If you would please excuse us."

Fred took the hint and moved on to film a napkin dispenser.

"Well, that was exciting," Bettina admitted. "I thought for a second we had been discovered." She laughed, and Marissa joined her.

"I froze and didn't say a word."

"What a hoot! I'll ask Ryan to look for us on YouTube when we get home. Your French toast might be famous someday."

Joe woke to banging on the adjoining door in his cabin. "Are you up? It's time for breakfast!" Evie was clearly ready to start her day.

"Not yet," Joe replied. "We're still sleeping." He glanced toward Jonah's bed to confirm that his son had indeed made it back to the cabin last night. "Give me ten minutes."

Trying not to wake Jonah, Joe dressed quickly and knocked on the connecting door. He sent a message to Jonah's phone telling him that he was eating breakfast with Elle and Evie and slipped out quietly. Joe knew better than to wake a teenage boy this early, even on a high-seas adventure cruise.

"I've been up for *hours*, Daddy," Evie exaggerated. "Mom made me wait till seven thirty to knock." Joe whispered "thank you" to Elle, who smiled back.

The adults were surprised to see so many people already dining at Blackbeard's Fortress. Young and old were darting about, filling their plates with pastries, eggs, fruit, and meat. Joe offered to help Evie with her plate while Elle gathered her breakfast.

Joe leaned into his wife before she grabbed a plate. "I have something to talk about."

"Me too," Elle added. And she was off.

Joe helped his daughter fill her plate with pirate waffles, extra syrup, and orange slices. He waited at a table with her until Elle arrived. Then he went straight back to the pirate waffle station to secure his own. A man with a video camera was filming the syrup station, so he added a few slices of bacon while waiting.

Back at the table, Joe noticed Bettina and Marissa sitting at a table near a window. They were talking excitedly and laughing together. He didn't remember ever seeing Marissa laugh like that. She was an upbeat and pleasant person, but she didn't show it on the outside like that. He smiled to himself at the fun the ladies were clearly having this morning.

As he contemplated a second serving of waffles, Elle spoke. "What did you want to talk about?"

"I'd like to wait until Evie isn't around. Maybe when she is playing later."

Elle raised her eyebrows. "Okay . . ."

"How about you? What did you want to talk about?"

"Her dance lessons," Elle started. "Anita said that the rate is going up this fall. Evie will go more often next year, and the price will reflect that. I'm wondering if we should stop dance now before she gets too involved."

Joe thought for a few seconds. "We can handle a little bit more."

"But what about your truck? It won't last forever."

"I may have an answer for that." Joe took his wife's hand. "God may be working this out." Before he could covertly mention the teaching opportunity, Evie spotted Jenny walking into the galley. She excitedly called the captain over.

"Good morning, Waller family," Jenny said cheerfully as she approached their table. "Are you all having fun?"

"I am!" Evie declared. "I made a new bestie at dinner, and we're gonna meet at the splash area after breakfast."

"That's wonderful!" Jenny asked if they had done the mixed dinner, and Elle shared that they had and that it was a wonderful success. The adults were hoping to meet again tonight after dinner for another show and more dancing with the kids. "What about the prom? That's tonight."

"Joe might be there," Elle explained. "At least for the beginning. I will take Evie for ice cream or something like that and get her to bed."

"So who's driving the ship right now?" Joe joked.

"You asked me that yesterday. And we have plenty of officers in the bridge handling our navigation. I'm on a break and am hungry. If you will excuse me, I see some bacon and eggs calling me."

"Of course," Elle offered. "Have a great day." She looked at Joe and back to Jenny. "And thank you for arranging this trip. It feels like a true blessing from God."

"I hope the kids are having fun. Take care."

Josh heard Ryan showering in the bathroom and jumped out of his bed. He had his clothes and shoes on before his friend finished.

"Ready to eat?" Josh asked.

"Always!" Ryan replied.

"Should we go to the gym first? I don't want to miss the clue."

Ryan thought for a few seconds. "Nah. Let's go with the rest of the gang." He checked his phone. Seeing no messages, he assumed that his friends were still asleep. "We can hang out at the buffet till everyone gets there."

Although he was eager to find the next clue, Josh didn't mind waiting. He was excited to see what was available at the all-you-can-eat breakfast buffet. The boys took the stairs two at a time and arrived on Deck Twelve slightly winded. They rushed toward the food and started filling their plates. When he sat down, Josh was surprised to see that his mother was talking excitedly with Ryan's mother. They hadn't even noticed their sons walk by as they discussed something funny.

"What do you think our moms are talking about?" Josh asked when Ryan sat down.

"I would guess shopping," Ryan said.

"Not my mom. She doesn't shop for fun. Do you think they found the next clue?"

"You're really into the hunt, aren't you? We can go to the gym if no one else shows up. I'm a little excited about it too."

Unfortunately for Josh, Hunter and Jandro walked up. The hunt would have to wait.

"Have you seen Zach?" Hunter asked.

"No," Josh answered. "What did he do this time?"

Hunter sat down at the table. "It's more like what *didn't* he do. He didn't go back to his mom's cabin last night. He messaged her that he was staying with me. I saw him write her when we were at the soda shop. We haven't seen him."

"Where do you think he went?" Ryan wondered.

"Who knows," Josh answered. "We can tell Jonah if we think Pastor Joe should know. But I think it's okay for now."

"I say we don't worry about it unless we hear something bad," Hunter suggested. "Wait for us while we get some food." Josh and Ryan waited and ended up getting extra bacon and donuts. They couldn't resist seconds for their first breakfast at sea.

Marissa and Bettina concluded that the next clue would involve a red flag planted at one of the beaches on Cutter Cay the next day. They had no idea what they would find on or near the flag, but until then clue-hunting was on ice.

Bettina "really, really, really" wanted to sunbathe on the top deck, but Marissa really, really, really did not. They decided to people watch for a little while and attend the "Meet the Captain" event in the theater at 11:30. After lunch, Bettina would sunbathe while Marissa napped. The day was a nice compromise for both women.

The two exited Blackbeard's Fortress and strolled toward the front, or bow, of the ship. The rest of Deck Twelve held the Ahoy Kid's Club complete with a mock pirate ship for children to climb over. The women could not enter the club without parental credentials, but they could see some of the facility through floor-to-ceiling windows.

Marissa took pictures of the science lab and was eager to show them to her work family back home. She took a close-up picture of a child's version of a microscope and a sand table with plastic beakers and test tubes. Dr. Schell might want to add something like this to his waiting room.

After visiting the kid's club, the women took the stairs down one flight to Deck Eleven. Bettina put her hand on Marissa's arm. "Let's check out the spa." Marissa agreed, and they walked through a doorway that played harp music as they passed.

"This is heavenly," Marissa noted as she looked over her head.

"It's sort of creepy." Bettina laughed. "The background music sounds like a funeral march, and the harps put it over the top." Both women were laughing now.

A woman dressed in a mint-green uniform with a mint-green beret and black wand walked toward them. "May I assist you?"

"No, thank you," Marissa replied politely. "We are just looking."

"Well, smells are free," the woman noted. "But services will be placed on your account."

Bettina tried to hold in a giggle but failed. "Could you please direct us to the smells?"

Marissa burst out laughing, and the woman "hmphed" before turning on her heels to walk behind a curtain. She tapped the wand on one of her hands as she left.

"I can't believe you said that!" Marissa chuckled. "I would have choked if we were drinking some of that apricot water over there."

"Let's try it. And look for a spray or something with the smell. It *is* divine."

"I agree!" Marissa wafted the air toward her nose. "Sort of like a mermaid."

"Exactly! The spa smells like a mermaid." The women laughed at Bettina's comment.

"And it's totally free," Marissa added with a finger pointed in the air.

At that comment, the women poured some apricot water into sparkly paper cups and walked toward the doors. On the way out, Bettina noticed the gym entrance. She quickly stepped in to see if the clue was still on the treadmill, and she spotted Ryan and Josh with some of the others. She pulled Marissa in too.

"I think they found the clue. Should we ask them about it?"

"Sure," Marissa replied. "Plus, I'd like to check in on Josh."

Josh spotted the picture of a flag first. "Look at this!" Hunter, Ryan, Jandro, and Jonah rushed over. Lena and Macy were on the other side of the gym scouring the yoga room. "That picture looks out of place."

"It does," Jonah agreed excitedly as he took out his phone to snap a picture of the mysterious image. "What is it?"

Jandro squatted down to get close to the clue. "It's a red flag sticking out of the sand. What could that mean?"

"There isn't sand on the ship," Jonah said. "So it has to be on an island. I suppose we should look for that flag tomorrow."

"That could take hours!" Hunter lamented as he sat on one of the exercise bikes.

"Nah," Ryan said. "We can just walk the beach. I bet it won't be far."

"What won't be far?" Lena approached the boys standing near the treadmill. Macy was walking behind her.

"Nothing," Ryan said, laughing. "Nothing at all." He looked at the other boys. "Let's go."

Josh turned to leave with the guys and bumped right into his mother. "Hi, Mom."

"Hi, Josh. How are you doing?"

Josh led his friends toward the exit. The mothers followed. "I'm fine. We just ate breakfast and are checking out the gym."

Marissa winked at her son. "We checked out the gym *before* breakfast. Have fun today. Use lots of sunscreen. And don't forget the big dinner tonight at seven."

"We won't. Love you!"

The last two words stopped Marissa in her tracks. Josh had told her that he loved her at least one thousand times. But rarely in front of his friends. And not unsolicited. She gave him a quick side-hug and told him she loved him too. Bettina hugged Ryan for good measure, and the women left the gym.

"Your moms are cool," Hunter told Josh and Ryan. "My mom would never take a week out for me like this. She's too busy."

Josh never considered his mom to be cool. She was a great mom, but not a *cool* mom. He also never considered that his mom might be making a sacrifice to spend a week on this trip. Didn't she want to take a break from work? He would have to remember to thank her later.

The group, including the girls, decided to get changed into swimsuits and meet up at the pool. No one had heard from Zach yet, but they decided it wasn't necessary to inform Pastor Joe of his disappearance. Jonah agreed to meet but said he would be a little late. He wanted to check in with his family first. "My dad was asleep when I got in last night, and I was asleep when he left for breakfast."

"No problem," Ryan said. "Tell Pastor Joe we said hi. And maybe we'll see Josh's new girlfriend at the pool." He elbowed Josh, who looked confused. "We saw you hit it off with that Winnie girl last night. I think she likes you."

Not knowing how to respond, Josh simply deflected. "C'mon, Ryan. I'm ready for the pool."

On their way to the stairs, the boys peeked in at the walking track. Several fitness-minded people were walking or jogging in the same direction. "Let's walk around," Ryan suggested.

They began walking and stopped at a point where they could admire the view. "There is so much water!" Josh noted.

"No kidding. It's the ocean."

"Yeah. But it goes on forever. And there's no land in site. Or other ships. Just us in the middle of all of this water."

Ryan chuckled. "Sounds like you are writing a country song, Josh."

"Maybe I am," Josh joked as they continued their lap around the track.

When they turned a corner at the end of the ship, they saw Ronnie and Mr. Morgan up ahead. They were walking quietly at a quick pace. Josh instinctively tensed his arms in anticipation of a punch from Ronnie.

"Wanna catch up to them?" Ryan asked.

"No way. Ronnie is always up to no good. I'm glad that Mr. Morgan is keeping a close eye on him. He's even making him exercise this morning."

"Fine by me. I'm looking for cute girls anyways." Josh laughed at Ryan's comment, and the boys finished a lap before taking the stairs down to their cabin.

Joe's phoned buzzed again. He quickly checked what he expected were messages from Dean Katz and was surprised to see that they were not from the dean but were from his father: *We are still praying for the safety of your group. The enemy doesn't let up just because you are on vacation.*

Joe thought the statement on their first morning was a little extreme but agreed. He was thankful that his father and his Sunday school class cared enough about young people to intentionally pray for their safety.

The second message from his father was more personal: *Have you told Elle about the job yet? It's a great opportunity. I can't help but think about the youth and the void you would leave behind though. I'm praying for the decision to be obvious. You are doing a great work now, son.*

Joe was nearly certain he would take the teaching position. There were too many signs pointing him in that direction. And someone would be hired to fill the void when he left Holy Cross. Right now, something miraculous would have to happen for him to change his mind. Of course, he needed to talk with Elle first. And she was currently splashing with Evie in the kiddie area. Stevie and Kate were playing along. Dave had taken Mary and Breezy to the big pool.

Joe had time to think and pray, but his mind felt numb. He had a decision to make, and it had to be made soon. Choice one was to stay at Holy Cross Church. The job was fulfilling, and the youth program was growing. Jonah was finishing the program, and Evie would be joining in a few years. Choice two was more of a challenge. He would have to develop syllabi and lecture notes quickly. He wouldn't be able to attend all the youth events with Evie, and more of his time would be spent away from the family. But the pay would be greater, and he would impact more students on a regular basis. *Pay?*

Joe felt a slight conviction. Was he making this decision solely on the pay increase? Sure, his family budget could us a boost. But salary had never been a priority for Joe and Elle. Following God's lead had always been their number-one goal.

But what about the signs? Did God arrange for him to eat with a college professor last night? And the classes were already full. Someone needed to teach them. *Is that supposed to be me, Lord?*

As Joe was silently praying, Dave sat down in a nearby lounge chair. "I'm officially old. Those girls are wearing me out. And today is only Monday. I'm not sure I will make it the entire week."

Joe laughed. "No judgement here. I've been sitting in my chair the whole time. You are a beast."

"Well, I don't know about beast. But I am having fun. I hope I get a chance to thank the captain for including our family. We know of another foster family who got to sail on *Plunder*, and their kids are still talking about the treasure hunt. The girls were so excited when we were invited to sail *Bounty*. Of course, Breezy started to panic when she saw the ship for the first time. But she challenged herself to 'be brave.' Those kids have been through a lot, and their resilience is truly inspiring."

"So Breezy and Stevie are foster children? I can't imagine what it is like to bring their storms into your home," Joe shared. "I've seen some heartbreaking situations. But we didn't bring them to our kitchen table."

Dave was nodding. "You hit the nail on the head. Our family routine is always disrupted. But those kids are worth it. Their situations are not their fault. I'm thankful that my job gives me a little flexibility to help with parent meetings and doctor visits. Kate still does way more of that than I do."

Seizing the opening, Joe switched the conversation to Dave's profession. "The flexibility sounds great. I have that in the ministry somewhat. But not regularly. What else do you like about teaching? What are the pros and cons, if you don't mind me asking? I would love to hear your thoughts, you know . . . if an opportunity ever comes up for me."

"Well, I meant what I said about it being the greatest job in the world. At least for me. I am fascinated by eye care and vision science. Each semester, I meet a new group of students to teach the field. They keep me young. And I know they will go out and help others using something I taught them. That is fulfilling."

"Sounds a lot like my job," Joe added.

"I guess it does. But to be honest, the students have become less interested in learning over the years. Some of them have a consumer mentality rather than a learner one. I guess that happens in the ministry too. But the grading . . ." Dave shook his head. "The grading never ends. That is probably the worst part about my job. Ha!"

"I never thought about the grading."

"It's brutal," Dave joked. "What about you? What's the worst part of being a youth pastor?"

Joe thought for a few seconds. "I'm not sure. I would expect that the long hours and the pressure of discipling young souls would be a common answer. But those haven't affected me yet. I love my job. It's the salary that is my issue. That sounds so shallow. But we just don't make enough to do what we want with our kids. This is the first vacation we've taken in five years. But God has provided all our needs, so I can't complain. I am truly blessed."

"I hear what you're saying," David responded. "Teaching and the ministry aren't always lucrative professions, but your rewards in Heaven will be worth it."

CHAPTER SEVEN

Today was Jenny's first Meet the Captain event. She had watched Captain Barone overcome his uneasiness week after week and answer the questions of hundreds of passengers. He usually invited a few senior officers to join him on the stage, and Jenny decided to do the same. Today, she would have Staff Captain Aksel Borg, Cruise Director Shawna Thames, and Chief Medical Officer Manny Cruz joining her. The four crew members were seated in tall chairs as passengers were steadily filling the ship's theater. As customary, Jenny was wearing her white uniform and navy stilettos. She had a commanding presence despite her petite build.

At 11:35, Jenny stood and spoke into the microphone. "Good afternoon, everyone. I hope you are enjoying *Buccaneer Bounty*. She's my baby. And I'm very proud of her." The audience clapped. Jenny then introduced her fellow officers and opened the floor for questions. About forty hands lifted into the air. "And don't worry about who is driving the ship while I am down here. We have a very capable bridge staff." A third of the hands dropped.

As expected, most of the questions were centered around the treasure hunt. Jenny handled them with humor and competence as she commended the purser and his staff. She revealed that six months of clues had been recorded, and that the staff was excited for the first treasure to be found. The remainder of the questions Jenny fielded were about her training and her time spent with Luca Barone.

Shawna answered two questions regarding the training of the entertainment staff. She shared that the cruise line hosts worldwide casting calls in eight major cities. The chosen talent then works together on land before they board the ship for six-month contracts. "The mischievous puppy," Shawna added, "is played by a world-class gymnast. She brings a playfulness that even the writers had not expected."

Next to field questions was Aksel. He began by touting the modern technology found only in *Bounty*. The intra-ship communication was based on a new dynamic system not available on any other ship. Also, *Bounty* was equipped with an artificial intelligence–based assistant accessible to all senior officers. AI was being used to aide navigation, entertainment, and safety. Aksel elaborated on the safety aspect. "We have every inch of the public spaces on the ship covered by AI surveillance. Security officers are alerted of anything suspicious. Soon we will have this technology on the islands as well."

An aging veteran raised his hand. "Who maintains the integrity of the passengers exiting and reentering the ship at the islands? And what happens if someone does not get back onto the ship?"

Aksel looked at Jenny. She stood and took the microphone. "That is an important question, sir. As you will see, passengers and crew are only permitted to exit the ship through one debarkation point. Each person is scanned so that we have a record of who has left *Bounty*. They are scanned again upon return. And they must complete a security check to return to the remainder of the ship. We have trained security personnel for each step of the process."

"Sometimes people miss the all-aboard time," Aksel added. "They fall asleep or have the wrong time on their watches. But our ports are all owned by Jewel, so we can quickly canvas the island and round up the missing people. That is not a problem with our ships."

"That's tighter security than when I was in the Navy," the veteran responded. The audience laughed and the man sat down. But not before he commented on the captain's "rocking shoes."

Before Jenny returned to her seat, two teenagers ran through the back of the seated area wearing bathing suits. Jenny was shocked to see that Zach was one of the teens. He stopped and waved at her. "Hey, Mom! Tell Laney that you are my mom. She doesn't believe that my mom is the captain."

"Yes, dear," Jenny replied with concern. "I am your mother. And I am the captain. You should get back to the pool now." The crowd remained quiet. Jenny had a sinking fear that Zach would get into trouble this week. He wasn't behaving normally. He wasn't behaving civilly. But she had a job to do now. So she handed the microphone to Dr. Cruz and returned to her seat. Thankfully, Zach and Laney left the theater without any further disturbance.

Lastly, Manny greeted the crowd. He described the medical facility and preemptively answered the most anticipated question. "The most common ailment we see is severe sunburn. So please be careful out there. If you run out of sunscreen, you can purchase more in the ship's canteen on Deck Five. You can also purchase bandages, which are our most requested medical aid."

A flurry of questions was then directed at the doctor. He answered them calmly and with genuine concern. After reassuring the passengers that the onboard morgue would rarely be used, Manny lightened the mood with a funny story about a man who got a foot stuck in a ship's toilet. He then listed some of the serious emergencies he had dealt with, including a shark attack, and ended with the story of a man who had been gambling in a casino for hours without his wife's "approval." She had been looking for him for over an hour and finally found him near the craps table. When he saw her, he quickly swallowed the dice so she would not know he had been gambling. The dice got caught in his esophagus, and the man struggled to breath. Thanks to the ship's medical staff, the sneaky gambler ended up fine. His wife forgave him and planned to mount the dice and display them in their home.

Manny's final story was about a woman who was rushed to an examining room with severe abdominal pain. "The X-rays showed her stomach excessively distorted. We were considering the possibility of gall bladder surgery or an intravenous pain treatment for pancreatitis, when she started retching. I will never in my life forget the sight of three pounds of bacon spewing from one of our precious passengers. The woman had allegedly eaten three plates of bacon an hour earlier and suffered serious abdominal distress from her questionable diet choice." The audience began laughing. "She liked pig butts and she could not lie."

After his final comment, Manny returned the microphone to Jenny. The audience was roaring with laughter. "I hadn't heard that story, Dr. Cruz. But I will now consider cutting back on the bacon tomorrow morning. Trust me . . . I could give that woman a run for her money." The officers on stage nodded in agreement. Jenny turned to the audience. "Please help me thank our stage party. As you can see, you are in good hands aboard *Buccaneer Bounty*."

The crowd applauded and began to slowly exit the theater. As soon as Jenny was backstage, she called Zach's number. As usual, he did not answer. She left a message for him to return her call and headed back to the bridge.

"Maybe we should go back and apologize to the woman at the spa," Marissa said to Bettina as they returned to their cabin after lunch. "I feel a little guilty about teasing with her."

"High. Low. Buffalo," Bettina responded while staring blankly at a wall.

"What? Buffalo?"

Bettina looked at her with a sly smile. "High. Low. Buffalo. It's a game."

Marissa understood. "Oh, you want to play a gabby game. Are you feeling edgy right now?"

"I am. Can we play?" Bettina pleaded. "Lunch was fun, but I am missing Jason and Ben. What if they are hurt right now? What if something is wrong? I can't be there for them if something bad happens."

"Now, you don't need to worry about that. I'm sure they are fine. And Jason would contact you if there was a problem." But Bettina was not convinced. So Marissa sat on her bed and complied. "How do we play?"

Bettina immediately relaxed and looked happily distracted. She sat on her bed facing Marissa with her legs crossed. "Tell me one thing that is going well in your life. One thing that is not going well. And one random thing."

The questions felt like plain and simple gossip-seeking to Marissa. Was Bettina really this anxious? Or was she playing a joke to get juicy dirt that she could share with the others later? Marissa decided to play along but with vanilla answers. "Um, this cruise is one thing going well. I am having fun. The dessert at lunch did not go well. I should have added more strawberries to my cheesecake. And my favorite color is yellow."

Bettina smiled widely. "You are good. I feel better already. Now I'll tell you mine. Let's see . . ." She grabbed a pillow off her bed and hugged it tightly. "You are my going well. I made a new friend without even trying. My hair is my bad thing. I should have had my roots done last week. And I hate turtlenecks. They look so weird."

Not sure how to respond, Marissa ignored the comments. "Are you feeling better?"

"I am! Do you really have to take a nap? Come sunbathe with me. We can get some more cheesecake on the way. And I know where we can get more apricot water."

"That sounds fun, but I'd rather stay in this afternoon. I'm enjoying my book."

Bettina made a pouty face. "Okay. Toni and Pam are at the pool already. I'll try to find them." She pulled a bathing suit out of a drawer. "And the mint chocolate chip woman was smiling when she went behind the curtain. I don't think we need to apologize."

When Bettina left, Marissa settled on the bed with her book. She expected to fall asleep within minutes but did not. After a while, she decided to slip out and take her book to one of the garden path benches. They had been luring her ever since she first saw them. If she didn't stay long, Bettina would never know she had left their cabin.

Marissa made her way to Deck Seven easily. She surprised herself by mastering the layout of the ship so quickly. Well, some of the layout of the ship. She walked through the lively Shipwreck Boulevard and marveled at the activity. Parents were giving their children a break from the sun; teenagers were enjoying milkshakes;

and senior citizens were playing card games. The area was ideal for socializing, but too noisy for reading.

After pondering her choices, Marissa selected the far-left garden path. She considered getting one of the famous Dagger drinks to take with her but decided it would be too much to carry. Toni had informed the women at dinner that the Dagger was "vital." Marissa was not sure what that meant exactly, but did want to try one. It was marketed similarly as the Cutlass on *Golden Fortune* and the Saber on *Plunder*. The former was made with cherries and limes, while the latter was made with bananas and coconut. According to Toni, the Dagger would be the best because it was made with pineapple and mangoes.

As Marissa was looking for an empty bench, she noticed her lookalike; Marley was sitting alone on a bench near an enchanting water fountain. She was reading intently and did not notice Marissa. Normally, Marissa would not start up a conversation, but she was intrigued by her alter ego.

"Marley?"

Marley's head jerked up. When she recognized Marissa, she smiled. "Hi, twin. How are you?"

"I'm great. And I'm Marissa, by the way."

Marley smiled shyly. "Thanks. I knew it started with an *M*."

"Looks like we had the same idea," Marissa said as she held up her book. "Quiet time."

"Well, we are twins. So I'm sure we are in the same boat. No pun intended. Even though I'm a travel agent, this cruise is overwhelming. I'm used to traveling with my husband. This sisterhood bonding is a little bit much. I've had more 'gal time' in the past two days than I have in the past two years."

"I totally agree." Marissa sat at the other end of the bench. "I was not made for a weeklong slumber party." Both women laughed. "But I must admit that everyone has been much nicer than I expected. I think I've been a little quick to judge by outward appearances."

"Same here. The group has gone out of their way to include me. But I am just happier with a book. So, how many children do you have?"

"Just the one son, Josh. He's great. And you?"

"None. We did the infertility thing for a few years and finally gave up."

"Oh, I'm so sorry," Marissa said as she patted one of Marley's arms.

"I'm okay. We have accepted it. Our family is small, but that's okay. We have three dogs, so I get to give out lots of love each day."

"That's great. I'm really glad I met you. And I'm having a lot of fun on this cruise. I actually considered getting out of it but am enjoying myself."

"Same here."

Marissa stood. "I will leave you to your solitude and find my own bench. Maybe we can meet for lunch sometime."

"That sounds nice. May I get your email address?" Marissa was wary of giving it out but felt an unspoken connection with her new friend. They exchanged information and even made plans to get Dagger drinks together on their next sea day.

"Cannonball!" Ronnie Ledbetter jumped right on top of Hunter. Both boys came up from the middle of the swimming pool coughing.

"Why would you do that?" Hunter yelled.

"Because you were there." Ronnie swam off and left the others mumbling complaints about his rebellious behavior.

Hunter climbed out of the pool and sat on the side. "I'll be glad when he moves to Tallahassee, or wherever he's going. He's a jerk!"

"I still can't believe Pastor Joe let him come on this trip," Ryan added.

Josh had to agree that Ronnie was unnecessarily nasty, but he still felt sorry for him. Who wouldn't act like that with Ronnie's homelife? As he was about to climb out of the pool, a wave of water crashed over his head. "Ronnie!"

"No, I'm Winnie." His new friend was laughing about her prank.

"Uh, oh . . ." Josh stuttered. "I'm sorry I yelled."

"No worries. I was being a jerk and shouldn't have splashed you. And I would love to meet this Ronnie guy. He sounds cool."

Josh rolled his eyes. "Trust me. He's not."

The two joined the rest of the youth group and spent two more hours at the pool before leaving to get ready for dinner. Once again, Winnie asked Josh if he was going to the prom. And once again, Ryan teased him for admitting that he was.

Back in their cabin, Ryan was more serious about Winnie. "She's really cool, dude. And I think she likes you."

"I'm not sure about that," Josh remarked quietly. "But she is really cool. I kind of wish we weren't wearing Hawaiian shirts tonight."

Ryan chuckled. "It will be fine. You aren't exactly James Bond, you know?"

Josh threw a pillow at his friend and began getting ready for the big formal night dinner. Ryan wore a ridiculous bright-blue shirt with a large parrot on the back. Josh's "formal" shirt was less flashy. It was black with rows of small, white hibiscus flowers. Neither wore a necktie as they had originally planned.

"Perfect!" Josh declared. "Let's go."

"I just love getting dressed up," Bettina squealed. "It's like we are going to the ball." She was pacing by the desk in a Jewel bathrobe.

"Calm down, Cinderella," Marissa joked. "We're just having dinner."

"No. We are having a *formal* dinner. There's a difference."

"Oh, really?"

"Sure. Everyone will be dressed up. And the food will probably be a little fancier." She sat in the desk chair. "Jason never takes me anywhere formal."

"We don't do anything fancy either. Well, unless it's a wedding. That's all we ever get dressed up for." Marissa expected Bettina to request a gabby game, but she was handing the excitement well tonight. "What are you doing over there?"

"Oh, I got these new travel curlers. I'm planning to roll this mess and wear my hair down. They are almost heated."

Marissa wore one of her new dresses and the pearl necklace. Thankfully, everything fit and matched. She pulled part of her hair back with a small clip and added gold loop earrings and off-white sandals. "Do you need any help?"

"Thanks, but I've got it. They just clip up." Bettina became alarmed. "Wait, where are the clips?" She tossed everything around on the desk. "I can't find the clips."

"Maybe they are in your suitcase." Bettina jumped up and knocked the chair over, then pulled the suitcase out from under her bed.

"They aren't here. I can't find the clips!"

"Calm down," Marissa said softly. "We can find something else to work. And you always look gorgeous. Don't worry."

"But I bought these rollers for tonight. I wanted soft curls for my new dress. It has tiny roses on it. It needs curls." Bettina began softly crying.

"Wanna play High, Low, Buffalo?"

She instantly calmed down. "Thank you. I feel better for you offering. But I'm okay for now. What can I use instead?" The women looked around the cabin but couldn't find anything suitable.

"What about Sunny?"

"What?"

"Our room steward. Maybe he can find something for you." Marissa didn't quite understand her friend's need to roll her hair, but she did want her to be happy. "How do we reach him?"

"I'm not sure. Should we call Guest Services?"

Marissa thought for a moment and quickly peeked out their door into the passageway. By some small miracle, Sunny was folding towels on a cart nearby. "Excuse me. Could you please help us?"

The attendant rushed to their cabin. "Of course, ma'am. What can I do?"

Both women were taken aback at the man's kindness and dedication to his work. He had other responsibilities but dropped everything to help two of his guests.

"My friend cannot find her curler clips." Marissa began pointing toward the now overheated curlers. "Do you have anything we could us instead?"

"Ah, yes. I have the perfect thing. I'll be right back."

When Sunny darted away, Bettina sat on her bed. "I'm sorry for causing such a panic. I have everything planned in my head for tonight to be perfect. Now we are going to be late, and Sunny is having to run all over the ship looking for makeshift curler clips. I'm such a problem."

"The way I see it is that we are all human. And it is not only a duty, but a privilege to help other humans."

Bettina's eyes widened. "Wow! You are a great bestie. Thank you."

"Of course. I'm having a lot of fun with you."

Sunny knocked on their door, and Marissa answered. He was holding his hand out with a dozen rubber bands. "Here you go. My wife uses these hair bands." Bettina couldn't mask her disappointment but gratefully accepted the bands and thanked their steward.

As she was about to close the door, Marissa popped up and handed the man a few dollars as a tip. "Thank you. They are perfect." Sunny walked back to his towel cart with a smile.

"What now?"

Bettina looked at the rubber bands. "I think they will work." She began rolling her hair and carefully securing each curler with two rubber bands. "Now we wait."

"Looks like they are working. And you handled the crisis quite well, I must say."

"Thank you, roomie. You and Sunny saved the day. I owe you."

Bettina finished dressing and sat at the desk to remove the bands. "Oh no! Oh no! Oh no! They're stuck!"

"What?"

"The rubber bands melted to my hair!" Marissa was frantically pulling at the bands. Two curlers fell onto the floor. The remaining six were dangling at different lengths from her head.

Marissa hurried to the desk. "Sit down. I'll look at them."

"My hair is ruined. The dinner is ruined. The entire cruise is ruined!"

"I don't think it's that bad. Let me look." Bettina quieted as her friend began picking pieces of rubber out of her hair. "It's coming out. See? Wanna play a game?"

"No. I'm fine. Thank you." Marissa continued to work on the rubber band/curler mess on Bettina's head. "Why does this stuff always happen to me?"

"Oh, goodness. Things like this happen to everyone. One time, I was walking into my office and one of my heels completely fell apart in the parking lot. No warning. I had to call Gene to bring me another pair of shoes. And of course, he brought pink tennis shoes that looked ridiculous with my skirt. Stuff just happens."

"I guess so. I don't like it though."

"Yeah. I imagine no one likes it. I'm almost done. Do you have a wide-tooth comb?"

"No. I'm a disaster." Tears began to fall down Bettina's face.

"That is not true, my dear. You are beautiful in every possible way. Let's see."

Bettina turned to face the mirror. The room was silent for ten seconds before she burst into laughter. "Ba-ha-ha! My hair! It looks like a bird's nest exploded right on top of me." Marissa joined the laughter.

"Are you okay?" Marissa finally asked.

"You know what? I am fine. Best day ever!" Bettina continued to laugh as she finger-combed her hair into a quick chignon. "Let's go, bestie. I'm getting hungry."

CHAPTER EIGHT

To accommodate the party of fifty-four, the maître' di reserved seven neighboring tables. Jenny arrived early to ensure that the group would have sufficient seating. She greeted the first ones who arrived and was relieved to see Zach enter with six of his friends. Each was wearing a colorful Hawaiian shirt with dress pants. She wasn't crazy about the informal shirts but had to admit they were original. They were festive and, thankfully, clean.

Zach rushed to his mother and gave her a hug. "Mom! I've missed you. But I'm having a great time." Jenny did not notice the eye-rolling by Zach's friends.

"We need to talk about this morning," Jenny whispered. "Your behavior was inappropriate. You've been on enough cruises to know proper decorum."

"Yes, ma'am," Zach answered sheepishly. "We were just joking. It won't happen again."

"Well, I'm glad you are having fun. Those shirts are a bit much."

"It was Hunter's idea," Zach blurted, throwing his friend under the proverbial bus.

"No, it's fine. Let's see where Pastor Joe has us sitting. I believe he has you with your friends. And I'll sit with some of the parents." Jenny recognized the relief on Zach's face when he discovered he wouldn't be sitting with her during the meal. Something was clearly up. She would pray about it and have a serious talk with her son when they returned to their cabin.

As the tables were filling, Jenny marveled at how mature the group looked. Gone were the T-shirts and flip-flops. In place were flowy skirts and sharp dress shirts. Even Ronnie dressed for the occasion, although Jenny noticed that he was wearing tennis shoes instead of dress shoes. She also noticed Laney walk up to Zach and put her hands on his shoulders. He gave a broad smile and said a few words to her before the girl walked away.

Lena looked like a young model in her strapless jade-green gown. Her mother, Toni, looked equally beautiful in a silver sequined dress. Lauren and Macy were wearing different shades of purple, while Kinsley's loose sheath had every color of the rainbow. Joe was wearing a tuxedo and a top hat. Jenny was thankful that she opted for her navy cocktail dress rather than her formal uniform.

Once everyone was seated, Joe stood in the middle of the group of tables and offered a blessing for the meal. "Father, thank You for the food You have provided us. Bless the hands that prepared it and those that will serve it. I am in awe of Your beautiful Creation. Thank You for letting me experience it on this ship. Please give Ms. Jenny wisdom and strength to lead our voyage. And as my father reminded me, 'deliver us from evil' whenever it approaches. In Jesus' precious name we pray. Amen."

Jenny was seated next to Marissa, who looked striking in a floral print dress and matching pearl necklace. Next to Marissa was Bettina, who always looked like a beauty queen. Her hair was up in a loose twist that added to the woman's attractiveness.

"My bestie and I are having the greatest time," Bettina told Jenny, who was a little surprised by the 'bestie' classification. Both women began giggling.

"I am so glad," Jenny exclaimed. "You ladies look beautiful."

"Thank you for arranging everything," Marissa added. "Josh and I would never have an opportunity like this otherwise."

Jenny clasped her hands together near her chest. "Well, it has been my pleasure." She looked toward Zach's table and noticed that he looked tired. He never looked tired. It couldn't be the sun because he was accustomed to spending hours at the beach. He must have not slept much last night. She made a mental note to text him a suggestion to keep up his sleep this week.

Efficient servers took food orders for the large group, and as expected most ordered the lobster dinner. A few selected the steak option. Bettina squealed when she ordered the chocolate treasure cake. The menu promised a "chocolatey surprise" inside the dessert.

Trying to be "in the moment," Jenny scanned the tables. She knew and loved each person seated in the group. The young people were at a critical age. They were about to launch out of their nests into adulthood. Her church had prepared them well—she hoped. It was time for them to soar on their own. Jenny offered a silent prayer for the futures of the teens seated at the seven dinner tables. As she was praying, a chill ran down her spine.

Watch and pray.

Jenny heard the words as if they had been spoken aloud. But it appeared no one else had heard. Silently, she asked the Lord to protect the youth from evil. Then she prayed for all the passengers and crew on *Bounty*. Evil was all around. Jenny prayed that Zach and the others would distance themselves from sin and wickedness.

"Earth to Captain Jenny." Shae patted Jenny's arm. "Your plate is here. But you seem to be a million miles away."

"Oh," Jenny remarked. "I apologize. Lots on my mind."

Shae smiled. "I forget that this is not a vacation for you. Thank you again for organizing everything. We are having a blast. Macy wants to live on the ship now."

The remainder of the meal was uneventful. The lobster was a hit, and the desserts were blissful. The treasure cake held molten chocolate and miniature dark chocolate gold coins. A few of the women asked for a second one.

The ship's photographers roamed the dining room and took plenty of candid and posed shots of the group. Jenny could tell that Joe was enjoying every minute of the meal. He was made for his job. She couldn't imagine any other man leading the students at Holy Cross.

After dessert, the other women at the table excused themselves. Most were planning to get coffee at the soda shop and spend some time people watching. Jenny smiled when she saw Bettina loop her arm through Marissa's. A new friendship was clearly blooming.

Joe was going from table to table, reminding the students that the prom would start at ten o'clock back in the dining room. It would be transformed with decorations, mood lighting, and a large dance floor. The theme was "Deserted," and a DJ would be stationed near the back of the room. Jenny reminded herself to briefly check in on the activities before she went to bed.

On her way back to the bridge, Jenny stopped at Zach's table. The boys were talking about how to spend the next hour while they waited for the prom to start. Zach jumped up and gave his mother a hug. He didn't seem tired and thanked her for planning the fun week. The boys added their thanks and asked who was driving the ship.

Jenny concluded that she was worrying about nothing and walked toward the elevator bank relieved.

All was well on the bridge when Jenny returned. The ship was slightly ahead of schedule for its arrival at Cutter Cay the next morning. Paul, the chief engineer, reported that the reflective tape in the cabin bathrooms was working well. No more falls had been reported.

Next, Peggy, the human resources director, delivered the timely news that two shark scrubbers had just been hired to man Cutter Cay. Security would not have to run the double red flags on the beach.

"Whew!" Jenny replied. "Just in the nick of time. Thank you for working so diligently on this."

"Of course, Captain," Peggy answered. "It's my job."

Jenny was technically off-duty for the remainder of the evening, but she chose to stay on the bridge for a while longer. She watched the competent officers manage the ship's navigation and told herself that this is where she was meant to be. At the helm of an ocean liner. She felt at home here. And she couldn't imagine living her life with a land-locked job. To Jenny, a ship's captain was the best job in the world.

After dinner, Elle and Evie met the Munsons on the top deck. The girls wanted to watch the movie, and the parents were happy to oblige by resting in lounge chairs for a while. Joe decided to check in briefly with Jonah and some of the students, so he headed for Shipwreck

Boulevard with a promise to catch the end of the movie with Elle and Evie.

Deck Seven was alive with activity when Joe arrived. Children were racing around with balloon animals, and parents were casually browsing the various shops. Photographers were taking carefully posed photographs of the well-dressed passengers. Joe looked for his students and found Jonah and a dozen others standing near one of the garden pathways. They were considering their entertainment options.

"What's kickin', fried chickens?" Joe joked. Most of the kids groaned.

"We're just waiting for the prom to start," Jonah said. "There is so much to do here."

"How's the day been?"

"Great!" Josh answered quickly. "I love this place."

Others added similar responses.

"So much fun."

"I love the unlimited bacon."

"Having a blast."

Joe nodded. "So, has anyone gone nuts yet?" Joe noticed a few glances in the direction of Zach and was surprised. He would have to keep an extra eye on the boy, especially at the eleven o'clock check-in time.

"We're good, Dad," Jonah added with a sigh. "I promise."

Joe talked with the students for a while, trying to compliment all of them on their appearance. "We clean up well, if I do say so. And the Hawaiian shirts are *gold*. I wish I had thought of that myself."

"It was Hunter's idea," Jonah added.

"Well, you all look great. Have fun at the prom. And remember . . ."

"No purple," the group said in harmony.

As he was leaving, Joe noticed Ronnie and Jim Morgan sitting with a group of older men. He walked over to say hi.

"Pastor Joe!" Jim called out. "It's good to see you. Ronnie and I were talking with these gentlemen about the Vietnam War. Each one of them served our country. Three of them were Ronnie's age when they fought."

Joe reached out and shook each man's hand. "It's a pleasure to meet you. And I thank you for your service." He noticed that Ronnie was smiling and listening intently to everything being said.

"It was our honor," one of the men said. "We have enjoyed getting to know this young man right here. Ronnie has represented your church well. Poor thing has listened to at least a dozen of our old stories."

Ronnie looked surprised. "I like the stories, Sergeant Jack. Thank you for telling them to me."

"Any time, boy. Not too many people like to listen to us blab on and on about the war. You are all right, Mr. Ronnie."

Joe noticed Ronnie duck his head down shyly. His behavior was unusual and refreshing. Jim Morgan was a godsend.

"Well, I'm missing a movie on the top deck," Joe said. "I will let you men continue your discussion. It was great to meet you, and I hope to see you around this week."

"Same to you," Jack replied.

Josh and his friends decided to hang out in food court area of Shipwreck Boulevard while waiting for the prom to start. Zach found Laney as soon as they arrived at the tables and left with her without saying goodbye to his friends.

"What's up with him?" Ryan asked. "It's like he doesn't even know us."

Hunter nodded in agreement. "And he's been on lots of cruises before. He should be hanging with us."

"It's probably better that he's not," Josh added. "He's looking for trouble."

Jonah stood tall and imitated his father by pointing a finger. "Remember boys, no purple." The rest of the boys doubled over in laughter. "If Zach doesn't watch out, he'll look like Barney."

The group made a beeline to the food court and secured cookies all around. They found a table near a jewelry store and continued to discuss Zach's strange behavior. Ronnie and Mr. Morgan walked by and seemed to be in a serious discussion.

Hunter changed the subject. "What about you, Josh? Any chance you'll go purple this week?"

Nearly choking on his macadamia nut cookie, Josh began shaking his head. "No way, man. I don't even have a pink." He took a sip of water. "Why would you say that?"

"We all saw how you acted around Winnie," Hunter replied. "She had no problem splashing you at the pool. Calm down. She's cool."

Ryan came to his friend's aid. "Yeah. She's cool. What about you and Makenzi? She's fine."

Hunter looked down. "She has a serious boyfriend back home."

"Brutal," Ryan responded. "But we aren't here to meet girls. We are here to have fun before our grown-up lives begin. Let's get more cookies." The guys agreed and went back through the snack line. They joined the girls from their group and decided to walk the garden paths before heading back to the dining room. Eventually, Lena complained that her shoes were too tight to walk around in, so the group sat on the benches for a while and then headed back to the dining room.

"Wow!" the girls gasped in harmony when they entered the prom.

"This is fun!" Lena squealed. The dining room had been transformed into a deserted island complete with dozens of palm trees and large LED SOS letters. The entrance was draped with netting and held a mock plank for partiers to walk over. A colorful, mechanical parrot welcomed each person to "walk the plank."

"This is cooler than our prom back home," Ryan added. "Only my school would have a Winter Whimsy theme in South Florida."

"Yeah," Lena said. "We had Candy Land as our theme. How do you dress for that?"

"I can't believe this is on a cruise ship," Josh remarked. "Let's find some tables to park at." The group found a few others from their church and sat at nearby tables. All marveled at the high-end decorations and fancy outfits of their shipmates.

"Those Hawaiian shirts are perfect," Lauren declared. "Did you know that we would be shipwrecked on a deserted island?"

Jonah laughed. "No. We just wanted to do something different."

After half an hour some of the boys decided to get some snacks. The DJ was spinning modern tunes, but no one was dancing.

A few girls were standing conspicuously close to the dance floor but did not have the nerve to step on it.

"Anyone seen Zach?" Hunter asked.

"Nope," Ryan replied. "And I don't expect to. He's off with Laney somewhere."

Josh's eyes widened. "I don't see how he can get away with it. Won't the leaders be checking up on him? Surely Ms. Jenny will figure out that he didn't come here. I say he shows."

Ryan chuckled. "Watch and learn, ole boy. Watch and learn."

The crowd was growing, and a few girls were bravely dancing in one corner of the dance floor. Eventually, the DJ started a popular line dance song, and the teens finally flooded the floor. Even Josh and Ryan joined the fun. At the end of the second line dance song, a slow song was played. Nearly every person dancing quickly exited the stage.

As Josh was walking with his friends to their table, he felt a tap on his shoulder and turned to see Winnie standing behind him.

"So how many left feet do you have?" Winnie asked as she pointed to his shoes.

"Ronnie, I mean Winnie?" Josh could feel his face reddening from his chin to his forehead. Winnie looked amazing in an emerald-green dress that nearly touched the floor. She was wearing makeup and large, silver hoop earrings and was barefooted.

Winnie put her hands on her hips. "You didn't answer my question."

"Uh . . . two," Josh answered. "Definitely two."

"Well, let's see about that." Winnie grabbed one of Josh's hands and pulled him to the center of the dance floor. He couldn't look back at his friends, but he knew that each one was staring at him with their jaws hanging down.

When Winnie stopped pulling Josh, she faced him and put her hands on his shoulders. She kept an "air cushion" between them, as Pastor Joe called it. Josh put his hands loosely on her hips and began swaying.

Years later, Josh would still remember his first dance with Winnie. He couldn't explain this feeling at the time, but he *knew* that the dance was a life-changing moment for him. She felt like a longtime friend. "Perfect" by Ed Sheeran would be their song, and they would tell their kids about the "two left feet" joke. When the prom was over, his friends would tease him relentlessly, but he didn't care. Winnie felt true, and while it didn't make any sense, she was worth the ribbing.

When the song ended, Josh and Winnie shuffled quickly to the tables held by the Holy Cross crew. Mercifully, none of his friends commented on the dance. Winnie took a seat, and Josh offered to find some snacks.

"Grab some chips if they have them," Winnie requested.

"And more of those tiny sandwiches," Ryan added. With that comment, Winnie was officially grafted into the group. Josh's mind was whirling. As he attacked the food table, he looked at his feet. They hadn't let him down—yet.

The entire group was eating at their tables when Jenny walked up. "Hey, everyone. Are you having fun?"

"We are," Hunter responded. "I thought grown-ups weren't supposed to crash our prom."

"Ha!" Jenny laughed. "The captain of the ship gets to crash all the parties. I'm just checking to see that everything is going smoothly. Is Zach around?"

The group became silent and then Jandro spoke up. "We haven't seen him. He must be running late."

Jenny looked at her watch. "It's almost eleven. I hope he doesn't forget to check in with Joe. And be sure to check in with your chaperones too." Phones appeared, and hasty messages were sent to adults. Jenny said goodbye and walked around, greeting other teens. She occasionally looked back to see if Zach had appeared. As Josh expected, he had not.

"Zach isn't the only one MIA," Ryan noted. "I haven't seen Ronnie either."

"I don't think a teen prom is exactly his bag," Hunter replied.

Lena, standing nearby, heard the comments. She and Macy were with Makenzi and Lizzy from the previous night's dinner. "We saw him again when we were coming up. He and Mr. Morgan were talking with some of the veterans back in the Boulevard. One of the old men had a box or something with a bunch of medals."

Macy was nodding. "Ronnie seemed really interested. I think he likes that kind of stuff."

"As long as he isn't tormenting us, I'm happy," Hunter declared.

"Oh, he isn't that bad," Macy added. The boys rolled their eyes. To them, Ronnie Ledbetter *was* that bad.

The night ended with a few more line dances and a group celebration on the dance floor to Kool & the Gang's "Celebrate." Josh said goodbye to Winnie and promised to look for her at noon for lunch the next day. Ryan had a lot of questions on the way back to their cabin, but Josh didn't have many answers. He wasn't sure himself what was happening with the spunky girl from Wonder, Alabama. But he liked it.

"That was fun," Bettina remarked. "How often do you get to watch a superhero movie under the stars. That makes me want to set something up in our backyard."

"It was fun," Marissa agreed. "I think I would have fallen asleep if we had stayed any longer."

"Me too." Bettina opened the cabin door and walked in. She abruptly turned back toward her friend. "Perfect pitch!"

"What?"

"Perfect pitch," Bettina begged. "Now."

"Do you need a gabby game? What's wrong?"

Bettina slowly turned to the room and pointed to the beds. On each bed was a carefully prepared towel animal. Bettina's bed had an adorable dinosaur, and Marissa's had an elephant.

"Pitch!" Bettina squeaked.

Marissa walked to her bed and sat beside the cloth creation. "These are just towels. And they are adorable. There's nothing to be anxious about." Bettina put her hands on her hips and did not move. "Okay. Okay. How do we play?"

With a sigh, Bettina explained the rules of the game. "You must try to sell me something in the room. It's friendly marketing."

Marissa laughed at this crazy idea. She even snorted. "Really? You're going to buy something in the cabin from me?" Bettina burst into tears, and Marissa immediately regretted her giggling. She patted Bettina's bed and coaxed her to sit down.

"I'll play," Marissa conceded. "Should I start?"

Bettina nodded.

Despite the utter ridiculousness of her situation, Marissa felt for her new friend. She hoped the antics weren't a big joke but couldn't take a chance. Marissa looked around the room. What could she possibly promote? She spotted her new flip-flops near the bed and picked them up. "How about these shoes? Would you be interested in buying these?" Bettina smiled slightly. "They are an attractive shade of brown. They should fit your feet perfectly. And look at how bendy they are. I'll take a thousand dollars for them."

"You don't say a price," Bettina said softly.

Good grief! "I tell you what. If you buy this left flip-flop, I will throw in the right one for free. And they can be called sandals, thongs, flappers, or foot clappers. Whatever you choose." *Please let that be enough.*

"Thank you, Marissa. I feel a lot better. And I know that towel animals cannot hurt me. But I didn't expect them. We didn't have them last night. That seems odd to me. Why did we get the animals tonight and not yesterday?"

Marissa put her flip-flops back beside her bed. "No problem. I'm glad to help. I'm not sure why the towel animals were brought in tonight. But I think most guests find them cute. It's been a long day. Aren't you looking forward to bed?"

"Wait. I didn't have a turn." *Double good grief!* Bettina spent the next five minutes promoting a bottle of water she had found in the refrigerator. Marissa did her best to not laugh, because the entire episode was so outrageous that it was beyond comical. But Bettina was not laughing. She obviously had a control issue. When she didn't have control in a situation, she created something she could control. Marissa wished Gene were here. He was great for crystallizing her concerns into a big picture. He would know if she should discuss counseling with Bettina or simply go along with her silly games. The gabby games were probably more serious than Bettina realized. Marissa decided to let the week play out and seek Gene's advice when she got home. She might even suggest that Bettina meet with one of the church pastors about her anxiety. In the meantime, she would become an expert gabby game player.

The day finally ended, and both women slept soundly, not knowing that the next day would bring a life-threatening crisis.

CHAPTER NINE

Tuesday, June 16
Cutter Cay

Once again, Zach did not sleep in Jenny's cabin. She assumed that he stayed with his friends again but was becoming concerned. She had already sent two messages to him and decided to wait before sending another. It was too early to ask Joe if Zach had checked in the night before, so Jenny readied herself for the day. *Bounty* would dock at Cutter Cay in two hours.

On the way to the bridge, Jenny stopped at the coffee shop on the Boulevard and briefly spoke with an older couple celebrating their forty-fifth wedding anniversary. She then ordered a double latte and a muffin to go and headed to the command center. Food would be available at the bridge, but Jenny wanted to eat as she was walking. That would keep her from worrying about Zach.

At the bridge, Jenny found bright-eyed officers already in place. Everyone was eager to dock the ship for the first time with passengers. They could see the local pilot's boat approaching *Bounty* from a distance. The pilot would precariously enter *Bounty* as she was moving and join the group on the bridge. He would assist with the navigation of the intricate waterways near Cutter Cay. Once the ship was docked, the pilot would disembark and later return to assist with the departure. Ship's pilots were unnoticed heroes to cruise ship industry.

"Good day, Jacks!" Tito, the local pilot, announced. "*Yinna* picked a beautiful day to bring your *t'ing* to our island. Welcome to Cutter Cay."

Jenny knew Tito from her recent time on *Golden Fortune* and was delighted to see him again. "I am so happy to see you, Tito. How have you been? And how's Myrna?"

"We be good, Captain. Milady's leg is causing trouble, but the Lord is blessing. Always blessing."

Jenny smiled. "I love your spirit, Tito. Let's park this big tub." Tito assisted the bridge crew as it docked *Buccaneer Bounty* smoothly at Cutter Cay. The ship approached the pier efficiently, and Jenny was pleased. She checked her phone twice, but Zach had still not responded.

Once the ship was tied and documents were submitted, Tito said goodbye for a while. He hugged everyone in the area and promised to return "*terreckly*," or right away.

As Tito was leaving, Zach walked in. Jenny audibly sighed with relief, although her son looked a bit disheveled. "I was getting a little worried."

"Why?" Zach asked sharply. "I was just eating breakfast with the guys. We're waiting for you to give us the okay to get on the island. I'm gonna show everyone around. What's taking so long?"

"Good morning," Jenny added. "I didn't see you at the prom."

"Were you checking up on me, Mom?"

"No. But I did expect to see you there."

Zach rolled his eyes. "I was there. Laney and I were hanging with her sister. You must have missed me."

Jenny had a strange feeling in her stomach. She knew she hadn't overlooked her own son. "And where did you sleep last night? That's two nights in a row."

"Some of the guys and I slept on the top deck last night. It was really cool. We used towels as blankets."

Jenny suspected this was another lie. Crew members weren't supposed to allow passengers to sleep on the pool deck. But they may have conveniently ignored the captain's son and his friends. "Who slept up there? Ty? Hunter?"

"Geez!" Zach answered in a heated tone. Two nearby officers turned toward them at his remarks. "This isn't the FBI. I'm not on trial. You know what? I'm out of here." With his hands balled into fists, Zach marched out of the bridge. Jenny could hear him stomping down the adjacent stairs.

What just happened? Zach had never responded to her questioning like that before. Well, maybe a few times. But never in front of her crew. Something was definitely wrong. Jenny let him go and made a note to seek out Pastor Joe and ask if Zach had been checking in nightly at eleven o'clock. She might even ask for advice on this awkward stage in her teenager's life. For now, Jenny had a ship to command. Next up was the customs documentation and then her morning announcement. She would inform the guests as soon as they were clear to disembark the ship and visit Cutter Cay.

"Was that Jenny on the speaker?" Bettina asked as she poked her head out of the cabin bathroom.

"Yes," Marissa answered. "We are allowed to get off of the ship now."

Bettina gave a cheer and walked out, holding her hairbrush like a microphone. "You may now exit the building."

Marissa chuckled. "Something like that. I think my bag is ready. Sunscreen. Towel. Book. Hat. Water bottle. Am I missing anything?"

"What about snacks?" Bettina wondered. "We might get hungry or thirsty out there."

"Oh, they have snack shacks and beach restaurants on the island. We can get something when we get hungry."

Bettina tossed her hairbrush onto the bed. "Perfect. Do you know where we are going?"

"Goodness, I thought you would know." Marissa sat on the small couch and pulled up the handy app. "It says there are three beaches: Emerald, Pearl, and Jade. Pearl is the farthest from the ship. I'm fine with whichever one you'd like."

"Hmm." Bettina put a finger on her chin. "How about Pearl? That's the only gem created by a living creature. Isn't that cool?"

"Very cool," Marissa answered with a smile. "Have you heard from the boys? Their cabin sounds quiet. They may be still sleeping."

"I bet they stayed up late after the prom. I'll tell Ryan to check in with us at Pearl Beach. You know, the one made by living creatures. And I will let Toni and Pam know where we will be." Bettina began typing furiously on her phone. She then looked up at Marissa. "A little girl time on the beach. What could be better?"

Marissa could think of dozens of things better than "girl time" on the beach. Reading alone on the beach was one of them. But spending time with Bettina was not that bad. She honestly enjoyed spending this vacation with her new friend—quirks and all. Marissa planned to bury her nose in her book to avoid the beachy "girl time." She would tolerate the excessive giggles and fashion talk during lunch. The weather was perfect. And Josh would be on the island somewhere. What could go wrong?

"They are meeting us at the elevators," Marissa announced. She dropped her phone and a bottle of water into her beach bag. "Oh, my goodness, bestie. We forgot about the clue!" Surprisingly, the women hadn't discussed the treasure hunt in nearly a day.

"I forgot about it too," Marissa remarked. "Can you pull up that picture again?"

"Sure." Bettina fished her phone out of her bag and found the blurry picture of the last clue. "Okay. It's a triangular red flag. And it'll be in the sand. That should be easy to spot."

"Since Pearl Beach is on the other end of the island, we should probably walk along one beach going there and the other coming back. That way we will see all the beachfront. A red flag should be easy to spot."

"You sound like Fernando Magellan, the famous map maker."

Marissa wasn't sure if Bettina was joking or serious. "Ha! I'm certainly not *Ferdinand* Magellan, the famous explorer. But I am getting more comfortable with this app and the layout of the ship."

"Gellin' like Magellan," Bettina said with a giggle. Marissa could only laugh at the funny comment. The women left their cabin with beach bags on their shoulders and were still laughing when the arrived at the elevator landing.

"Oh my," Marissa declared while trying not to laugh as she spotted Toni and Pam waiting.

"What are you wearing?" Bettina asked. "Pearls? To the beach?" Both women were wearing pearl necklaces. Toni's was shorter, while Pam's went down to her waist. Pam was also wearing oversized pearl earrings.

Pam looked confused. "Toni said we should wear our pearls. You said it's a 'pearl beach.' I even have the pearl clutch handbag that I bought for my nephew's wedding."

Bettina put one of her hands on her chest. "I guess that is a little confusing." She explained the names of the three beaches and reassured the women that they looked fine. The pearls were no problem.

"I'm not wearing this to the beach!" Toni shouted as she rushed back down the passageway to her cabin.

"We'll be right back," Pam added.

Bettina began laughing again once the women were out of sight. "What a hoot, Magellan! And it's not even nine yet."

"I think it's going to be a great day, Marco Polo. Pearl Beach today and a cute show about a puppy tonight.

"Plus, a treasure hunt. Best day ever!"

Marissa nodded. "Best day ever."

"What is the best day ever?" Josh rounded the corner. Ryan was behind him.

"Your mom and I are having a girl day," Bettina told Josh. "And nothing is going to ruin it. Not even creepy towel animals."

The women peppered their sons with questions about the prom and remainder of the evening. Ryan showed them a few pictures of the decorations. The boys promised to be careful exiting the ship after they ate breakfast. And they agreed to check in with their mothers at Pearl Beach at least once. When Pam and Toni returned, the boys took the stairs up to the buffet and the women took the elevator down to the gangway. Marissa chuckled to herself when she noticed that Toni was now wearing emerald earrings.

Joe waved to Ryan and Josh as they entered Blackbeard's Fortress for breakfast. The boys quickly grabbed plates and began filling them with pancakes. Several of the other students from their group, including Jonah, were sitting on the other side of the buffet.

"Did you hear me, Daddy?"

"I'm sorry, Evie. Ask me again."

"Can we sit by Stevie's family at the beach?"

Joe sat up straighter. "Sure, honey. Do you know how to find them?"

"No," Evie answered as she shook her head. "We're just meeting at Cutter Cay."

"That's a pretty big island, Evie," Elle added. "We'll just have to look out for them."

"And don't forget about the clue," Joe whispered. Evie smiled. She was enjoying the treasure hunt. "Do you remember what it was?"

"Yes, Daddy." Evie was whispering also. "A flag."

"Then we are ready for the hunt," Joe declared. "Is everyone finished eating?"

"Yep," the girls answered together.

The family walked around and checked in with the students. Jonah looked sleepy, but so did the others. He promised to be careful on the island and to check in with his parents on the beach at least once.

Joe was looking forward to some "beach chair time" at Cutter Cay. He had messaged Dean Katz an hour ago, assuring him that he would have an answer before the day ended. All he needed to do was get the "okay" from Elle. He planned to talk with her while Evie was playing with her friends. Elle would surely come to the same decision as he had. God was steering Joe to teach, and he couldn't wait to tell his wife.

Joe, Elle, and Evie returned to their cabins and packed for the beach. Evie looked for her "cruise bestie" as they made their way to the exiting gangway but did not spot Stevie. She assured her parents that they would cover the entire island to find her friend. Both parents rolled their eyes at the plan.

Elle decided that Jade Beach would be the best choice for the day, and Joe secured two chairs with an umbrella for the family when they arrived. As Elle plopped their beach bag onto her chair, she looked toward two jet skis zooming off the shore. It looked as if teenagers were racing them in a zigzag pattern. She also noticed flags in every color of the rainbow sticking out of the sand in front of them, placed about five feet apart. Blue ones. Yellow one. Orange ones. Squares. Rectangles. Crosses.

"Do you see those?" Elle asked.

Joe and Evie noticed the flags at the same time.

"It's the next clue!" Evie shrieked.

Joe held a finger to his mouth. "Shhh! Now everyone knows."

"But that is the clue," Evie whimpered. "I just know it."

"You are even better at clue hunting than I thought you would be. What are we supposed to be looking for?"

"A red triangle. May I go look for it?"

"I'll take you in a little bit. Let's get settled for a bit."

"No, Daddy. We have to go now!"

Joe raised his eyebrows at his daughter.

"I'm sorry. May we go now, Daddy?"

After smiling at Elle, Joe lifted his shoulders. "I guess we can look for treasure if you want. But only for a little bit. I need to talk to Mom about something important. If we look for the flag, you will give me a few minutes to talk with her."

"Yes, of course!" Evie jumped up and pulled her father's hand to get him to stand as well. Elle promised that she would be fine lounging in her chair while they were searching for the gold. Evie brought one of the shovels, just in case.

After ten minutes, Joe and Evie returned to the chairs.

"No red triangle?" Elle asked.

"One," Joe replied, frustrated. "But Evie claims that the stick was the wrong color. I think that flag over there looks exactly like the picture. But she says that the stick in the picture was 'woody,' not 'brownish.' And each flag has a small arrow at the bottom. They are pointing in different directions. That must mean something." Evie sat down in the sand.

"So, what next?" Elle asked.

"We will have to scour this entire island to find the correct flag." Joe looked at Evie, who was now smiling. "Ms. Jenny did not make the gold easy for us to find, did she?"

"I could find it if you would just let me walk around the whole beach," Evie announced.

"That's not a good idea," Elle answered. "Even this beautiful island has some dangers. I say we enjoy the sunshine for a bit and check out the other beaches after lunch." Joe nodded in agreement. Reluctantly, Evie accepted the plan and began building a sandcastle in between her parents' chairs. Joe would have to wait for lunch to talk with Elle.

Around eleven thirty, Evie heard Stevie calling her name. The Munson family was on their way to the nearest food station and spotted the Waller family. Evie begged to join them, and Joe was more than happy to agree. Beach cheeseburgers were difficult to resist, especially with the scent off the grill drifting toward his chair. Evie tossed her shovel and ran to the other girls.

"Isn't this island beautiful?" Kate Munson asked as the families were walking to the nearest food station. "I know we aren't that far from Fort Lauderdale, but the landscaping on this island is just so beautiful. I could stay right here all week."

"It really is lovely," Elle agreed. "Did you notice the sea grape plants? I wonder if we can grow them back in Florida?"

Kate looked back. "No, I didn't. I'll have to look for those before we leave."

The families got in line together for the food buffet. They had a choice of grilled hamburgers and hot dogs, crispy fries, fresh fruit, chocolatey brownies, and four varieties of cookies. Three separate tables held condiments and fixings. Joe laughed at the massive ketchup dispenser. Something like that would be great to have at home.

When the Munsons sat at a picnic table, Joe strategically sat at a separate one and asked his wife to join him. He was running out of time to speak with Elle. As expected, Evie asked to sit with her friend. Joe agreed and gathered cups of Caribbean punch for his family.

Joe placed his hat on the bench beside him and said a blessing over the food. Elle spoke next. "What is it that you wanted to speak about? By the way, this cheeseburger is out of this world!"

"No kidding," Joe agreed. "I may have to get another." Joe took another bite of his hamburger. "I got an unexpected call two weeks ago."

"Two weeks? Is it something bad?"

Joe took a sip of punch. "No, I think it's good. Do you remember Faith Community College? Near the bypass? It has that huge eagle statue by the entrance?"

"Yes." Elle tilted he head. "Mindy Schell went there for a year."

"Well . . ." As Joe began speaking, two boys came running toward their table with an overflowing tray of French fries in each hand. The first was looking behind him and crashed straight into the edge of the picnic table. The second child collided with the first. In what seemed like slow motion, four servings of French fries rained down on Joe and Elle. The boys started howling, so the adults attempted to stand and help them. But they were thwarted.

From the edge of his vision, Joe noticed the sky grow dark. Dozens of seagulls descended on their table to devour the fries. All Joe and Elle could do was cover their heads with their arms. Dave Munson attempted to wave the flying pests away but had little success. For some reason, he was yelling, "Elope! Elope!" to the birds. They did not elope.

Feathers and wings were flapping everywhere. Elle wasn't sure if she should laugh or cry. She peeked to her left and noticed Evie and the Munson children staring in horror. Joe was trying to stand but had to remain seated to avoid the attacking birds. The gulls were not only eating the loose fries but were also demolishing their burgers and desserts. Both of their drinks were knocked over.

At some point, a bird flew off with Joe's hat. He waited patiently at the table until beach workers shooed the birds with a broom and a towel. When the coast was clear, Joe ran off to retrieve his hat. The bird had landed with it on a branch about eight feet off the ground.

As Joe was developing a plan to rescue his hat, Elle sat quietly at the table and surveyed the aftermath. Surprisingly, only the fruit and shredded paper plates were left on the table. A large amount of bird droppings was now in the place of the food. And the careless boys were nowhere to be found. The "Bird Armageddon," as it would forever be known, had ended.

"Good grief!" Kate declared as she patted down Elle's hair. "That was almost spiritual."

Elle began laughing. She knew her response was inappropriate. In her defense, this was her first live seagull attack, and she had no idea what an appropriate response should be. So, she laughed. Evie and the Munsons began laughing too.

Joe returned with his hat, which now had a hole in the top. He and Elle cleaned up the mess and washed up in a restroom. They decided to skip the rest of lunch for now. Evie was thrilled and begged to go clue hunting. Joe looked at his wife and grinned. "Care to look at a bunch of colorful flags with me, Milady?"

"Yes, of course, Captain." Elle looped her arm with Joe's and began walking toward Emerald Beach, holey hat and all. "What could go wrong?"

PART TWO

Stormy Seas

For He will command His angels concerning you
to guard you in all your ways
Psalm 91:11

"There they are!" Ryan shouted as he pointed. "Our moms are over there, Josh." The group of six boys—including Josh, Ryan, Jonah, Jandro, Zach, and Hunter—rushed over to the chairs where Marissa and Bettina were sitting. They noticed Lena and Lauren's mothers were in the next set of chairs.

"We've been looking all over for you." Josh was winded. "We're going around checking in with all the parents before we find a place to park. Are you okay?"

Marissa appreciated that Josh was being thoughtful in front of his friends. "I am. I'm having a lot of fun. We were just about to get some lunch."

"I'm fine too. How are you boys?" Ms. Pam interrupted. "Did everyone have fun at the prom? What kind of music did they play?"

The boys agreed that the prom was a hit. Marissa noticed Zach elbow Josh like he had done earlier by the elevators. He was clearly joking, but Marissa worried it might be more. "Do you have your sunscreen, Josh?"

"Yes, ma'am. Ryan has all our stuff in his backpack. After we find Jonah's parents, we're gonna find some chairs together and get lunch."

"We need to check out the flags too," Hunter added. "They are all over the island."

"We do too," Bettina added with delight. She put her hand on Marissa's shoulder. "Let's go treasure hunting, bestie."

Josh had never heard anyone call his mom "bestie" before. And his mom didn't shirk away from the attention. She just might be having more fun this week than either of them expected. Josh wished his dad could see his mom socializing with the other moms. She seemed almost cheery.

The boys walked on in search of Pastor Joe and found him on Jade Beach. There was a section of empty chairs nearby, so they set their towels and shoes on them and hustled over to their leader.

Joe spotted the boys walking toward him. "Ahoy, mateys!" He stood up and side-hugged Jonah.

"What happened to your hat, Dad?" Jonah asked.

"Would you believe that a seagull tried to take me out at lunch?" All the boys gasped and then listened to the animated version of the attack. Jandro mentioned that a video of it was probably on YouTube already.

"You might be famous, Pastor Joe."

"I haven't heard about the prom yet," Joe said. "Anything to report?"

"It was fun," Jonah answered. "Josh slow danced with a girl."

Joe high-fived Josh. "Nice!" Josh looked down at the sand, and Joe quickly changed the subject to minimize the boy's discomfort. "Don't miss sail away. You have to be back on the ship by four o'clock. We're gonna eat at the buffet tonight if you want to join us."

"Some of us want to eat in the dining room. Some want to eat the buffet. And some want pizza," Jonah explained. "We'll be split up. But we're meeting back at the theater at nine thirty to watch the puppy-dog show. Lena and Lauren begged us to go."

"Then we will see you there." Joe saluted. "Dismissed."

As the boys were walking to their beach chairs, Winnie approached. She had been walking the island, looking for Josh. "Hey, there."

"Hey," Josh stammered. His friends were looking at flags and intentionally ignoring them.

"I was about to go flag hunting. Wanna come with me?" All the boys accepted the invitation meant for Josh. "Great! Let's go!"

The group moved closer to the water and began walking on the sand to the right. They passed a few flags that did not match the clue and stopped when they saw two jet skis zooming around.

"I wonder what they are doing?" Jonah asked.

Winnie spoke up. "My mom said they are shark scrubbers. They keep the sharks from eating all the kids."

"That's crazy!" Jonah declared. "I want that job."

"Me too," Zach added. "And the taller one looks like me."

Jonah stopped and looked at the scrubbers. "He does. Weird! And the other one looks sort of like Josh."

The group continued to walk the perimeter of the island in search of the flag that matched the picture in the gym. Several flags were red and triangular, but they did not have the correct stick—or at least the group *thought* they weren't correct. Finally, on Jade Beach, most of the teens agreed they had found the correct flag. It was red and triangular and had a stick with the right shade of brown to match the clue in the gym. The stick had a small black arrow pointing perpendicularly out from the stick, as did all the other flags. This arrow was pointing inland toward a walking path.

"The arrow must mean something," Zach announced.

"Where is it pointing?" Josh asked. He walked directly behind the arrow and sighted in the direction it was pointing. "It's aiming for the towel hut. Should we go look over there?"

Without a response, the group walked toward the towel hut. It was a simple structure with cubby shelves below a large, wooden counter. Strangely, there were no towels in the cubbies nor on the counter.

"There is nothing here," Jonah remarked. "Just a bunch of shelves. No towels. No clue."

"Maybe the sign means something," Winnie said. She moved closer to the hut and casually looked at the sign above it. Josh noticed that two families with small children were watching them. They must have discovered the same red flag. "Notice that it reads '*Buccaneer Bounty*' towels," Winnie whispered. "Not 'Cutter Cay' towels. I think that's the clue."

"Good work!" Jonah hooted excitedly. He lowered his voice. "Let's walk back to the chairs. Too many people are watching us." The group nonchalantly moved away from the towel hut. Winnie kept looking back to see if anyone else noticed the wording.

"Hey, I'll meet you back there," Zach said casually. "The guys on the jet skis are taking a break. I want to talk with them." Josh figured that Zach was up to something, but didn't say anything to stop him. Neither did anyone else.

Back at their spot, Josh and Winnie sat side by side in beach chairs while the others tossed a foam football around in the shallow water. Some of the girls from their group were standing in the ankle-deep water watching the guys.

After a few minutes of awkward silence, Winnie spoke. "I didn't expect to meet someone like you."

Heat flashed through Josh's face. "What do you mean?"

"I don't know. It's just comfortable, you know? Like we've been friends for a long time. And we just met two days ago."

Josh realized he had two choices: Admit to Winnie that he felt the same way, or play cool and act like he didn't feel the instant connection too. He took a chance. "Yeah, I know what you mean. You're easy to talk to. I certainly didn't expect to meet someone like you . . . ever."

"Cool. What are you doing tonight?" The days were running together, but Josh remembered something about the puppy-dog show and told her. "My parents want to see the ice show at nine thirty. Want to meet after the shows?"

"Sure," Josh squealed excitedly, then quickly regained his composure. "The dance hall?"

"How about on the pool deck?" Winnie suggested. "We could stargaze. My mom said that we can get hot chocolate and bring it to the chairs."

"That sounds like fun. I'll look for you after the show."

Winnie smiled. "And bring your friends. I don't mind."

Josh was a little disappointed at her willingness to share the evening with his friends but realized that Ryan and the others might like to stargaze too. "I think Ty has an app that identifies the stars and constellations."

"That will be cool."

"If something comes up, you can text Ryan. He'll get your message to me. As soon as I get home and start working, I'm gonna get my own phone."

A seagull flew close to their chairs, and both teens flinched. "That will be great. Do you start working as soon as you get back?"

"Yep," Josh answered. "Adulthood officially starts on Monday."

"Don't take this wrong, but do you eventually want more from life?"

Josh nodded. "As soon as I can afford it, I'm getting my own apartment. And a dog."

"No. *More* more?" Winnie sat up in her chair and turned to face Josh. "Do you want to do more? I don't want to just clip along with the American dream like my parents and my sister and brother. I want to do more."

"That sounds great to me. But I wouldn't even know where to start."

Winnie dug through her beach bag and found her sunscreen. She held it in her hand but didn't open it. "I get that. But I think I know where I'm going to start."

"Oh really?" Josh chuckled.

"Yep. Honduras." Winnie became animated while speaking about Honduras. "Our church had a guest speaker from Honduras last year. He showed some pictures of an orphanage that desperately needs help. Those kids got into my heart. I can't explain it. But I'm going. My parents won't take me, so I'm saving up to go next summer."

"Wow!"

Winnie put the sunscreen back into her bag without using it. "I'm serious. My brother said he will go with me if he can. He's starts pharmacy school in August. I wrote the speaker. His name is Buddy Nolan. He said they have mission teams come to the orphanage every summer. I want to stay for a whole month, but my mom talked me into starting out with a week. She's hoping I'll get over my 'obsession' once I get there." Winnie made air quotes at the word *obsession*.

"That sounds incredible."

Winnie pulled up pictures with her phone and showed Josh the children in the orphanage. Before she said anything, he wondered if he could save enough to go to Honduras next summer.

"It's about seven hundred dollars to fly from Birmingham. Miami might be cheaper." Winnie smiled as she spoke. "We just have to pay for our food. The rooms are free."

Josh was nearly speechless. "Wow!"

"I can tell you more about it tonight. I really think that God wants me to do this."

The football landed near Josh's foot. He and Winnie jumped up and joined the group in the water. Winnie had to leave around two forty-five because she was to meet her parents at three o'clock. Josh offered to walk her to their chairs.

"Thanks for the offer," Winnie said. "I can make it by myself."

Jonah rescued his friend. "Take her, Josh. We'll wait for you."

Josh grabbed his backpack. "Don't worry about it. I may take a few minutes. Don't wait for me. See you later." He and Winnie held their shoes in their hands and slowly walked through the sand toward Winnie's family.

"He's a goner," Ryan joked to his friends. "I didn't see something like that coming before this week. But he's a goner."

As he was walking back, Josh noticed Zach standing in shallow water still talking with the two boys acting as shark scrubbers. The jet skis were bobbing in the water, and Zach looked like he was in a serious conversation. Josh didn't like the look of the whole thing.

"Winnie! Over here!" Winnie and Josh had walked past her parents. They had been talking about their high school graduations and were completely unaware of their surroundings.

Winnie rolled her eyes at herself and backtracked. Her mother was still waving her arms. "Hey, Mom. This is Josh. We met at the meet-a-friend dinner on the first night. He's from Miami."

Winnie's mother perked up. "Hi, Josh. It's nice to meet you. Call me Anna. Do you have a parent in the travel business?"

"No, ma'am," Josh answered. "We go to church with the captain, and she arranged a trip for the seniors."

Now Winnie's father perked up. "You know Jenny Lu? She's famous. We were hoping to get picked to eat at the Captain's Table."

"Yeah," Josh added. "She's really cool. In fact, her son is over there by the jet skis. I'm gonna go check on him."

Winnie looked relieved for Josh to manage to avoid her mother's further scrutiny. "See you later, Josh."

"You too."

As Josh was jogging towards Zach and the shark scrubbers, he heard Winnie's mother call out. "Oh, Josh . . . ?"

"Yes, ma'am?"

"What is your last name?'

"It's March." For some reason, Anna high-fived her husband.

When Josh approached Zach, he saw him shake hands with one of the scrubbers. The three boys seemed like longtime friends. Zach was clearly up to something.

Zach spotted Josh and stopped smiling. "Hey. I'm just meeting these guys. They were born in the States, but they know all these islands. This is Charles, and this is Anthony, my 'twin.' Their dad is in the U.S. Navy, and they live in Freeport."

"Hi," Josh said awkwardly.

Zach cheered up. "They were just telling me about the underground tunnels and caves on these islands. What are they called again?"

"Karst holes," Anthony answered.

"They were gonna show me one at the back of the island." Zach put his arm around Anthony. "Can my friend come too?"

Anthony looked at Charles, who was smiling. "Yeah, yeah. You both can come."

Josh took a few steps back. "No, thank you." He looked at Zach. "We need to get back. The ship sails away in an hour."

"We have plenty of time," Zach pled. "C'mon. When will we ever get a chance like this? We could cover the entire island in twenty minutes if we had to. I promise we won't be late." Zach put his hand on his heart. "My very own mother would never leave me."

Josh knew that visiting the karst holes was a bad idea, but he didn't want to leave Zach alone. Pastor Joe had instilled in them the importance of the buddy system. "Okay. But quick. Just look at it and head back."

"Scout's honor." Zach was now holding up three fingers.

Charles and Anthony left the jet skis without securing them, and Josh and Zach followed them toward Pearl Beach. They passed dozens of passengers heading back to the ship. At a large grouping of bushes, they left the path and walked between two tall shrubs. Josh noticed a small pond with murky water just past the shrubs. Anthony led the group past a "Do not enter!" sign and beside the pond toward a mound of grass. They walked around the mound and stopped.

"The hole is behind the tall weeds," Anthony announced while pointing to the grass. "Put your bags here." He took off his shoes, and Josh and Zach dropped their backpacks.

"Wait!" Charles spoke up. "Leave your hats. The bats will try to steal them."

Josh instinctively put his hand on top of his head. "I think I will keep my hat on."

"No way, mon," Charles insisted. "That is too dangerous. Seriously, the bats come after hats like that."

The entire quest was becoming ridiculous, and Josh knew it. He reluctantly put his hat on top of his backpack as Zach did the same. Charles and Anthony left their red lifeguard hats on the grass.

"And those bracelets set the bats off," Charles added. "But that is up to you. We don't have them."

Zach began taking his ship bracelet off. Josh looked at him in frustration. "I'm not taking my room bracelet off. What if it gets lost?"

"My mom can get us another one. But suit yourself." Zach zipped his bracelet into his backpack. "I'm not rescuing you from killer attack bats though."

Josh reluctantly removed his bracelet and placed it under his hat.

Anthony walked toward the hole. "The ground is soft, so be careful. It could cave in at any minute."

Josh really did not like this impromptu adventure, and he planned to tell Zach that on their way back to the ship. The nonsense had to stop. Zach was becoming more and more careless. As if he were trying to get in enough trouble that he wouldn't be allowed to leave for college.

"Where's the cave?" Zach asked.

Anthony pointed. "There. Look over the edge. But be careful. The bats might stir."

Josh and Zach carefully stepped to the edge of the karst hole. They saw a dark opening near the bottom of the mound. Josh heard something moving and could only assume it was a bat. Or possibly many bats.

As Josh was leaning to look closer, he felt someone shove his back. He stumbled to the opening and fell into the karst hole. The bottom of the cave was about twenty feet below the opening, and he crashed into it with a thud. Zach landed with a howl at the same time.

"Hey!" Josh shouted. "Get us out of here!" The sound of Charles and Anthony running away echoed through the cave.

"They tricked us," Zach muttered. "I think my arm is broken. It's totally smashed."

"If we ever get out of here, I will break the other one." Josh was angry. He tried to stand but fell back into the mushy ground.

"I didn't know they were gonna push us. Honest."

Josh weakly sat up. "We never should have left the group. How bad are you hurt?"

"I'm afraid to move it. But I think it's pretty bad. I landed on my elbow."

"Hand me your phone. I'll try to call Pastor Joe." Josh tried to stand but fell back into the muck again.

"My phone is in my backpack," Josh sighed. "The battery's nearly dead anyways."

"Are you serious? We have no phone and no light." Josh looked around. "I'll try to climb out of here. Just sit still. The ship hasn't left yet." He tried to climb one of the walls, but the sandy limestone simply crumbled whenever he touched it. "We're stuck in here. It's impossible to climb."

"What's the plan now?"

"I have no idea."

"You shower first," Marissa told Bettina. "I don't mind waiting."

Bettina grabbed her clothes. "Thanks, bestie."

Bestie? Marissa was still amazed that beauty-queen Bettina was even talking to her, much less calling her "bestie." Despite her anxiety issues, the woman was very friendly. And honestly, she was fun to be around. Marissa let her mind explore the option of going to lunch with her new friend when they were back on land. Or even playing "picklesball," as Bettina called it. Would having a girlfriend be so terrible? She would have to see how the rest of the trip went.

Marissa heard the boys in the hallway opening their cabin, so she opened her door. Ryan was standing alone. "Hey, Ms. Marissa."

"Hi, Ryan. Is Josh around?"

Ryan grinned slightly. "He walked Winnie back to her parents. He should be back soon."

"Winnie?"

"Yeah. She's from Alabama. They hit it off at the prom last night."

Marissa's head was spinning. Josh met a girl on the ship. That didn't seem like him. Should she worry? "Will you ask him to check in with me when he gets back? We're gonna clean up and eat dinner in a little while. I would like to know that he made it back on the ship."

"Sure thing." Ryan opened his cabin and waited to be dismissed. Marissa walked back into her cabin and sat on her bed. Her mind was still swirling, and she began to feel a dread building.

To worry or not? That was the question. Josh was a good kid. But he didn't have much experience with girls. Anything could happen on a megaship. Anything. Marissa could hear the water in the shower still running, so she decided to send Gene a quick email. She told him about Cutter Cay and then cut to the chase. *"Josh met a girl from Alabama. Should I be worried?"* She knew that she was overreacting, but something did feel right. She hit send and found some dinner clothes. When Bettina finished her shower, Marissa told her that Ryan was in his cabin. But she didn't mention that Josh was with a girl. That would have to wait until she met Winnie.

Later, as they were leaving for dinner, Bettina knocked on Ryan's door. He answered with wet hair. Jandro and Hunter were standing near the desk. They were talking about towel huts, and Josh had not returned yet. Marissa reminded Ryan to let Josh know that she was looking for him and followed her bestie to the elevators. She checked her email and was relieved to see that Gene had written back. *"Only if she plays linebacker. Those kids from Alabama are intense. Seriously, Josh is a good kid. No need to worry, Maisy. I just finished the pot pie. Hurry back!"*

Marissa silently scolded herself for agonizing without a reason. She put her phone away and challenged Bettina to a reverse dinner. Both women quickly agreed to eating their dessert first. Bettina even began whistling when they exited the elevator and saw the entrance to the Fortress.

Both women went straight for the bread pudding. Tonight's variation was chocolate walnut. A woman dressed as a pirate was serving vanilla ice cream to go on top, which both women opted to have.

"This is crazy," Bettina announced as they sat at their table. "I would never eat something like this for supper back home."

"Me neither. But it looks so good."

"That it does, Marissa. That it does." Bettina said a blessing, and the women enjoyed their chocolatey dessert. "I'm too full to eat anything else. How silly is that?"

Marissa smiled. "Probably a bad idea, but I don't regret it."

"Neither do I. Let's find some protein to add some sort of nutrition to this night."

As they searched the meat options, a woman approached Marissa. "Are you Josh's mother?"

"Yes. Is everything okay?" Marissa was instantly concerned.

"Oh, yes. He's fine. I'm Winnie's mom, Anna. I saw Josh talking to you at lunch, so I figured you were his mother."

For the second time tonight, Marissa heard Winnie's name. But she hadn't met the girl. She didn't know how to respond.

"I just wanted to say hi. In full disclosure, I haven't seen Winnie interested in a boy like she is with Josh. She's back in our cabin getting ready. I think she might take all night to pick out her outfit." Anna laughed at her own joke. "And she didn't pack that much."

"She's back at the cabin?"

"Yes, we got back a little while ago. My husband and I were hungry, so we left her to get dressed. Are you on an all-protein diet?" Anna said as she looked at Marissa's plate of two chicken breasts.

"Oh, no. My friend and I had a reverse dinner tonight. We ate dessert first. Now we are trying to get some protein."

Anna's eyes widened. "Dessert first? I could never go out of order. I don't think you are supposed to do that."

"Well, we may regret it. But it was fun. And it was nice to meet you, Anna. If you see Josh, would you ask him to check in with me? I haven't seen him since the beach."

"Sure. I think the kids are planning to stargaze tonight on the top deck. I'll tell Winnie to have Josh check in."

"Thank you." Marissa walked back to her table. She had a very bad feeling about Josh. It wasn't like him to be off on his own. Of course, there were two dozen students in their group. The chances of Josh being alone were very small.

Watch over him, God. Please!

CHAPTER ELEVEN

"Can we do the pirate buffet tonight?" Evie was changing into a sundress.

"Sure," Elle responded. "As long as Daddy doesn't need to be somewhere else."

"Stevie is gonna ask her parents to go too. They are going to the ice show tonight. I think. And we need to look at the towel huts sometime."

"Sounds like a plan." Elle was secretly hoping she would have a chance to talk with Joe at dinner. He was acting like he had something important to tell her. It was probably that the price on the new-to-them truck on the Penny Car lot had dropped. If it dropped enough, it would be difficult to pass up.

Joe knocked on the adjoining door and asked the ladies if they were ready to eat, and they yelled back that they were. Jonah was in the shower, and Joe reported that Jonah had gotten a little sunburned but was "alive and well." He also reported that most of the youth were also eating at the buffet. Joe asked Elle if she would join him in sitting with them. He wanted to hear how the trip was going so far from their perspective.

So much for a serious conversation tonight, Elle thought.

"Can we look for the clue first?" Evie asked. Joe thought for a few seconds and decided that it was a good idea to look while they still had sunlight, so the threesome made their way to the pool deck.

There were two towel stations on the top deck—one on each end of the pool. Evie led the way to the closest one. A group of about twenty people were walking around it, inspecting every inch. It appeared that no one could spot an obvious clue. So the group, including the Waller family, moved to the other station. Once again, there did not seem to be a clue on the station.

Maybe the arrow was pointing at something else. Or we got the wrong flag. Or the clue isn't out yet. The others expressed their apparent mistakes and gave up on the search, but Evie was not ready to call it quits.

"Can we go back to the first one?" Evie asked.

"Of course," Joe answered. "Lead the way."

Evie scoured the hut while Joe gave Elle an eye roll. There wasn't a clue to be found.

"I found it!" Evie whispered to her parents.

"I don't see anything, hon," Elle whispered back.

"That tiny sticker." Evie was pointing to a sticker on the back of the towel hut. "It looks like it belongs. But it says, 'Hands off!' That seems strange."

Joe discretely looked at the sticker. "I agree that is strange. But what in the world could it mean?"

Evie pulled her parents toward the kiddie splash zone. "It's soccer. You don't use your hands in soccer."

"That's true," Joe added. "But it could also mean lots of other things."

"I'm sure it's soccer, Daddy. Is there a soccer field on the ship? Or a soccer game?"

Joe looked at Elle. "I guess that's better than nothing. Let's eat dinner. Then we can go to the arcade and look for a soccer game." Evie was content with the plan and followed her parents to the stairs.

Blackbeard's Fortress was bustling with hungry passengers. Apparently, many of the travelers were opting for the convenient buffet after a fun-filled day on Cutter Cay. Joe did not spot Stevie's family, but did find a large group of his students. He helped Evie gather food while gathering his own, and they sat with his teenagers. Elle let him know that she was going to join Marissa and Bettina for a little "girl time."

"Let's see . . ." Joe started when he approached the teens. "How many of you got sunburned?" Two of the boys, including Jonah, raised their hands. "Not bad, team. I expected it to be worse. So, tell me about your day."

The group ate and shared stories of beach volleyball, unlimited snacks, and the "bird Armageddon." Joe noticed that Zach and Josh were missing.

"Not sure about Zach, but Josh is probably eating with Winnie's family," Ryan shared. "He met her parents at the beach, and they probably invited him to eat with them."

Joe raised his eyebrows. "Should we start planning the wedding?"

Jonah laughed. "We might, Dad. He's smitten."

"First," Joe added, "you are too young to use the word 'smitten.' And second, I think cruise ship romances get washed away like sandcastles. It is nice for him to have a new friend to text over the summer though. Where is Winnie from?"

"Ala-bama," three of the boys said in a singsong drawl.

"Then we better not challenge her family to a pickup football game," Joe joked. He then challenged the boys at his table to make the grossest dessert they could without wasting food. They had to eat what they made and not make too much mess.

The boys finished their food and rushed to the dessert section. Joe followed. Ryan returned quickly with chocolate ice cream topped with ketchup. Jonah added pickles to a piece of coconut cake. Jandro mixed chocolate pudding with salsa and added shredded cheese sprinkles. And Joe put a piece of grilled fish on top of a small piece of cheesecake. Jandro was declared the winner, and Joe watched to make sure that everything was eaten. Or mostly eaten. Evie watched the entire spectacle in horror as she ate very large and very pink cupcake.

When they finished eating, Joe and Evie joined Elle and the women at their table. They were talking about Josh's new "girlfriend." Elle was reassuring Marissa that Josh would be fine. He had never given anyone a reason to be concerned. Joe listened to his wife's wise advice and nodded in agreement. Marissa was also concerned that she hadn't seen Josh since the beach.

As they were talking, Jenny walked up. She was looking for Zach, who wasn't answering his phone.

"He was with the guys at the beach," Joe said. "I saw him."

"Do you think he's made some friends on the ship to hang out with?" Elle asked.

"Probably." Jenny sighed. "He's been running around with that Laney girl a lot. Did he check in last night?"

Joe took out his phone to confirm. "He did. Let me see . . . He texted at eleven sixteen, 'okey dokey.' That was it."

Jenny smiled. "That was him. I guess I shouldn't worry. Thank you for checking."

Evie spoke softly. "Ms. Jenny?"

"What is it, sweetie?"

"Is there a soccer field on the ship?"

Jenny thought for a few seconds. "I'm not sure why we are whispering, but no. There isn't a soccer field on the ship. Are you missing the game?"

"Not really," Evie answered. "I was just wondering."

"You know," Jenny thought out loud, "there is a small soccer field on Treasure Island. It isn't used much. Maybe you could play when we dock there on Friday." Evie looked at her father and smiled.

The captain excused herself to chat with the teens from their group for a few minutes before returning to the bridge. Joe wondered if she ate dinner. A ship captain's life was certainly a busy one.

Joe started to text Zach to check on him but decided against it. Zach was an adult and could take care of himself. He was on the ship somewhere. That was enough for now.

"The water's getting deeper!" Josh sloshed back and forth in the dark space.

"No kidding?" Zach moaned sarcastically. "What should we do? The tide is coming up. What if the cave fills with water? We'll drown."

For the tenth time, Josh tried to lean against a wall but couldn't. The loose limestone crumbled easily. "We won't drown. In fact, we may be able to swim out if the water gets high enough."

"I'll drown for sure. I can't even move my arm." Zach was holding his right arm securely with his left. Thankfully, he had lost feeling in the wounded limb. But that only made him more concerned that he could have permanent damage. "What should we do?"

"I'm not sure. We're trapped down here." Josh trudged through the water, looking for anywhere to sit. "But the ship can't leave without us. They will know that we didn't check in and will come looking for us. It must be nearly five by now."

Zach agreed but did not move. He simply held his arm and stared into the darkness.

Tooooooooooot!

The ship's horn let out a loud blast signaling that it was sailing away. Away from Cutter Cay. Away from Josh and Zach.

Josh lost his temper. "This never would have happened if you had stayed with the group! Why did you even go over to the shark scrubbers? Beer?"

"No!" Zach shouted. "It's not like that. I just wanted to meet them."

"Not buying it." With folded arms, Josh turned to Zach. "I deserve the truth. This is all your fault."

"My fault? I didn't push us into a hole. I didn't steal our stuff. I'm innocent."

Josh had heard enough. He moved away from Zach and began praying. Then he told his friend to pray. "God is the only One who can help us now. You better start praying. It's about to get dark. There must be animals on this island. We have no protection at all."

"What good will praying do?" Zach answered hostilely. "We need to do something. We'll have to rescue ourselves."

"Are you serious, Zach? Don't you pray?" Josh folded his arms.

"Not really. And my life is great as a result." Zach moved a little and winced from the pain. "Well, until now."

Josh rolled his eyes. "How rich . . ."

"Look, I believe and all. God made the entire universe, even this hole. And I believe that Jesus died to take the punishment for my sins. But that's enough. I don't need to pray about it every day. I'm good."

"What about the spiritual warfare that Pastor Joe was telling us about? Satan's not *good* with you. He's prowling around like a lion trying to destroy you every day."

"Well, it doesn't feel like it to me. My life is sweet."

Josh thought about Zach losing his father at a young age but didn't mention that. "Maybe that is the point. Maybe Satan is leaving you alone because you act like you don't need God."

"What are you now, a preacher? I saw you with that girl. You mean to tell me that you are going to take her out and *pray* all night?"

"I'm done talking. Why don't you just go ahead and get us out of here? You are the reason we are in the mess. So fix it!" The boys stood on separate sides of the area. Josh sent up a silent prayer for help while Zach stood there, silent.

After ten minutes of silence, Zach spoke up. "You're right. This is my fault. I've got a problem. And I don't need you preaching to me about it."

Once again, Josh saw the two choices he had in front of him. He could ignore Zach and leave him to his consequences. Or he could coax the truth out of his friend. The right choice was obvious but not easy. "Tell me about your problem."

"I'm good, preacher man," Zach snickered. "Worry about yourself."

"Hey, I'm not perfect. I don't think we're supposed to be judging anyone. You can tell me. Maybe I can help." Josh cringed at the last sentence. Even he knew that he probably couldn't help with whatever Zach was caught up in.

"Nah, I'm fine."

"Suit yourself. I'm gonna try to get us out of here. The water is past my knees now." Josh walked the perimeter and felt the walls of the cave. Pieces of limestone slid into the water with loud splashes. At one area near the water's surface, Josh's hand pierced the wall. Rocks rained into the sea water below.

Zach slogged to Josh. "There's a light in there. It's a tunnel. See it? Should we try to go through?"

"It's just a hole," Josh remarked. "I don't think it's a tunnel."

"Let's try. Start digging!"

Zach was no help with the digging. He needed his working arm to hold his broken one. Any movement at all caused pain to shoot to his shoulder. So Josh stood, centered in front of the hole, and began digging. The hole widened, but not enough for either boy to crawl through. The other side of the opening was filled with knee-deep water also.

"It's a dead end," Josh muttered. "We're stuck. Our only hope is for someone to notice that we're missing."

"I told Laney to lie to my mom about tonight. We were gonna sleep on the pool deck again."

The pool deck? Josh was supposed to meet Winnie after the show. But that would be hours from now. She will think that he stood her up. Josh begged God to save them. *Please let someone notice we're missing, Lord. Before the ship is too far away.*

Josh was able to sit sideways in the new hole, but he had to sit in the water. Tired of standing, he opted for a wet bathing suit. Zach, on the other hand, continued to stand with one arm wrapped around his body.

The sun had set, and the sky was fully dark. Crickets and katydids were conversing with frogs and birds like they must every night. Josh had never felt so helpless. And alone. He pictured his mother quietly eating supper. And his father back home was probably watching *Jeopardy*. Neither had any idea that their son was in trouble. Water began dripping into the cave. It made a loud, echoing sound. Thankfully, the sea level had not risen much more. Josh could tell that his feet were becoming swollen. They hurt when he walked around.

"I'm sorry," Zach spoke out of the darkness. "You are right. This is all my fault."

"Yep," Josh added bluntly. "All your fault."

"Do you ever get these thoughts to do bad things? Things you know are wrong?"

"What do you mean?"

"I get thoughts. They pop in my head. I know I shouldn't do them. But I can't stop. It's kinda fun, you know?"

Josh tried to think like Pastor Joe. How would he answer Zach's confession? "Isn't that what Pastor Joe has been warning us about. The devil makes sin seem fun. He tempts us until we cross the line. Then he becomes an accuser."

"That's a churchy answer. Do you know what I'm talking about?"

"Sure. I'm tempted. But it sounds like you are getting bombarded."

Zach leaned his shoulder against the rock wall and winced. "That's what it feels like. I'm bombarded."

With sudden clarity, Josh knew what to say. "You've lowered your hedge of protection like Pastor Joe said. You did something to lose your connection with the Holy Spirit."

"Do you really believe all of that?"

"Yes, of course I do. That's in the Bible."

The dripping water stopped, and a brief sulfur smell passed through the cave. "I'm not going anywhere. Explain."

Josh shot his eyes upward. He was asking Jesus to give him the right words. "As believers, we have the protection of the Holy Spirit. From temptations and evil and deception. From spiritual attacks. But we can give up that protection voluntarily when we aren't strong in our faith. That doesn't mean that bad things will never happen. But we don't want to run around disconnected from the Holy Spirit at any time."

"What do you mean by 'strong in our faith?' I believe. Why isn't that enough?"

"Well, sin for one. We can lower our hedge with alcohol, drugs, pornography, gambling. Weren't you listening to Pastor Joe last week?"

"Not really. I didn't think it applied to me."

Josh shook his head in the darkness. "That sounds like pride. Here's the thing. We are in a war, and Satan is always on the attack. It doesn't seem like it because we are teenagers just finishing high school. But he knows our ancestors and our family weaknesses. He knows where we are weak. He knows exactly how to tempt us." Josh moved out of the hole and stood. "And I think we really don't want to give up any protection from the Holy Spirit."

"I guess the Holy Spirit hates me."

"Why do you say that?"

"My mom doesn't know anything. She thinks I've been studying with Jandro back home. That's what I tell my Lao Lao. But I've been going to the ridge. I only drink beer, but I go every weekend. Some of the guys there smoke dope. I've done it a few times. But it leaves a nasty smell. My mom would slaughter me if she knew."

"That's bad, Zach. You just turned eighteen."

"It hasn't caused any trouble yet," Zach snapped back. "Well, until now. I was asking those jet ski guys where I could get some weed. Laney wants to try it."

"Wow! How do you afford that? You don't have a job."

Zach paused. "My Lao Lao has a stash of cash in a jewelry box in her dresser. Don't ask me how I found it. I've been taking money without her knowing. But I'm gonna put it back when I get a job."

"When you become a lawyer? Eight years from now? That's low, Zach."

"I know. It didn't seem that bad until I just told you. Ty's been doing some sports betting, and he lost a lot of money right after graduation weekend. We've been trying to get it back, but he's getting more and more in debt."

"How can he do that?"

"He got a credit card that his parents don't know about."

"Do you see now that Satan has been playing you, and you are falling for it? Both of you. Exactly like Pastor Joe said. And you pulled me into your trouble. I knew better but fell for it myself. We're in a pretty big mess right now."

"Did you pray?"

"I did," Josh said confidently. "You should too. And you better start soon. It's only getting darker in here."

CHAPTER TWELVE

Wednesday, June 17
Sea Day

"May I get some more pancakes, please?"

Elle looked at Joe. "Where does she put them?" Then she looked at her daughter. "You may get two more, but that is it. You've had six already. We are at tummy-ache level today."

"And hurry," Joe added. "We need to see Ms. Jenny after we eat." Evie walked leisurely to the pancake station.

"Still no word from Zach?" Elle asked as she piled their used plates into one neat arrangement.

"No. He never checked in. We need to tell Jenny. In person."

"Why don't you go, and I will take Evie to the pool?"

Joe added his fork to Elle's dish pile. "That's a good idea. And I really need to talk to you. It's important."

"That's what you keep saying. Tell me now. Evie will take a few minutes."

"Well, I got a phone call—"

"Pastor Joe!" Ryan and Jandro called out as they walked to his table.

"What's up, boys?"

"Josh never came back to our room last night." Joe's eyes widened at Ryan's revelation. "He was supposed to meet with Winnie, so I didn't think anything about it. But he wasn't in his bed this morning. And I don't think he slept in it."

Joe looked at Elle. "I need to find Jenny." She waved him off. "Ryan, text me immediately if you see Josh or Zach. Neither one of them checked in last night."

"Woah," Ryan added. "Do you think they stayed with the girls?"

"I don't know, but we need to find out." As Joe stood to leave, Winnie walked toward the buffet. Ryan rushed over to her.

"Winnie, have you seen Josh?" he asked.

"Nope. And tell him to leave me alone. He bailed on me last night."

"What do you mean?"

"We were supposed to meet on the pool deck, but he didn't show. I waited over an hour." Winnie rushed off, trying not to burst into tears.

"Wait!" Ryan caught up to her. "He's missing. He never came back to our cabin. Neither did Zach."

"What?"

"Pastor Joe is going to check with Ms. Jenny."

Winnie walked toward Elle. "Do you think something happened to Josh?"

Elle patted Winnie on her shoulder. "I'm not sure what's going on, but I'm sure he is fine. We just need to let Jenny know that they haven't checked in. Please let someone know if you see him."

"Yes, ma'am."

Jenny was getting worried. Zach hadn't replied to any of her text messages. And he didn't sleep in her cabin again last night. She wanted to find Joe and ask for help, but she had a lunchtime meeting at the bridge. The veterans from the embarkation dinner were expecting a tour. Jim Morgan was also bringing Ronnie Ledbetter. The boy had become interested in the Vietnam War after listening to a dozen of their combat stories.

Wearing white pants and white button-up with officer epaulets, Jenny rushed to her cabin and checked Zach's bed again. She put her hand on the pillow and prayed for his safety. Today, she missed Brian more than usual. Her husband should be helping her raise their son. He was better at communicating with people than she was. He would have been a great "teenager dad."

Jenny skipped lunch in the dining room and returned to the bridge. She made a cup of coffee and sat in her command seat. The ship was traveling at nine knots. It was basically coasting around the islands in a designated pattern until it could dock at Mermaid Cove tomorrow.

At precisely one o'clock, the four Vietnam veterans arrived. They were joined by Flying Fred. Jenny smiled as she realized that the newlyweds wouldn't make it to the bridge tour. She smiled again when she saw Ronnie arrive with Jim Morgan. The boy was wearing a set of dog tags around his neck.

"Good morning, gentlemen," Jenny said cheerfully. "Welcome to my office, the nerve center of the ship." No one spoke. "Why don't you get some coffee and cookies. We are well fed up here." Flying Fred put two cookies on a napkin, but the rest stood still.

"How about I show you around the bridge?" Jenny asked. "Let's start with the radar screens." The captain went over the instrument panel, explaining how the GPS navigation system works. She explained what each steering joystick did and detailed the intra- and inter-ship communication systems. "Most people are interested in our weather sensors when they visit the bridge. We have an entire station set up to predict weather from five minutes to five weeks out. The staff captain keeps in regular contact with Jewel's chief meteorologist. If anything pops up, we will evaluate our current path and adjust if necessary. You may remember last year when *Golden Fortune* arrived in Miami a day late. They were rerouted to avoid a developing tropical storm."

Flying Fred pulled out a small video camera and began filming. "I am here live at the control center of the deadly ship, *Buccaneer Bounty—*"

Before Jenny could speak, Aksel Borg stopped Fred. "You need to turn that off. We do not allow filming in the bridge."

Fred did not stop. "Then why did J-Lu invite me up here?"

Jenny walked toward the influencer and took the camera out of his hand. She pressed Stop. "You will have to leave now. This is a matter of safety for the entire ship. Staff Captain Borg will see you out."

After considering his options, Flying Fred grabbed his camera and his cookies and walked out.

"Well done, Captain." Robert Thomas shook Jenny's hand. "You took command."

Jenny moved on with the tour. "Would anyone like to sit in my seat? The 'captain's view' it the best on the ship."

Jim Morgan encouraged Ronnie to try the seat. Before the boy could sit down, Pastor Joe walked in and announced, "Zach and Josh aren't on this ship! We can't find them anywhere."

"What?" Jenny said, her fear rising. Subconsciously, she picked up the interphone to call security. "That's impossible. We scan everyone. I would have been told if someone were missing. How could they be missing?"

"Ryan said that Josh never returned to their cabin last night. Have you seen Zach?"

Jenny looked at Ronnie. "No, I haven't. Have you seen them, Ronnie?"

Ronnie shook his head. "No, ma'am. But we don't usually hang out together."

Someone on the other end of the phone answered, and Jenny asked if there were any missing passengers. After the negative response, Jenny ordered Aksel to take charge as she went to the security station on Deck Three. Without asking, the visitors followed her.

On the way down, Jenny bombarded Joe with questions, but he had few answers. The boys hadn't been seen since the beach the day before. Jenny tried to think of a reason for both of them to be missing. All she could come up with were girls. They must be off with some girls somewhere. But where?

"I'm sure he's fine, Marissa," Bettina reassured. "This is just a big mix-up."

"Where could he be?" Marissa was pacing in their cabin. Ryan was sitting on his mother's bed. He had been reluctant to worry Josh's mother but decided that she needed to know. He finally told her that

Josh never made it to their cabin last night. At his revelation that he hadn't been seen all night, Bettina tried to reach Joe. He didn't respond to her text right away.

Bettina walked to her friend and put her arm around her. "Sit down. You need your strength right now. Joe will find Josh, and we will all laugh about this soon enough. That boy may need to be grounded after his shenanigans." Ryan cringed.

Marissa kept pacing. "Something isn't right. This isn't like Josh. Should I notify Gene?"

"Let's wait a little bit before we tell Gene. We don't have any solid information." Bettina turned to her son. "Ryan, can you get us something to eat? And two waters?" Relieved to leave the room, Ryan rushed to the food court on Deck Seven. He looked at everyone he passed, hoping to find his friends amongst the crowd.

"We shouldn't have come on this cruise," Marissa said. "Everything was fine back home."

"Do not get ahead of yourself, bestie. Let's play a gabby game. That will help. Hmm. How about Common Thread? Name ten things you have in common with Prince Charles."

Marissa snapped. "Stop! I don't want to play one of your stupid games. I want my son to come back." As soon as she yelled, she regretted her outburst. Bettina walked to her bed and sat down. "I'm so sorry, Bettina. That wasn't me. I'm just so worried. Please forgive me."

Bettina bounced up. "Of course. Maybe I should start. I will list ten things I have in common with Saturn."

Marissa began laughing. "Go ahead. I can't wait to hear this. But can we pray first? We need to pray."

"Of course! Let's hold hands to make it stronger." Marissa agreed, and the women prayed for Josh and Zach's safety. They acknowledged that God knew exactly where they were and pled for Him to protect the boys from any danger or threat. Immediately, Marissa's spirit calmed. She thanked her friend for her intercession.

"Sure thing, bestie. Now let's get on with it. Number one, I have rings on my finger like Saturn . . ."

As Bettina was pondering her Common Thread list, the cabin phone rang. Marissa quickly answered, and a security officer introduced himself. He asked for details of her missing son, but the anxious mother had very little to offer. Josh was last seen walking on Jade Beach with Winnie to meet her parents. That was all she knew. She didn't even know Winnie's last name.

"We are meeting at the security station on Deck Three, Mrs. March. You are welcome to join us." The officer explained how Marissa could enter the crew-only area and then hung up.

"I need to go to Deck Three," Marissa said in a shaky voice.

Bettina put her arm around her friend. "Let's go together."

"My feet are peeling pretty badly," Zach said worriedly.

"Mine too." Josh was trying to hold his feet up and out of the water one at a time, but balancing was difficult without some sort of support. Both feet were peeling from being wet for so long. The sea water had retreated sometime after midnight, and the boys were able to sit in the wet mush for a few hours. They tried to sleep but heard too many noises to feel safe letting their guard down. The water had risen above their knees and was now slowly lowering again.

"If we ever get out of here, I'm gonna sleep for a week," Zach announced.

"I'm gonna eat five pizzas," Josh countered.

"You know, it's possible they will never find us. We have no food and no water. How much longer can we last?" Josh did not respond. "I doubt my mom even knows I'm missing."

Josh looked at Zach. "Why would you say that? She's probably got the entire crew looking for you right now."

"Nah." Zach sighed. "She's too busy. She's gone all the time. And I give her a lot of grief. She's probably enjoying the peace right now."

A small fish swam past Josh's legs. He casually dodged it. "I don't believe that. And even if it's true, my mom is going nuts right now. I'm sure of it. Surely Ryan has told her that I didn't come back to the cabin. She knows."

"What if something happened to Ryan?"

Josh hadn't thought about any of his friends being harmed in addition to them. Or Winnie! "Don't think like that. Either way, we didn't check in last night. Something has triggered them to look for us."

"I'm gonna go crazy if we are stuck here any longer."

"We need to be tough. They are looking for us. I promise. Can you feel your arm at all?"

"Nope. It's a little achy. But that's it. If I hold it tight, I can manage."

"Tell me more about the voices you hear telling you to do bad things."

Zach turned away from Josh. "It's not voices. Just thoughts. And I don't want to talk about it." The conversation stopped for a full minute. "If you tell anyone what I said, I will make up a lie about you and Winnie."

"You're a jerk. And I will never forgive you for getting us into this mess."

"I didn't push you, remember? Anthony did. And I didn't ask you to come over and bother us."

Josh stopped talking. He plopped down into the shallow water and made another attempt to dry his feet. Through the opening above him, he could see that the sun was shining brightly. Was it possible that the ship was still sailing without them? Had it turned around to rescue them? Not knowing was brutal. Josh asked God again to rescue them—quickly.

The boys remained quiet for nearly an hour. Both were sitting in the chest-deep water. Josh decided to break the silence. "When do you leave for Gainesville?"

"August thirteenth," Zach replied matter-of-factly. "I didn't sign up for summer registration, so I have to go the week before classes start."

"What classes will you take?"

Zach snickered. "Oh, I don't know. I don't really care. I'm more interested in the parties."

Once again, Josh was taken aback by Zach's attitude. "Ms. Jenny is paying a lot of money for you to be down there. Don't you want to get a degree and go to law school?"

"I'll finish. But I'm not gonna miss any parties. This is my time to have fun. I'll have the rest of my life to pay bills and be a grown-up."

"That sounds about right."

"What does that mean? We only get to be young and free once. I'm not gonna waste it. You do you, preacher man. I'm gonna do Zach."

Josh thought carefully about his response. "That attitude sounds like those bad ideas in your head again. Your mom is trusting you. Pastor Joe has invested in you. Heck, I want good things for you. Why would you want to waste this opportunity?"

"You don't get it," Zach blurted.

"No, I get it," Josh replied. "If I had the chance to go to college, I wouldn't blow it. I'll think of you living the dream while I'm checking out old ladies at the store." Zach chuckled at Josh's final comment. "I'm serious. This is another example of spiritual warfare. It's right before your eyes, and you don't even see it."

A dark-gray bird flew into the cave and somehow perched on the far wall. The visitor heralded the end of their conversation. Neither boy wanted to continue down that serious path. Although it was quiet, the bird provided a much-needed distraction for the hungry and dehydrated boys.

After what seemed like hours of silence, Zach became restless. "We need to get out of here." Light was still shining outside, and he began kicking at the small hole he could see.

Josh walked to the hole. "Stop kicking. It's gonna cave. I'll dig it out. That light is still there, so we might be able to get out of here. But I seriously doubt it." He clawed at the opening with his bare hands for a while. Every few minutes, he would try to fit through the opening. Eventually, he was able to squeeze through.

"Go to the light, Josh. And find someone who can get me out." Zach watched Josh crawl on his knees through the water and disappear through the hole.

"I'm stuck!" Josh cried out.

"Dig yourself out!" Zach ordered forcefully.

"I can't," Josh moaned. "It just a bunch of rock. And I can't turn around. It's pitch black in this tunnel. Help!"

Zach tried to help Josh get free, but he couldn't use his arms. He needed to hold the broken one with the healthy one, so he began kicking around Josh again.

"Stop! You're pushing me farther down. I'm gonna drown in this mud."

"We're doomed." Zach kicked some dirt and walked away from Josh.

Jenny rushed into the security center. The six bridge visitors followed closely behind. "Update!"

Tyler Wayne, the security officer, stood. "We've spoken with the two employees on Cutter Cay. They did a sweep of the island and didn't find anyone. Megan is pulling up the gangway camera right now. The boys scanned in at three forty-two p.m. We can see that on the log. But I want to see the video to verify."

"I want to see it too," Jenny shared. "Thank you, Wayne."

The four veterans, plus Ronnie Ledbetter and Jim Morgan, found nearby chairs and moved them into the hallway outside of the security center. Each wanted to help with the search in any way he could.

"There has to be some sort of reasonable explanation," Jenny wondered aloud. "Maybe they lost their phones."

"It is possible," Tyler answered. "But they haven't been seen since yesterday."

Jenny walked out to the hallway. "Ronnie, are you sure you haven't seen Zach or Josh? Try to think back to yesterday and last night. Were they at dinner?"

"I didn't see them. I promise," Ronnie answered.

As Jenny began pacing the passageway, Marissa arrived. She was followed closely by Bettina. "Any word? Are the boys really missing?"

"It seems that they are. Come with me." Jenny took Marissa's hand and walked back into the center. "This is Josh's mother. Any progress with the video?"

Megan spoke. "We are almost there. Let's see . . . three forty-two p.m. There! I see them." The mothers leaned in to see the video footage more clearly.

Marissa gasped. "That's not Josh! I can see Zach, but that's not my son!" She looked closer.

"No!" Jenny squealed. "That's not Zach either. Look closer. That's his hat, but it's not Zach." Both women looked at the screen, then at Tyler. "What does this mean?"

"Well, Captain, we now know with certainty that the boys did not get back on the ship. And it seems we have two stowaways."

"Call a triple Charlie," Jenny demanded. "Now!"

Tyler quickly called a "Charlie, Charlie, Charlie" emergency code. He used the intra-ship line so passengers did not hear. Eventually, they would be notified of the security threat onboard as well. But for now, only the crew knew something was amiss.

While the security officers were communicating with their team, Marissa began crying. "How could they be lost? How could this happen?"

Jenny put her arm around her friend and walked into the hallway. She addressed the concerned bystanders. "It seems that two boys fraudulently scanned in as Zach and Josh. We don't know who or where they are. And we don't know where our boys are."

Immediately, Robert Thomas spoke up. "I'd like to help." The other veterans agreed.

"Me, too, Ms. Jenny," Ronnie added as he stood. "I want to help find Josh and Zach."

Jenny shook her head. "Thank you for your offers. But we have professionals already on this. We don't need added hands complicating the efforts."

Ronnie sat down, but the veterans remained standing. Robert spoke for the group. "With all respect, Captain, I believe we can help. We will wait one hour for your newfangled technology to find your son. If he hasn't been found, we insist that you take advantage of our expertise. Two of us are well-trained in the location of captives in this type of terrain."

At the word *captives*, Marissa gasped. Bettina walked her to the chairs and convinced her to sit down. The women listened as Jenny spoke with Robert. She hastily agreed to their timeline and returned to the command center.

Robert rapidly crafted a plan while they waited. "Ronnie and Jim, can you contact some of the boys' close friends? Ask them for any details they can think of. And write them down. Come back in thirty minutes." As the two darted away, Robert turned to the other veterans. "Let's move our chairs to the end of the hall so we don't disturb the crew. Jack, we were rats. We can help find the boys if they are underground."

Jack nodded. "If they weren't found by a sweep, they very well may be underground. These islands have karst holes just like in Vietnam."

"Let's start a list," Robert suggested. "We'll need flashlights, a map of the island, ropes, first-aid supplies, oxygen . . ."

While the men were planning, Jenny was pacing in the command center. "Any word?"

"No, Captain," Tyler replied. "A thorough search of the ship for the stowaways is underway. And the island employees are searching Cutter Cay right now. They are focusing on the beaches. One reported that there were two unmanned jet skis floating about a hundred feet off Pearl Beach. He is acquiring a boat to get to them to look for clues."

"The shark scrubbers!" Jenny blurted. "There were two young men just hired to man the jet skis. Call Peggy. Get her to track down their information."

"Aye, Captain."

As Tyler spoke on the phone, Jenny walked to the hallway toward Marissa and silently prayed. *Father, you know where they are. Please keep them safe. And show me the way to bring them back.*

"Jenny!" Marissa rushed to her, anxiously awaiting news. Her left sandal was unbuckled, but she didn't seem to notice. "Do you know any more details?"

"We think the two shark scrubbers scanned in with our boys' security bracelets. With the boys' hats, the crew member at the kiosk did not notice a difference in their faces. Amazingly, the stowaways look very much like Zach and Josh. We have an alert out and are scouring the ship to find them."

"What about Josh and Zach? Where are they?" Marissa's voice faltered.

"Workers are searching the entire island now. The boys couldn't have gone far. I am about to put in a notice of route deviation with the line. Aksel is already turning the ship around to head back to Cutter Cay. No other ships are set to dock there today, so we can get close to the dock. One of the officers is contacting the Royal Bahamas Defence Force. And the U.S. Coast Guard."

Bettina spoke for Marissa. "How long will that take?"

"We will be back to the island in a little over two hours," Jenny shared. "To be honest, the government agencies take a little longer. But they will have the resources and equipment that we'll need to find the boys."

"What equipment?" Robert Thomas overheard the conversation.

"I don't know," Jenny admitted.

Tyler appeared in the command center doorway. "A decent map would be nice. Plus drones. Infrared cameras. And I have requested a Cavefinder. Our UAV drone probably won't work too well on the land. Too much iron in the soil."

Robert's eyes widened. "We are cave finders, sir."

"I appreciate your willingness to help, Seargent Thomas. But we have access to the most advanced terrestrial and subterranean search and rescue equipment around, in addition to our cutting-edge marine search technology. Once it gets here, the boys will be found. I promise."

Robert looked at the other men, then to the captain. "Jenny, we don't have time to wait for the fancy equipment. The boys could be injured. Put us on the ground; we'll find them."

"That's absurd! I can't have passengers conducting search and rescue missions." Jenny turned to return to the security center.

Robert spoke softly toward her direction. "Is there actually a policy stating that volunteers *cannot* search for missing passengers? Are you really pulling rank on us with two young men in danger?"

Jenny looked at Marissa, who was huddled with Bettina behind Robert. "Tyler, come here." The officer approached. "How long are we talking?"

"I don't know, Captain. I put in the request, but it could take hours. We've got about five or six more hours of daylight. And we won't get to the island for at least another two hours."

"Okay. Keep working your plan. You are the best, Tyler. But I'd like you to bring the men in the hall in on the operation. They have specialized experience that we just might need."

Robert heard Jenny's request. "All right, men, let's put together an operational plan. I'm calling it Operation Bounty Runner."

"Quiet, quiet," Joe bellowed to the two-dozen students gathered near the gym. "Thank you for rushing here so quickly. And so calmly." He paused and scanned the crowd. The youth and many of their chaperones were staring back at him. He was their leader, and he knew that he was prepared for this moment. "As you probably know, Josh and Zach are missing."

"Is it true?" Lauren Lu blurted. "I thought it was a joke."

"Yes, it's true," Joe answered somberly. "They haven't been seen since yesterday at the beach." Joe noticed Winnie and her parents standing near Ryan and Jonah. "I am going to use our birthday plan, so listen up. This will be different from dividing teams for gaga ball, but it's still the birthday plan."

The gym was quiet. A few strangers joined the back of the crowd. Joe communicated the plan methodically. "Those of you with January, February, and March birthdays will pray for Zach and Josh's health and safety. For their protection. And for their mothers' peace of mind." A few students began to move. "Hold up. Not yet."

"Hold on, everyone," Jonah pled. "He's not finished."

"The April, May, and June birthdays will pray for the boys to be found quickly. Without any delay. Those with July, August, and September birthdays will pray for Ms. Jenny and the security team. You will ask for them to have wisdom and clarity. And for them to understand God's plan. Finally, the October, November, and December birthdays will deliver the knock-out blow. You will pray that Satan's plans will be revealed and uncovered. And most importantly, that those plans will be derailed. This is serious. You will pray for victory over the evil forces. And protections from any attack."

Elle stood next to her husband. "Ephesians chapter six verse twelve tells us that 'our struggle is not against flesh and blood, but against the rulers, authorities, and powers of this dark world and against spiritual forces of evil in the heavenly realms.' Today, we are standing firm against these evil forces."

Joe squeezed Elle's hand and continued his charge to the group. "We will use the walking track to cover the ship in prayer. Walk laps at your own pace. We'll stop when God tells us to stop. These are individual prayers, so no talking to one another. Each one of us is calling on God's mighty power to return our friends safely. Please take this seriously." The group began shuffling about, eager to get started. "One more thing! I wrote my father, and he has members from our church praying back home. We are calling an army of angels to battle for us." Joe had planned to lead a group prayer, but the students were already dashing off toward the track before he could speak. Joe reached for Elle's hand and began silently walking beside her. Evie followed behind.

"Gene? Are you there?" Jenny arranged for Marissa to call her husband on the ship's satellite phone system.

"Marissa? Are you okay?"

"Yes," Marissa answered shakily. "But Josh is missing."

"What?! Josh is missing? What do you mean?"

Marissa began sobbing, so Bettina took the phone. "Gene, this is Bettina. Josh and Zach did not return to the ship last night. Jenny has it under control. The whole security team is looking for them."

"How did that happen?" Bettina shared all the details available. Gene was silent while he processed the disturbing information. "Would you please put Marissa back on the phone?"

"Sure. Here she is."

"Gene. . ." Marissa began sobbing.

"Listen, Maisy. Josh will be fine. I'm sure of it. You stick with Bettina. I'm gonna call the cruise line and try to get to you somehow. I want you to stay strong until I see you. And call me when you get any new information. I will be praying for both of you."

Marissa stopped crying. "We can't afford a plane flight."

"Yes, we can. That is what our savings is for. Don't worry about me. Just call me whenever you get any new information. Okay?"

"Okay. I miss you."

"Josh! Get out of there!" Zach flinched as he bumped his arm on the limestone.

"I can't. I'm stuck." Josh tried to turn around, but any movement stirred up the mud on the ground and caused the tunnel to shrink. The sides were caving in. "The hole is filling with mud."

Zach moved to the tunnel and began kicking the bottom of the opening.

"Stop! It's caving in!"

"I'm gonna stick my leg into the hole. Try to grab onto it." Zach did not hear a response. "Grab my foot." He could hear Josh struggling but couldn't hear a voice. "Josh!"

"Ahhh!"

"Josh! Josh!"

There was no response.

CHAPTER FOURTEEN

"Thank you, Tito," Jenny said from her bridge seat. "Thank you for arranging our quick approach on such short notice."

"Of course, Captain. I am glad to help. Myrna is home praying. I'm sure she has our church interceding as well. Please do what you must. I will wait for your departure after successfully finding the men."

Men? Jenny hadn't yet accepted the fact that Zach was now a man. But he was. He was eighteen years old and would be moving to Gainesville in eight weeks. Somehow, the thought of her son being a man made the situation seem more dire. He shouldn't have been duped or tricked into staying on the island. He must have been taken against his will. Or something worse. "Thank you, Tito. I need to go to security."

"Godspeed!"

As Jenny made her way back to Deck Three, she spotted families and individuals enjoying the ship's amenities. They were laughing and eating and dancing, unaware of the crisis their captain was facing. An announcement had been made notifying the passengers that *Bounty* would be returning to Cutter Cay for an "urgent situation." But few knew the gravity of the matter. Few knew that her life was unraveling and out of control.

Her phone's ringtone shook Jenny out of the fog. "Hello?"

"Where are you?" Tyler asked. "We have an update."

"I'll be there in two minutes." Jenny rushed past travelers who readily recognized her. Thankfully, each of them understood that she was involved in a serious matter and did not attempt to stop her.

At the security center, Tyler was looking at his computer terminal. Peggy Davis was standing beside him. When Jenny arrived, he showed her photos of the two shark scrubbers. "Here are our stowaways. Anthony and Charles Martin. Ages sixteen and nineteen. Their father is stationed at AUTEC on Andros Island. He hasn't reported the boys missing but is being contacted."

Jenny stared at the photos on the screen. The boys resembled Zach and Josh, but not as closely as she first thought. "Why are they on our ship?"

"We have no idea, Cap," Tyler answered. "It could be a covert military mission. They could be transporting drugs. They could be joyriding."

"Drugs?! Joyriding?" Marissa had overheard the conversation.

Tyler turned to face the worried mother. "Yes, Mrs. March. We must consider every possibility. We will find them and get your son back."

"What is the status of the search?" Jenny questioned.

"We've checked the cargo holds and the void spaces. A team is checking the lifeboats as we speak. Don't worry. They can't hide forever."

Jenny sighed. "Thank you, Tyler. The Coast Guard will assist as soon as they get to the island. Have you met with the vets yet?"

"No, ma'am."

"Let's talk with them. Marissa, will you excuse us for a minute?" Jenny and Tyler moved into the hallway while Marissa remained with Peggy at the computer terminal.

The four veterans were sitting in chairs arranged in a square, while Ronnie and Jim Morgan were standing behind the chairs. Jack was writing on a notepad while the men took turns speaking. Jenny interrupted their discussion. "Gentlemen, Tyler would like to speak with you about the rescue plans once we reach the island."

Tyler's head shot up. "I don't think we should discuss our strategy with anyone, Captain. That would be a violation of policy, I believe."

Jenny put her hands on her hips. "I am aware of our guidelines, but this is an emergency. We can work around the policies." She looked at Robert. "Would you please share with us your ideas? Tyler can then work them into *Bounty*'s official strategy, if he sees fit." Robert nodded. "I will leave you men to discuss the rescue of my son. I would like to check on Josh's mother and visit the prayer walk. When I return, I would like a detailed line of attack." Jenny took two steps away and turned. Her tone softened. "And thank you. Thank you very much for helping me find Zach. All of you are heroes to me."

When she peeked into the security center, she saw Marissa and Bettina talking with Peggy. They seemed content for the moment, so she gave a quick wave to Marissa and made her way to the elevator bank. The walking track was on Deck Eleven.

As the elevator doors opened to the track, Jenny caught sight of a dozen people walking directly past her. She stepped out onto the edge of the track and watched the outpouring of love. Youth members, as well as total strangers, were walking in unity. Some were whispering. Some had their hands raised. An older woman was humming "Amazing Grace." The air around her seemed electric, and Jenny was overwhelmed by the love of her friends and passengers. Tears began flowing from her eyes as she stood, unable to move.

When Joe passed, he stopped and whispered. "Are you okay?"

"I don't know. But thank you for organizing this. You are doing more for Zach and Josh than my entire security team is. This is amazing! I can't thank you enough. I am so glad that God placed you as the youth pastor. Don't ever leave this role. You are exactly where you should be."

Jenny walked a lap in silence, begging God to give her team the wisdom to find the boys. She also prayed for Zach and Josh to be found safe. As far as she knew, they hadn't eaten or had anything to drink in over a day. Time was running out.

Joe couldn't believe what Jenny had just said. Was God steering him away from the teaching job? Jenny was blunt with her comment that he was where he should be. Joe felt the significance of his role this week and returned his focus to the prayer walk. He really needed to speak with Elle soon. But that would have to wait. Josh and Zach were the focus right now.

As Joe walked, he marveled at the diversity of the people walking the track. Young and old were praying together. Strangers and friends. Passengers and crew members. His spirit was lightened by the commitment of God's people, and he continued to walk and plead with God for the rescue of his students.

Bettina convinced Marissa to go back to their cabin to wait for updates. Tyler promised to call them with any news. Both women were lying on their beds, and Bettina was urging her friend to play a gabby game, but Marissa refused. She also refused any television or music being played. She needed her mind to be alert.

"They will find them," Bettina reassured as she fluffed her pillows for more support. "We will get back to Miami as a big group and have a great summer. You'll see." Marissa wasn't convinced. "Would you like a snack or coffee? We could order room service."

"No, thank you. I couldn't eat right now." Marissa fluffed her pillows also. "I'll be better when Gene gets here." On cue, the cabin's phone rang. "Hello?"

"Maisy, it's me," Gene bellowed. "I've been on the phone with Jewel Cruise Line all morning. I can't come out there because I don't have a passport. I knew I should have gotten one when you and Josh did. But I didn't think I would ever need it."

"Oh no," Marissa whispered. "But I need you here."

"I will be at the port to pick you and Josh up as soon as the ship arrives. And they gave me a number to call whenever I want to talk with you. They will patch me into your ship phone. If you don't answer, I can call a security center for updates. I also got Josh two weeks off, so he won't have to start at the store next week."

"Thank you, Gene. Thank you for thinking clearly."

"Of course, Mais. Josh will be fine." Gene's voice quivered. "Donna at the church called and said that a prayer chain has been organized. People are praying in the sanctuary for an hour at a time. Satan won't win this battle. I promise."

Marissa felt lighter while talking with her husband. They talked for a while longer, and she shared about the activities she had done so far. And the food. So much food. Finally, Gene suggested that they clear the lines in case someone had an update. Marissa agreed and promised to write him any updates she had. "I love you, Gene."

"Oh, my dear, I love you a million times that. Goodbye."

After the call, Marissa folded her hands over her stomach and tried to get some rest. Thankfully, Bettina was doing the same. The room was eerily quiet except for some minor creaking of the walls. Marissa was comforted realizing that the noises were caused by the ship traveling at full speed to return to Cutter Island.

They haven't eaten all day. They could be hurt. Or worse. Scary thoughts were disturbing Marissa. She tried to think on pure, lovely, and true thoughts. But images of Josh shaking and scared kept returning. Finally, she spoke. "I think I would like to play a gabby game. The quiet is too scary."

"Of course." Bettina sat crisscross and scooted back to her pillows. "Let's play the Alphabet Game. I'll pick a topic, and then we go back and forth with items in alphabetical order."

Marissa chuckled. "You are good at this."

"I've had lots of practice. Hmm. How about ice cream toppings? You start with something that starts with *A*."

Marissa stood, walked over to the couch, and sat down. "Almonds."

"Good. That was quick. I'll say bananas."

"Chocolate."

Bettina struggled for a minute. "Dough. People put cookie dough on ice cream."

"I will allow it." The women laughed and continued with espresso, fudge, and gummy bears. Then the phone rang, startling both.

"Hello!" Marissa answered quickly.

"Mrs. March, this is Tyler. Can you make your way back to Deck Three? We'd like to share our plans with you and the captain before we arrive to Cutter Cay."

"Of course! I'm on my way." Marissa hung up and passed on the information to Bettina, who was looking at her phone.

"Let's go." Bettina jumped up from her bed. "I think we should make a quick detour to Deck Eleven on our way. Ryan just texted that we need to see the jogging track."

"Okay, but I'd like to hurry."

"And buckle your shoe. Didn't you notice it flapping like that?" Marissa obliged.

The women rushed to the jogging track and were amazed at what they saw. At least one hundred people were walking solemnly around the track. Marissa knew instantly that they were praying for Josh and Zach. A tear fell down her face as she watched not only friends but complete strangers praying for her son. She recognized Winnie walking near Ryan and Jonah.

Bettina took Marissa's hand. "Let's do a lap." Without responding, Marissa walked beside her new friend. The air became cool, and she could hear soft mumbling from some of the prayer walkers.

Marissa prayed silently. *Thank you, Lord, for these people. Please hear their prayers. And please protect my son. Help the crew find the boys as quickly as possible. Let us be a family again in our cozy home.*

When the women completed a lap, they traveled to the security center on Deck Three. Marissa took a minute to send a message to Gene telling him about the prayer walkers.

Tyler was sitting in the hall with the four veterans, plus Ronnie and Jim Morgan, who were now sitting in chairs. "Mrs. March, please join us. We are waiting on the captain to arrive."

Ronnie and Jim stood and offered their chairs to the women. "Thank you, Ronnie." Marissa patted the young man on his shoulder.

"We're gonna find them, Ms. Marissa," Ronnie said earnestly.

"Thank you." Marissa looked at Tyler. "Are they hurt?"

"We don't have any information about their condition at this point." Tyler paced beside the chairs. "As soon as we find the stowaways, we will question them. Until then, we have a rescue plan in place."

Marissa's shoulders sank. "Thank you," she answered softly. Jenny rushed to the group and did not interrupt.

Three security team members, including Megan, appeared and stood behind Tyler. "Here is the plan, everyone." Tyler referred to a table with more detailed notes. "When we dock, we will implement a four-stage approach."

"We're calling it Operation Bounty Runner," Robert added.

The security members rolled their eyes at the name, but Marissa felt strangely comforted that the veterans had given Josh and Zach's rescue an official title.

Tyler continued. "First, we will secure the area. As far as we know, the Defence Team and the Coast Guard have not arrived yet. Both are securing thermal imaging search equipment. We can search for individuals in the water but not on land. Until they arrive, I am in charge. I will authorize access to the island. Peggy informed me that the island employees who initially swept the area have gone home. We should be the only personnel on Cutter Cay.

"Second, we will establish a search area after an initial assessment. Twelve members of our team will conduct a grid pattern search of the entire island. They will begin with the last known location. We should have enough daylight to complete the hunt before dark." The two women shivered at the word *hunt*.

Megan spoke up. "I brought the two-way radios. Each person on the ground will have one. Plus, Captain Jenny. And the group sitting here." She looked at Robert. "You may listen, but you cannot get involved."

"We respectfully request to *be involved,*" Robert pled. "We were trained in this sort of rescue and—"

"I appreciate your offer, Sergeant Thomas." Jenny stood and wiped her hands on her pants. "But I cannot have passengers interfering in the mission."

The veterans looked at each other and then at Tyler as he continued with the plan. "Nelson over here will be running the drone throughout the ground search. We will have members on the ship surveying the aerial data." He looked at Marissa. "We will also be running a water rescue simultaneously. As soon as we dock, RIBs will be deployed to search for bodies in the water." The hallway became still as Tyler resumed. "Those are rigid inflatable boats. We have submitted missing persons reports to alert the Bahamian Island and Turks and Caicos of our mission. If the boys have left Cutter Cay, we will find them."

Tyler returned to the security center without offering to answer questions. The group looked toward Jenny, who tried to comfort them. "Tyler is the best. He will find Zach and Josh. They will be back on the ship by suppertime."

Marissa could only smile at Jenny's promise. The lump in her throat was about to choke her.

"We appreciate the intel, Captain," Robert said. "And we will be ready to provide any assistance you may need. We have gathered supplies and are ready to take action."

"What do we do now?" Marissa asked with a shaky voice as she stood.

"We will be waiting right here, Mrs. March," Robert answered. "You need some rest, but we can keep you better informed if you stay here with us." Marissa nodded and sat back down.

"Have you all eaten?" Jenny asked the group.

"We are fine," Robert replied, "but the ladies need to keep their strength up."

"Without waiting for a response from Marissa and Bettina, Jenny called the ship's room service number and asked for a tray of light snacks to be brought to the security center. The group would have a long afternoon, and possibly an even longer evening.

Jenny found a seat in the security center and called the bridge. Aksel reported that they were twenty-five minutes from Cutter Cay. *Bounty* had received permission to approach, and Tito was assisting with the navigation. They would be anchoring offshore, since no dock workers were available to assist with the mooring lines at the pier. Jenny commended Aksel for taking command without warning.

When the food arrived, Jenny joined the others in the passageway. She chose crackers and hot coffee. The smell of her drink calmed her nerves slightly. She was trained in crises like today's, but not for the rescue of her own son. Her only son. Her mind quickly went to the group praying on the jogging track. Their intercession meant everything to her.

Marissa needed the same hope. "Did you get a chance to see what is happening on the track?" Jenny asked her friends.

"We did," Bettina answered. "We even walked a lap with the others. I cannot tell you how thankful Marissa and I are that people are praying for the boys while the search is underway." Bettina side-hugged Marissa, who was peeling the wrapper off a blueberry muffin. "Did you organize the walk?"

"No," Jenny said. "Joe got that started. And I heard there is a group praying at the church as well."

Bettina refilled her coffee and offered more to Jenny, who politely declined. "I'm thankful for Joe. Both of my boys grew spiritually when they were in high school. That discipleship is invaluable."

"I agree," Jenny added. She looked over at Ronnie, who was sitting silently next to Jim Morgan. Clearly, the boy considered himself part of the rescue team. Jenny knew that Ronnie would jump in to help if he were needed, and the idea surprised her. Everything she knew of him was that he was selfish and rude. Perhaps she had misread him. Or perhaps Ronnie was seizing an opportunity to show his true character. Whatever it was, he fit in with the older men perfectly.

Jenny could feel the ship slowing and knew they were about to anchor. She was torn between commanding the bridge and assisting in the security center. She was the ship's captain. But she was also Zach's mother. Her maternal role won out, and she found a chair in the hallway to sit with the group. From the corner of her eye, she noticed Marissa let out a soft sigh as if to thank Jenny for remaining close by.

"Two RIBs have been deployed, Captain," Tyler yelled from the entrance of the center. "The waters are now being searched."

Jenny felt a chill run up her spine. "Thank you for the update."

The hallway was silent for five minutes before Tyler bellowed another update. "A tender boat carrying the search team is on its way to the island as we speak." He looked at Robert and Jack. "You may listen on the two-way, but I wouldn't recommend it. The incoming exchange will be unfiltered."

Robert looked around and saw nods from his fellow veterans and both mothers. He turned the radio on and sat it on a small table so everyone could hear. Jack adjusted the volume to lower the static noise.

It didn't take long for the first transmission to come through: "Sea glider in the air. Confirm transmission."

Jenny stood. "That's the drone. I'll check on it."

Ronnie spoke and startled Marissa. "Wouldn't Zach and Josh just wait at the dock for someone to come back for them? Why would we need a drone?"

"Apparently, they weren't there this morning," Jack explained. "They are detained for some reason. A drone will provide quick coverage. But the boots on the ground will be our best hope."

Better understanding the gravity of the situation, Ronnie looked at the women. "I'm praying, Ms. Marissa." Josh's mother could only nod.

Jenny returned to the hallway. "The drone is transmitting. And the grid search is underway. It won't be long."

After thirty agonizing minutes, Jenny walked back into the security center. The radio had spit out numerous updates on the search, but nothing related to finding the boys. Marissa was sending email updates to Gene continually. She asked him not to call because the lump in her throat was still there. She could not speak. Not even to him.

Jenny had her full trust in Tyler and his team. She stood by the back wall and listened to their operation unfold as professionally as possible. But where were the boys? If they weren't on the island, how were they moved? She knew that the longer the search took, the harder it would be to find them.

"We are conducting the return sweep now, Captain." Tyler was wearing headphones and looking at his command console. "If the boys aren't found, we will wait for the Coast Guard. They are bringing infrared cameras, but I'm afraid they won't be much help. We will have to expand our search to neighboring islands."

Expand our search. The reality that Zach could be seriously hurt or kidnapped from the island hit Jenny like a moving freight train. Her mind froze, and her heart began to race. She slowly doubled over.

"Captain! Captain. Sit down." Megan held Jenny's elbow and walked her to a chair. The group in the hallway rushed to the doorway. "Get Doc!"

As Dr. Cruz was being summoned, Bettina rushed in and tried to comfort Jenny. She spoke softly to her and, thankfully, did not suggest a gabby game. The entire area was silent, except for the crackle of reports from the island search party.

Jenny's mind wasn't connecting. She usually had control of her thoughts and knew how to handle any situation. But it wasn't working now. She had let herself consider the worst-case scenario, and it sent her brain spinning. She could not make it stop.

"Let's pray." Bettina held her hands together and began asking Jesus for a miracle. Marissa moved closer, and the others in the hallway bowed their heads. Bettina continued to pray while the rest of the passageway remained eerily quiet.

"Thank you," Jenny murmured. "I feel a little better."

"Don't let your mind go there," Bettina warned. "I know what that is like. Just stop those thoughts from even popping into your mind."

Jenny stood and hugged Marissa. Both women had tears running down their faces. But they had a newfound strength to continue the wait.

"Let's go in the hall," Bettina offered. Jim, would you read from Psalms for us? I think that would be helpful."

Jim took his phone out of his pocket. "Of course." Before he could speak, an excited voice barked over the radio.

"A hat. We see a hat!" The group listened intently. "It's a red lifeguard hat."

Jenny's heart sank. That wasn't Zach's.

Surprisingly, Tyler requested the coordinates and ordered the four nearest searchers to move to that area. He then popped his head out of the doorway. "Our stowaways were wearing Zach and Josh's hats. This has to be one of theirs."

"Woo-hoo!" Ronnie hollered. "They found them." But the room remained silent.

"They just found one of the hats," Robert explained. "That doesn't mean that the boys are still there."

Ronnie looked at the ground. "I'm sorry."

Robert put his arm on Ronnie's shoulder. "No need to be sorry, young man. The world needs more of the gumption you young whippersnappers have. Let's keep listening."

The radio popped with a back-and-forth exchange. Jenny held her breath.

"Voice . . . hear a voice . . . found one. Repeat. We hear one of the boys answering us."

Tyler ordered the drone to cover that area immediately. Jenny and Marissa rushed to the screen.

CHAPTER FIFTEEN

"It's Zach! We have contact. He's stuck in a hole, and he's hurt. Bronski is dropping in with some rope."

"Thank you, Jesus!" Jenny fully exhaled for the first time all day. He had been found. She feared that he was likely beaten and battered, but he was found. She asked Manny Cruz, who had arrived earlier, to wait at the gangway deck where the tender boat would return.

"Aye, aye, Captain." The doctor rushed into action. Jenny began thanking God for her son's discovery.

"Captain," Tyler whispered. "May I speak with you privately." Instinctively, Jenny looked toward Marissa. The woman was pale and noticeably frightened. Bettina turned her away from Tyler.

Jenny followed Tyler to his seat at the console. "They are lifting Zach out of the hole now. One of his arms is injured, so the effort is a little complicated." Jenny was silent while Tyler continued. "Josh is not with him. Zach said that Josh tried to get out of the hole and fell farther into the cave system. He hasn't heard from him in hours."

"Oh no."

"We have to tell Josh's mother. Would you like to do it? Or should I?"

Jenny rubbed her forehead. "I will tell her. What is being done?"

"I haven't heard from the Bahamians since two o'clock this afternoon. The Coast Guard should be here in an hour or two. Maybe longer. They are bringing a Cavefinder detector. It will map out the system for us."

"An hour or two? Really? Josh may not have that much time."

"We must do this 'by the books,' Captain. I am following protocols."

"I know you are, Tyler. Thank you very much." Jenny turned toward the door. "I will tell Marissa, but it won't be easy." She walked into the hallway, and her face instantly betrayed her.

"Oh no!" Marissa wailed. "What happened to Josh?"

Jenny sat beside Marissa and explained that he had fallen deeper into the cave system. She added that the Coast Guard would be bringing cutting-edge technology soon. They just needed to pinpoint his exact location.

"Can they talk with Josh?" Marissa squeaked.

"No. Zach hasn't heard from him in a few hours."

Everyone in the room gasped at once.

"We have to get him out," Jack demanded. "Get us on the island, ma'am. We will get the boy out." The four veterans stood and demanded to be sent to Cutter Cay.

Jenny grimaced. "I appreciate your offer. But we have top-notch professionals on the case. The Coast Guard will be here soon."

"The tide is rising . . . close to high tide . . ." The radio squawked an alarm.

"He's going to drown!" Marissa was frantic. "Please let the men try. We can't just leave him down there without trying."

In fifteen years at sea, Jenny had never blatantly bucked the rules. She valued integrity and professionalism. Allowing passengers to conduct a search was not technically covered in Jewel's policy. But it was against the "spirit of the law."

Of course, Josh was in imminent danger. She would want everything possible to be done if Zach were missing.

What should I do, God?

Go!

"Let's go." Jenny heard God's answer as if He were speaking directly to her face. "I'm coming along. And we will not interfere with the security team."

The four veterans, Jim, Ronnie, and Jenny marched to the elevators. Marissa followed.

"You should stay here, Marissa," Jenny offered. "We will keep you posted with the radios."

"I'm coming. That's my son out there."

Jenny sighed. "Okay, you can come along. Bettina, please give Joe an update. Ask him to keep the prayers going." Bettina ran up the carpeted stairs without looking back.

When the group arrived at the gangway, the tender boat was unloading. Half of the grid searchers were returning to the ship. Zach had already been taken to the medical facility on a stretcher. Marissa wanted to offer for Jenny to go see him, but she knew that the captain was her only hope for the veterans to assist in the search. The security team would not violate policy without the captain's direct orders.

"Watch your step." A helpful crew member held Marissa's hand as she stepped into the boat. It was large enough to carry dozens of passengers but only held twelve this afternoon: Marissa, Jenny, Jim, Ronnie, the four veterans, a ship's nurse, and three people from

Bounty running the tender. Robert was carrying a duffle bag, which he carefully placed on his lap when he sat down. "We have life vests available. The trip should take about six minutes."

Marissa was too nervous to take out her phone to email Gene. The wind and the waves would make typing on the miniature keyboard challenging. Plus, her thoughts were scrambled. She probably couldn't make a complete sentence if she were ordered to.

Please, God. Please! she pleaded.

When the tender arrived at Cutter Cay dock, the employees jumped out and tied the mooring lines. Two members of the search party were waiting to bring the newcomers to the cave. The helped the party exit the boat.

"Have you heard anything from Josh?" Marissa asked hopefully as she and the group walked down a gravel path.

"No, ma'am. We haven't heard a thing. We've got two people in the hole, but they haven't gone far."

Jack jumped into the conversation. "Do you see any exit points? Where did he fall? How many chambers are we facing?"

The man tried to keep up with Jack's rapid walking pace. "The bottom of the hole is filled with water. We may have to wait for low tide."

"Unacceptable!" Jack declared.

Marissa's mind was whirling even more than it was before. Men were firing questions and answers faster than she could think. How could this be happening? The entire scenario seemed surreal. Was she really marching across an island in the Bahamas with a bunch of strangers looking for Josh? *Please let this be a dream!*

"Mrs. March?"

"Yes," Marissa responded. "I'm sorry. I'm not myself right now."

"That is understandable," Jack said somberly. "We would like your unofficial permission to search for Josh. This man here tells us that it is not safe to search for tunnels. They could cave in. We happen to know that the limestone in the karst holes is very much like those in Vietnam. They shouldn't cave."

Marissa stopped walking. "The hole could cave in on Josh?"

"It may have already collapsed," the search member reported. "We should wait for the Coast Guard to bring their equipment."

"Nonsense!" Robert interjected. "Let us take a look."

Jenny walked up to Marissa and put an arm around her friend. "This is up to you. We are in uncharted waters right now. I honestly do not know if the cave could collapse or not. The Coast Guard should be here in less than two hours. But these men are here now. What do you want to do?"

Gene would know what to do. Josh would know what to do. But Marissa did not. She could not think clearly. "I don't know . . ."

Before she could finish, a voice boomed over the group. Jim Morgan spoke. "Heavenly Father, we give you praise today. Jesus, we thank You for Your victory over principalities and snares of evil. Holy Spirit, we ask You to open our eyes to the enemies around us. Give each person here the wisdom to conduct this mission successfully. And do not let the Enemy hinder us in any way. In Jesus' name we pray. Amen."

"Get him now!" Marissa asserted.

The veterans began running. Ronnie and Jim followed closely behind. The search crew looked at Jenny. "Go! Show them the hole."

Marissa stood taller. "Thank you."

"Of course," Jenny replied. "Let's get your boy."

The women walked briskly toward the hole. Marissa thought about reaching out to Gene but left her phone in her pocket. She wasn't ready to communicate with him yet.

When they arrived at the grassy area, Marissa began crying. The group stopped and stared. "This isn't a hole. It's a cave entrance."

A man climbed out of the opening with the help of a rickety ladder. "It's full of water and mud. I don't see how we can go any farther."

Robert looked at Jenny. She nodded. "We'll give it a go, sir." The man looked confused but stepped aside.

The four veterans gathered around the duffle bag. Robert took out a flashlight and declared that he would "take the dive." The others volunteered but finally agreed that Robert was the smallest and likely the most agile of the "geezers." He removed his shirt and began descending the ladder.

"Shirts only get in the way," Jack told Jim and Ronnie, who were watching intently.

Marissa stopped crying and was now holding her breath. After a few minutes, Robert called for a shovel. One of the older men passed him a foldable metal shovel from the duffle bag. Marissa wondered where they had found these supplies. Perhaps they always traveled with their rescue equipment.

The group could hear Robert grunting as he tried to reopen the hole Josh fell through.

"How did he find it so quickly?" a crew member asked.

"There are lots of clues," Jack answered. "Odd-looking debris. Disturbed walls. Sounds. Smells. His eyes probably adjusted quickly."

"Smells?" Ronnie asked.

Jack nodded. "Yep. During the war, we could smell the enemy before we could see him." Ronnie raised his eyebrows.

Marissa watched the operation in amazement. So many people were working in the heat and mud to help her son. She felt completely helpless. As if sensing her thoughts, Jenny walked over to her. "Josh is in good hands. I can feel it."

"I know," Marissa answered. "But what if they are unable to find him?"

Jenny took a few seconds to answer. "The Coast Guard is on their way. We will find him. The nurse is ready to help him as soon as he comes out of the hole." Marissa didn't respond. She simply hugged her arms around her body and watched while she surrendered control over to God. It was all she could do.

"I can't get it!" Robert yelled from the hole. "The dirt is caving back in, and my blasted arthritis is acting up something awful." Marissa began crying again at this update.

Without saying a word, Ronnie ripped off his T-shirt and jumped into the hole. He barely touched the ladder.

"No!" Jenny rushed to the entrance. "Not Ronnie. I don't approve of one of our children taking this risk."

Jack looked at the captain. "With all respect, Captain, that boy is older than I was in Nam. He's not a child anymore."

"But he's under my care," Jenny declared. "I can't allow—"

"Woo-hoo!" Robert echoed from the karst hole. "Look at that boy go! He's got that tunnel nearly open. Someone toss down that second flashlight."

Jenny watched in amazement with the others. Robert announced that Ronnie was crawling through the opening on his own. Sea water was splashing everywhere.

"Tie this rope around your ankle." Marissa heard Robert instructing Ronnie to bring a rope with him as he moved. She hoped that Josh would be able to crawl on his own but appreciated the presence of the rope. "Put the radio in your pocket like this."

Eventually, the sounds from the hole grew quiet. The crew member who came out of the hole crawled back in. Everyone stood in silence near the entrance, listening for any sounds from Ronnie.

The nurse spoke up. "What would keep someone trapped in a cave like this?" Marissa did not want that question to be answered. She looked away and then walked back to the gravel pathway. Jenny followed her. The two women stood with their backs to the commotion, but they heard Jack's answer clearly: "A flooded tunnel. Deadly gases. Ground collapse. Traumatic injury." The list continued, but Marissa tuned it out. If she let herself go down that pathway, her mind would succumb to the darkness.

"Is there any word on Zach?" Marissa asked.

"The doctor sent a short report that he was dehydrated but fine. They were working on his shoulder, which might be dislocated. Thankfully, his arm isn't actually broken."

"That's good news."

"Let's pray," Jenny suggested. Marissa nodded and began walking away from the scene.

"I can't talk right now, but I want to pray," Marissa sputtered. Jenny squeezed one of her hands and walked beside her friend. They walked quietly about one hundred yards and circled back to the group of people standing outside of the hole. Jack informed them that they had heard nothing from the two-way radio.

Marissa thought of Josh trapped underground. She thought of Gene pacing frantically in their living room back home. How could this be happening? Then she remembered the faithful friends praying right now. Scores of people praying for her family. They were covered. She continued to give the situation over to God. *This is too much for me to handle, Lord. Please, take over.*

Suddenly, the radio that Jenny was holding began to crackle. "Flip flop . . . too dark." They heard Robert respond calmly. "Remember what I showed you, Ronnie. Keep your shoulders up. Carry the flashlight in your weak hand." The group above ground moved closer to the opening of the hole.

Josh was as good as blind. He couldn't see a speck of light anywhere around him. And he had no idea where he was. There was a fall. And another fall. Followed by some time that he wasn't awake for whatever reason. When he came to, he began frantically crawling. The ground was dry and he had no shoes, but he could move. Until he couldn't.

At some point, Josh became hopelessly stuck with his arms over his head in a crawling position. He couldn't move forward, and he couldn't move backward. He was stuck like Winnie the Pooh in Rabbit's doorway. The lack of food, water, and oxygen made his mind foggy. Josh thought of himself stuck like Pooh and laughed. *Silly old bear.* The words brought back memories of his mother reading that story to him. He tried to think of the name of the book but couldn't.

He just remembered that Pooh ate too much honey. How ridiculous! And oh, would honey be delicious right now.

Josh had no idea how long he had been stuck in the tunnel. Or was it Rabbit's doorway? He hadn't heard Zach in a very long time. And he was about to give up hope. No one would ever find him this far down in the cave—if anyone even knew to look here. He felt he should pray, but his mind couldn't put the thoughts together. His ideas were coming at him like pieces of macaroni in a food fight. Little did he know that scores of people were praying for him in intercession.

Both of Josh's arms were no longer tingling. They were painfully numb. He was totally and entirely trapped. Completely helpless. At God's mercy. The feeling was surprisingly freeing. He no longer had any control. Everything was in God's hands.

Help me.

The air was becoming warmer. Josh listened for sounds of help but only heard rushing water above him. He also heard wind echoing in front. The air smelled metallic—a smell he would never forget if he ever got out of this tomb.

Josh fell asleep on and off. He was physically exhausted and running out of life. Thoughts of Winnie began passing through his mind. He could remember exactly what her dress looked like last night. Or was it the day before? She felt like a best friend already. Of course, she was probably angry that he didn't show up on the pool deck. She might have met someone else. She likely had no idea that he was dying in a cave on Cutter Cay.

Cutter Cay. What kind of name is that? Josh pictured a huge letter *K* folding down like scissors cutting pieces of paper—and cake! It was cutting chocolate cake with extra icing.

What is that smell? Josh could smell something sour and medicinal. It was noticeably different. He tried to kick his feet, but he had no strength. They felt like they were weighted with lead. Never had he been in such a helpless predicament. He couldn't even call out for help.

After waiting a minute or two, Josh could still smell the strange smell. For a brief second, he saw a glow of light. It was coming from behind him. But it went away. Could it be Zach? Or someone from the island?

"Help! Help!" Josh gathered all of his strength and forced himself to call out. His voice echoed in front of him, and he heard something flap and fly away. *Please let that be a bird and not a bat.* "Help!"

"Josh?" Someone said his name. Was he hallucinating? The noise was warbled. But it was a noise. "Josh? Are you there?"

Relief swept through Josh, and tears involuntarily streamed down his face. He couldn't wipe his eyes, and they began to sting. The light became brighter, and Josh felt someone moving around his feet. Then a shovel was digging him out. The dirt was flying away at a superhuman speed. Eventually, Josh fell backward out of Rabbit's doorway. He slowly lowered his elbows to his hips. Feeling came back quickly as painful pins and needles.

"Thank you! Thank you for coming for me."

"No problem," the voice said. "I need to get this rope around you. Sit still." Josh knew that voice but could not picture the face. It wasn't Zach. "Can you crawl?"

"I'm not sure. I don't feel so well."

"Just lie still. I'm gonna drag you out. Keep your hands by your sides."

Josh did as he was told. His mind was still swirling. And he really wanted some honey.

"Found him!" Jenny listened closely to the update. Did Ronnie just say that he had found Josh? If so, could he get the boy out? And was he still alive? The group around the hole quieted as they listened to the two radios. ". . . gonna pull him out . . ."

Robert had climbed out of the hole and left the crew members to help the boys exit. He was giving advice to Ronnie on how to pull a body behind him. Something about intermittent pulls and small movements. Robert seemed concerned that too much movement could cause another collapse. They had to make the right moves to get both boys out of that cave.

The nurse stood closely by the entrance with her medical bag on her shoulder. Jim Morgan ran with one of the veterans back to the tender boat to retrieve a mobile gurney Dr. Cruz had insisted they bring. Marissa stood like a statue, staring at the karst hole. Jenny thought to herself that her maritime training had not prepared her for anything like this. But the Holy Spirit had His hand in her command. He was guiding Operation Bounty Runner.

It took Ronnie almost thirty minutes to reach the opening of the karst hole. Crew members took over and lifted him out of the cave. He was covered in mud and exhausted. Robert and Jack hugged him and led him to a grassy area. Someone handed him a bottle of water. Jenny noticed a relieved smile on Ronnie's face as he drank the water.

Marissa was standing still and quietly staring at the hole. Jenny watched eagerly as one of the crew members backed up the ladder. He did not have Josh and asked for help. Ronnie jumped up, but Robert put a hand on his chest to stop him. "Let them do it. You accomplished your mission, young man." Ronnie complied.

After a few attempts, Josh was finally lifted out of the hole. Marissa rushed to him but did not touch him. *Thank you, God!* He was wet and shaking. His face was covered in mud, and the skin on his feet was peeling. Jenny thought for sure she heard Josh saying, "Silly old bear."

The nurse pulled out a stethoscope and listened to his heart. She declared Josh strong enough to be moved to the tender boat. He was lifted onto the gurney and carried down the gravel pathway. Marissa walked beside him silently. Before the crew brought him onto the boat, the nurse inserted an IV to provide fluids and nutrition. Jenny relaxed when she saw the fluid moving into his arm.

An image of Joe entered Jenny's mind. She quickly fished her phone out of her pocket and sent him a message with an update. Five seconds later Joe texted, "Praise God!" Jenny then offered to help Marissa message Gene with an update. When they reached the ship, she would be able to call him.

"Will you type it?" Marissa asked. "My hands are shaking too much."

"Of course." Jenny typed as much as she could before she had to climb into the tender boat. She hit Send and prayed that the message would be sent quickly.

The ride to the ship was rockier than the trip from the boat to the island. Much rockier. Waves were cresting at nearly six feet. The driver was running the boat too fast for the waves. It would flip if it turned sideways even slightly. Jenny made her way to the helm.

The passengers were holding onto their seats. The nurse took out a few life jackets and began passing them out. As Jenny was rushing toward the operator, the boat turned sharply to the left. Marissa let out a yelp.

"Starboard, ho!" Jenny commanded as she stood. But the driver didn't react quickly enough. A massive wave crashed into the starboard side of the tender, causing it to list to the port side. Josh fell off the gurney, and Jenny tumbled into the water.

The waves slammed Jenny into the hull of the boat before she could emerge. Her hair was whipping in front of her face as she struggled to get her head out of the water. Once she surfaced, waves continued to crash over her head. She spotted an orange object flying toward her face and assumed it was a life jacket. Struggling to stay afloat, Jenny managed to grab the life jacket. But the boat was getting farther away.

"Turn around!" Jim yelled at the pilot.

"I can't! The boat will flip."

"We can't just leave her," Marissa pled from Josh's side. He was crumpled on the bottom of the boat now.

"We aren't. I've stopped the engines. The captain will have to catch up to us. Don't jump in or you will be struggling right beside her."

Three of the men rushed to the in-water stairs, ready to pull Jenny into the boat. She was swimming toward them but making no headway with the waves pushing against her.

"Where are you, God? Why is this happening?" Jenny was struggling and questioning. How did she end up in the water during Josh's rescue? She could see the boat when the waves ebbed. But she wasn't gaining on it despite kicking her legs continuously. She felt completely hopeless.

Be still.

Jenny knew instantly that God had spoken to her. She began crying in the choppy waters and stopped kicking. "Help me. I don't know what else to do. I'm drowning out here, and I've lost control of Zach. Please help. Please help."

The passengers watched as Jenny stopped kicking and began floating. She was holding on to the life jacket and bobbing in the water. But she was slowly getting closer to the boat.

Jim looked upward. "Father, we need another miracle. Please calm the waves so our captain can return safely to this boat and to the ship."

Everyone but Josh stared at Jenny moving closer to the boat. As they watched, the winds slowed slightly. The waves decreased. Jenny hooked her arm through the jacket and began slowly swimming to the boat. When she got close enough, Jim threw a life ring to her. She managed to grab it, and two of the men pulled her in.

"I'm fine," Jenny declared as she took off her wet jacket and shoes. "How's Josh?" The group turned toward the boy, and the nurse declared him "also fine and recovering." Jenny then staggered to the helm of the boat and took over command. She maneuvered it to the ship's launch site and waited for it to be lifted to the gang opening. No one said a word.

CHAPTER SIXTEEN

At the medical facility, Jenny rushed to see Zach. He was sitting on an examining table eating a banana. His right arm was wrapped in a sling. "We found Josh. He's all right."

Zach grinned. "That's amazing!"

"How are you feeling?"

"I'm fine. My arm hurts, and this sling is already annoying, but I'm fine. Why are you wet?"

"It's a long story."

Zach grew serious. "Mom, I'm sorry."

Jenny looked surprised. "Why would you be sorry? Those boys kidnapped you. You have nothing to be sorry about."

"No. It was my fault. And I'm very sorry. I spent a lot of time thinking, and I began talking with God. I'm not living right, and I need to change. You have been the best mom—and dad—anyone has ever had. I'm just really sorry."

Jenny was speechless. She did not quite understand how the kidnapping could be Zach's fault, but she was grateful that he recognized he needed a change. She hugged her son for an awkwardly long time. "I have to check on Josh and Ronnie and then get to the bridge. And I expect you to be sleeping in our cabin tonight."

"Ronnie?"

"He's a hero."

"Yes, ma'am."

At the bridge, Jenny was briefed on the ship's new sailing path to Mermaid Cove by Aksel. She was still in her wet clothes. *Bounty* would arrive one hour later than expected but would still make the stop. An announcement would be made to the passengers soon.

Tyler was also on the bridge. "I am working on a report to the line. Can you come to the security center tomorrow to help me fill in some of the details?"

Jenny inwardly sighed and rolled her eyes. "Of course. I will come by after we dock."

"There has been no sign of the stowaways. We think they exited the ship before we left Cutter Cay."

"That's odd but understandable. Thank you for your efficient work, Tyler."

"Yes, ma'am."

Good news messages continued to fill Joe's phone. Zach and Josh were back on the ship. Jenny was back in command. And Ronnie was a hero. They could not ask for a better outcome. Joe decided it was time to halt the prayer walk, so he stood near the back of the ship and stopped people as they walked by. He high-fived many of them as they approached.

When it looked like all the prayer walkers were gathered and listening, Joe shared the updates. "I am thrilled to say that Zach and Josh are back on the ship." A thunder of cheers rang out. "It turns out that they were pushed into a huge hole in a cave by the two jet ski operators. Security believes that those two boarded the ship but then left somehow. Your prayers worked!" Joe was about to share the medical condition of Zach and Josh but wondered if that would be considered a breach of privacy. So he announced that the boys were being seen by medical officials at that time. He added that Ronnie Ledbetter was crucial to success of their rescue and would share details if and when he were able to.

"The families affected today are very grateful for your intercession. You shook heaven's gates today. I suggest that we all take a few laps of praise and thanks before we go about our business." Joe made eye contact with Elle. "My family will be hitting the yummy buffet soon. Before we go, let's join hands and thank our Father for His blessings today. All of them." The group moved in tighter, and Joe led a heartfelt prayer of thanksgiving. Immediately after, he sent his father a detailed message with the good news.

As the crowd was dispersing back onto the walking track, Jonah ran up to Joe. He was joined by some of the other boys. "Can we go see them, Dad?"

Joe shook his head. "I don't think that is a good idea. I will text you when they are ready for visitors. I'm sure they are eager to share all the details from the past twenty-four hours with you. But they need to rest right now."

"Okay. We're gonna get something to eat. I'll look for you guys later."

"Aye, aye." Joe saluted. "And Jonah? Be careful."

Elle seconded the call for safety. "Would you guys mind taking Evie to eat? She's getting hungry, and we will be here on the track for a while longer."

Jonah responded quicker than usual. "Sure. C'mon, EV."

As the group walked away, Elle side-hugged her husband. "You are in your element, my love. Promise me you won't ever leave the ministry. It looks good on you."

Joe's eyes widened. But before he could speak, Winnie and her parents walked over to him. "Pastor Joe, these are my parents, Anna and Jude." Joe shook hands with Winnie's father. "Thank you so much for organizing this walk. I can't explain it, but I feel different. I feel energized."

"That's great, Winnie. I feel it too." Joe paused to look at the smattering of walkers still circling the track. "I suggest that you not go far."

Winnie looked uncertain. "Okay . . ."

"I have a feeling that Josh is going to be asking for you very soon." Winnie smiled broadly. Joe couldn't wait to ask Elle if she had seen the girl's joyous reaction.

When Winnie's family left to get supper in the main dining room, Joe and Elle decided to take two laps around the track. They held hands and prayed silently. At the end of the laps, Joe looked at Elle. "We really need to talk."

"Okay. Why don't we hit the buffet and talk while we eat?"

Joe laughed. "Nope. I've been trying to talk with you for three days. The buffet is the worst place to have a serious conversation."

"Serious?" Elle noted.

"Yes, serious but not *bad*." Joe pulled Elle toward the elevators. "What do you think about grabbing a pizza at Oro and taking it down to the garden paths?"

Elle giggled. "Sounds like a cheap date. I'm in!"

Opting for one large pizza and two bottles of water to go, the couple darted to a bench on the center garden path on Deck Seven. "This is exciting," Elle whispered. "I feel like a celebrity trying to avoid paparazzi."

Joe laughed. "We're not quite celebrities, E. But we better take advantage of our time alone."

"You have me intrigued. What is going on?"

Joe started at the beginning and told Elle about the unexpected message from Dean Katz and the generous job offer. He explained that he had attempted to tell her but was interrupted each time he tried. "When we ate dinner with Stevie's family, I became convinced that the teaching job was God's will. Dave told us that his job as a college professor was the best one in the world."

"Oh, wow!" Elle gasped. "I had no idea that was going on. You've had a lot on your mind."

"Yep, I have. And the decision was even heavier without your input." Joe put his paper plate on the bench beside him. "But you just gave me your input without even knowing it."

"I did?"

"You asked me to promise that I never leave the ministry."

Elle took a sip of her water. "But I didn't know that there was a job offer on the table."

"That makes it even better."

"I see what you are saying. When do you have to give your answer?"

"Yesterday." Joe picked his plate back up.

"Yikes!"

"I'm really torn."

"Why don't we pray about it and make a decision in the morning? I say don't jump unless God makes it clear."

"That sounds like a great plan. Thank you."

After finishing their pizza, Joe and Elle walked around the ship, checking on as many students as they could find. Today's scare was more than either of them had faced during Joe's ministry. They wanted to ensure that everyone was at peace. Thankfully, they were.

Later, Joe received word that Josh was up for visitors, and he quickly shared the news with Jonah.

PART THREE

Calm Seas

241

He will be the sure foundation for your times,
a rich store of salvation and wisdom and knowledge;
the fear of the LORD is the key to this treasure.

Isaiah 33:6

CHAPTER SEVENTEEN

Thursday, June 18
Mermaid Cove

Josh woke with a dull headache, and his shoulders hurt whenever he moved. It took a few seconds for him to adjust to his surroundings. He was in his mother's cabin. She had insisted that he sleep by her side last night, while Ryan's mother slept in the boys' cabin next door.

Dr. Cruz had given Josh the option to leave the ship on a helicopter or stay for the rest of the week. The choice was a no-brainer. He'd stay on the ship all summer if he could. Strangely, though, his first thought when given the choice was Winnie, not his friends. He wanted to spend more time with her. And he was thankful that she was among his friends when they were finally allowed to visit him in the medical center. Winnie stayed back as the others rushed in. But she made eye contact with him, and that was all he needed.

"Are you hungry?" his mother asked.

"I am. Can you tell if Ryan is awake yet?"

"I haven't heard anyone moving around. We can tell his mom that we are at breakfast."

"Sounds good." Josh groaned when he stood. His mother rushed over, but he insisted that he could dress by himself.

"A warm shower might help," Marissa suggested. Josh decided that he would take a quick shower—alone.

When Josh finished showering and dressing back into the clothes he had slept in, his mother was waiting to join him for breakfast. "Ms. Bettina texted. They are ready to go with us. You can go over there to get new clothes if you want."

"Nah, I'm fine. I'll change into a bathing suit after we eat." Josh looked for his shoes. "I'm meeting Winnie at ten."

"Please take it easy today. And Dad wants to talk to you again. You were kind of out of it last night."

"Sure. After we eat. I can't find my shoes."

Marissa started to look but quickly remembered that Josh's flip-flops were still in the cave. "You were barefoot when they got you. We can get another pair next door. Are your feet okay?" Josh was amazed that he lost his shoes. He didn't remember losing them.

"My feet are fine. It's my shoulders that hurt. And my head a little."

"I've got your medicine. You need to take it after you eat."

"Okay." Josh found Ryan and his mom in the passageway by their cabins. After getting some shoes out of his room, the group made their way to Blackbeard's Fortress. Josh could tell people were staring at him. He felt like a low-level celebrity and laughed at an image in his mind of signing autographs for adoring fans.

The buffet was busy with passengers fueling up for a fun day at Mermaid Cove. Josh and Ryan saw others from their youth group and went to sit with them. Marissa and Bettina sat separately at a table nearby. Josh had eaten some salty broth and three popsicles at the medical center last night. Now he was starving. But the rows of breakfast food did not look appealing. He walked back and forth and finally settled on a green apple.

Five minutes after he sat down with his friends, his mother handed him a plate with some toast and jelly and a scoop of Froot

Loops. *How does she always know exactly what I need?* Josh thanked his mom and devoured the toast.

"How long were you stuck in that tunnel?" Ryan was talking, but Josh barely noticed. "Josh? Did you hear me?"

"Sorry. I don't know," Josh answered. "I fell asleep a couple of times."

"In the cave?" Macy asked.

Josh nodded. "Yeah. It was entirely dark. Quiet. And warm for some reason. What else would I do?"

"That is so wild," Jonah remarked. "What did you say to Ronnie when he dug you out?"

Josh looked up. "Ronnie?"

Jonah snickered. "Yeah, when he dug you out of the hole." Josh looked confused. "Dude. Ronnie jumped in the hole and rescued you."

"You're lying."

All eyes turned to Josh. "Are you serious?" Jonah asked. "You don't know?"

"Know what?"

"Ms. Jenny gave the veterans permission to look for you while she waited for the Coast Guard. They were too weak to dig out the hole, so Ronnie jumped in and got you out. Didn't you see him pulling you out?"

Josh looked around the table. By the looks of the eyes on him, Jonah must have been telling the truth. "No. All I remember is that my shoulders hurt like crazy. And the sun was wicked bright when I came back out."

"That's wild," Jonah declared. "My dad said that the Coast Guard arrived about two hours after you got on the ship. They had a bunch of high-tech equipment ready to rescue you."

"Really?" Josh sighed. "I don't know if I would have made it two more hours."

Macy leaned forward. "I heard that Ms. Jenny might get in trouble for letting Ronnie and the veterans help."

"That stinks," Josh groaned. "I'm gonna say something. Those guys saved my life!"

"Yeah," Macy agreed. "We should all say something."

Josh looked around the dining area. "Has anyone seen Zach? I didn't get to talk to him last night."

"No," Ryan said. "I think Ms. Jenny is keeping tight wraps on him for now. He can't even walk around without her permission."

Macy pounded her fist on the table. "Good! Someone needs to get him under control. He's the one who caused all of this in the first place."

"Go easy on him," Josh said. "He's recognizing the consequences of his actions. I think we might see a different Zach going forward."

Macy rolled her eyes. "I'll believe it when I see it."

"What about Ronnie?" Josh asked. "I still can't believe he pulled me out of that tunnel."

Ryan smiled. "Face it, dude. Ronnie is a hero. I was joking about him hanging with the old guys, but him doing so ended up saving your life."

"That will never make sense to me," Josh admitted. "Tell me what you know."

The group shared the information they had, including the extensive prayer walk organized by Pastor Joe. Ryan teased Josh about Winnie walking with her parents around the track. And Macy teased him about losing his flip-flops. Josh was starting to feel normal until two other guys walked in.

"Charles!" Josh pointed to two teenagers eating near the entrance to the buffet. Everyone nearby turned to look in the direction Josh was pointing. "That's Charles and Anthony!"

The teenagers jumped up and began running. They exited Shipwreck Boulevard before anyone could react. Josh tried to go after him but could only wince as he tried to stand. His mother rushed to him and begged him to sit back down.

Ryan and Jonah bolted after the boys before Marissa had arrived. In less than three minutes, they returned.

"You'll never believe this," Ryan said as he was breathing heavily. "The guys turned the corner and ran smack into Ronnie. I guess he and Mr. Jim were coming to breakfast."

"Did Ronnie get them?" Josh asked, amazed at the events unfolding.

"Yep," Jonah added, also breathing heavily. "Three workers from the mall held them down. We told them they were the jet ski guys, and one called security with a walkie-talkie."

Josh sat speechless. His mother was patting his head. She suggested that the group stay put for a little while before they went to the pool. Josh might be questioned about the boys now that they have been found. Hundreds of guests were already flooding off the ship onto Mermaid Cove. The pool deck should be calmer today than on a sea day. Josh loved the idea.

The other teens agreed, and Marissa promised to find them with an update on Charles and Anthony. She and Bettina were heading to the security center immediately. When they left, Ronnie walked up to the group. He had a small cut on his chin and numerous scrapes on his arms. Josh just stared at him.

"Cleanup on aisle nine," Ronnie blurted out. None of the group knew how to respond. "Just joking, Josh. I'm really sorry that I've been such a pain to you. All of you. My brothers take it out on me, so I took it out on all of you."

Josh looked Ronnie in the eyes. "I can never thank you enough for saving my life, dude. You will always be my hero."

"It was nothing. Jack and Robert told me what to do." Ronnie grinned. "Those guys are really cool. I'm thinking about joining the Navy. I did get into FSU, but there's no way I can go. I haven't even signed up for a registration time."

"Are you sure about that?" Ryan asked.

"Pretty sure. Two of the guys think I should go into the Army, and two think I should go into the Navy. I've never been on the sea before this week. The Navy might be pretty cool."

Mr. Morgan walked up behind Ronnie and put a hand on his shoulder. "My nephew is a Coastie. I think Ronnie should consider the Coast Guard too." Ronnie grinned again.

An hour later, Josh and Ryan had changed into swimwear and were lounging in two chairs on the pool deck. They were waiting for others from their group to join them.

"Your arms look pretty gnarly," Ryan noted. "Do they hurt?"

"Nah, just a bunch of scrapes. My mom wants me to stay out of the sun today. Sunburn would make them worse. But I'm fine . . .

physically. My mind is still whirling with everything that happened. I can't think clearly. And I want to talk to Zach."

"He should be around sometime. I can't believe we haven't seen him yet."

"And Winnie."

Winnie appeared out of nowhere. "What about me?" she joked.

"Oh, I was just wondering what you thought about calculus."

"Very funny. How are you feeling?" Before Josh could answer, Ryan stood and offered Winnie his chair. She refused at first but eventually plopped down. Ryan graciously jumped in the pool. In a matter of minutes, Jonah and Jandro joined him.

"How are you feeling?" Winnie asked.

"I was just telling Ryan that I am fine physically, but my mind is spinning. I can't focus very well this morning."

"That's understandable. I got hit on the head last year, and I felt like my mind was spinning like that for two days. It will eventually go away."

Josh sat up on his elbows. "Wait, aren't you going to the island today? You're missing it."

"Nah. My parents just got off the ship, but I'm staying onboard today." She looked at Josh with a smirk. "Unless you want me to leave."

Josh rested back on his chair. "No. I'd like you to stay, but only if you want to stay." Winnie giggled, and Josh felt courageous. "Your sandals look nice."

Winnie looked at her feet. "That's a first. I've never been complimented by a cute guy on my vacation footwear."

Cute guy. Josh hadn't been called a cute guy before. Not to his face.

Marissa had called Gene twice already this morning. He was relieved to finally speak with Josh again during breakfast. But he could tell that Josh was having trouble concentrating on the conversation. When the boys went to the pool, Marissa excused herself and called Gene again. She shared that the ship's doctor expected Josh to be slightly unfocused for a day or two. She already made him an appointment with their family doctor for Monday. Dr. Cruz recommended an immediate follow-up.

"How are you, Maisy?" Gene asked. "You've had a stressful day."

"I'm surprisingly good. Just wish you were here." Marissa sighed.

"I know. But I'm not. God is watching over you and Josh, so you will be fine. You have three more days at sea. Go and live it up. Eat extra desserts for me."

Marissa giggled. "Don't worry. I've already been eating extra desserts. The food is so good. I haven't eaten much since Josh went missing, but I think that's about to change."

"Nice!"

Marissa gave Gene more details about Josh's rescue and the trip so far. Both were thankful for the organized prayer walk. "I wish you could have seen it, Gene. The Holy Spirit was there on the walking track. It was amazing."

"Oh, I'm sure it was something to see. And don't forget that the Holy Spirit's protection is always with us. We just need to be careful not to quench it."

"I'd like to talk more about that as a family when we get home. Josh is so vulnerable."

"I agree. So, tell me more about this Winnie girl."

Jenny's morning started in fifth gear and had only gotten crazier. The ship had docked at Mermaid Cove as expected and without issue. While she completed numerous questionnaires regarding the missing passengers, Aksel had handled all the paperwork necessary for their revised itinerary. To add to her stress, Jenny had a virtual meeting with officials from the cruise line tomorrow at nine o'clock. They would be discussing possible sanctions over her actions. The word *termination* was even mentioned.

Zach was not helping with Jenny's nerves. She ordered him to stay close by, and he complained about his restrictions continuously. He was already asking to have his shoulder sling removed. Thankfully, he fell asleep early last night and stayed in the cabin. But his first thought when he awoke was Laney. Jenny officially declared him to be "on restriction" until she had the time for a lengthy discussion about his actions, and she prohibited him from contacting the girl. Jenny made Zach eat breakfast with her on the bridge and remain in the area until at least lunch. Zach was clearly not happy about his new imprisonment.

After an hour of problem-solving, good news began to trickle in. The purser reported that the treasure hunt was not affected by the interruptions and was on schedule. Dr. Cruz reported that Josh and Ronnie were cleared to resume normal activities with caution on Zach's shoulder before normal activities. And Guest Services reported that they had only received a handful of complaints about the return to Cutter Cay.

The good news deserved an extra banana nut muffin, and as Jenny was peeling off the wrapper, Tyler from the Security Center rushed in. "We've got them."

"Who?"

"Anthony and Charles Martin. The stowaways."

Jenny sat her muffin down. "I thought they left the ship."

"Apparently, they have been hiding in plain sight. Josh recognized them while they were eating at the Fortress. They were apprehended by crew members and are in the brig right now."

"Good work, Tyler." She patted him on the shoulder.

"Full disclosure. I did absolutely nothing to capture them. But I do have them detained."

"I can't believe they were running around the ship like that."

"Me neither. We are about to question them, and I wanted to update you in person. Hank Popovich from legal will be supervising the questions from Miami. They will start soon, if you want to observe."

"Are we allowed to question a minor? Without a lawyer?"

"According to the international law, we are allowed to question each of them. They have been advised of their right to counsel. The Bahamian authorities are on their way and will take over from here."

"So the boys will probably clam up."

Tyler nodded. "Yep. They probably won't speak. But we will still ask."

"Okay." Jenny looked around the bridge. "As soon as we finish today's docs, I will head down to the center. I'm sure I don't have to say this, but please ask why they pushed Zach and Josh."

"Will do, Captain. See you soon."

When Tyler left, Jenny rushed around the bridge, completing her duties. She thanked her officers for their exemplary service on the inaugural sailing and then finished her coffee. Not wanting Zach to face the Martin brothers, she gave him a temporary reprieve. "You may hang out with your friends until six o'clock. I expect you to be in our cabin by the end of the first dog watch. You know when that is, don't you?"

"Yes, I know." Zach rushed away without saying goodbye.

When Jenny entered the Security Center, she saw Charles, one of the Martin brothers, sitting in a side room with two crew members sitting on either side of him. He was wearing a Nike T-shirt and red bathing suit. The other brother, Anthony, was currently in another room being questioned.

Megan noticed Jenny and walked up to her. "Captain, come this way." She led her to a one-way window. On the other side, Anthony, Tyler, and a security colleague were sitting around a square table. "Anthony has spilled the beans," Megan said, hoping Charles would overhear. "He's told us everything that happened."

Jenny was confused. Anthony remained silent while Tyler repeatedly asked him why they attacked the passengers. He was not spilling the beans. She looked at Megan, who quickly winked. She was attempting to trick Charles into confessing when it was his turn to go in. Was that ethical? Jenny had a weird feeling about the manner of questioning but said nothing.

After ten minutes, Anthony was led out a back door and Charles was brought to the table. He looked down at his feet the entire time.

Tyler shut the door. "We'd like to get your side of the story, son. Is there anything you would like to tell us? And remember, you have the right to have an attorney present."

"It was Anthony's idea! I didn't want to do it." Charles set both hands flat on the table. "We didn't want to ride jet skis all day, but our mom made us take the job to give us something to do this summer. The tall guy walked up and asked if we had any weed." Jenny winced. "Anthony lied and told him that we could get some. We had seen the karst hole that morning and joked about pushing someone in it. The crazy thing is that the dude's friend walked up as we were leaving, and we both realized that we looked like their twins. So we tricked them into leaving their hats and arm bands before Anthony pushed them into the hole. Then we walked right onto the ship."

Tyler spoke calmly. "So this wasn't planned? You just did this on a whim?"

"Yeah. I guess so. Tony wanted to go back to Miami and see his girlfriend. And this pirate ship is a sweet ride. It worked perfectly. Is that what he said? If he said it was my idea, he's lying."

"I can't tell you what your brother said. Have you heard from your parents?" Charles shook his head. "Where have you been hiding?"

"Nowhere. We took some shirts from the chairs by the pool. We've just been hanging out around the ship. We slept in the chairs by the outdoor movie screen last night. Nobody bothered us."

Jenny couldn't believe what she was hearing. Two teenagers evaded their state-of-the-art security system. The cameras. The security officers. The personalized arm bands. If Josh hadn't noticed them, they would still be running loose on the ship. For the first time today, Jenny feared for her job. For her career.

After the questioning, Charles was led through the back door where Anthony was waiting. Tyler walked through the other door into the hub of the area. "Unbelievable," he said, shaking his head. "They were just hanging out with the passengers."

Jenny stood taller. "Call a meeting with your team. Thirty minutes." Tyler nodded as she left the area. Jenny needed to clear her head, so she walked to the garden paths on Deck Seven.

How could her life turn upside down like this so quickly? Everything was a mess. Jenny missed Brian and the life they had before he died. Commanding a megaship was demanding, but raising a teenager alone was even harder. She felt so lacking and had to do something. But what?

Be still.

What was that? Jenny turned her head and looked over her shoulder. But there was no one nearby.

Be still.

Now she knew she was going crazy. She was hearing things again. Jenny rushed from the bench back to the security center. She was not going to sit around and watch her future crumble away. That worked in the high seas, but not on the ship. Now was the time to take charge.

Back on Deck Three, Jenny found Tyler and the security team sitting in a makeshift conference room. "Update!"

Tyler raised his eyebrows briefly and began speaking. "It looks like this was a spur-of-the-moment act by the two boys. The FBI has been informed of the latest intel."

"FBI?" Jenny asked. "I didn't realize they were involved."

"The kidnapping of American citizens on foreign land is a big deal." Tyler looked around the room. "The U.S. Embassy has also been updated. We are awaiting the Bahamian police to arrest the boys. As soon as they dock, we will escort Anthony and Charles from the ship."

Jenny sighed. "Thank you, Tyler. Thank you, everyone. I'm sorry for snapping. I have a meeting with the cruise line tomorrow morning. If I still have my job, we will meet to discuss the breach in our security protocols—both on the ship and on Cutter Cay. This never should have happened."

"Why did you say *if*?" Megan asked.

"Two people were kidnapped on my watch. My own son, for goodness' sake! This is serious."

"Nonsense," Tyler said. "This was not your fault. I won't let you take the fall for this, Captain."

Jenny smiled. "Once again, thank you. But that decision may have already been made." She stood. "I need to get back to the bridge. Please message me when the boys are off the ship."

"Will do." Tyler saluted, and Jenny left the security center. She had a job to do and had no time to worry. She let out a silent plea to God to fix the situation. To watch over Zach. And Josh. And the Martin brothers. And *Buccaneer Bounty*. And her position as Captain. And so much more.

Help!

CHAPTER EIGHTEEN

"How did Dean Katz take it?" Elle asked Joe as they were walking to dinner. Jonah had agreed to supervise Evie tonight so their parents could have another impromptu date. Evie wasn't entirely thrilled with eating with the teenagers, but Joe promised her that they would be one of the first people to leave the ship for Treasure Island tomorrow.

"I don't know. He hasn't replied to my message yet." Joe held the elevator door as Elle entered. "I wish I could have called him in person, but I'm sure he understands that I am out to sea."

"That is a little awkward. But you've been messaging all week. He must understand."

"As soon as I hit Send, a weight was lifted off my shoulders. I didn't want to leave the ministry. This is my calling. But the offer was so lucrative. How could I turn that down? Now I see that God wants me here with the students. The youth. At Holy Cross."

Elle side-hugged her husband. "I'm proud of you. And you never know what God might do in the future."

"Ha! I may be one of the dancers in the puppy-dog show on a cruise ship. You never know."

"Let's not go that far, Pastor Joe."

When the elevator door opened, Elle stepped out without looking. She ran smack into Jenny, who was rushing out of an adjacent elevator car. "Oof!" Both ladies hit hard.

"I am so sorry, Elle," Jenny said, sobbing. "I can't do anything right these days."

Joe walked the women away from the elevator doors. "Goodness, Jenny. What is wrong? This isn't like you. Is Zach okay?"

"I honestly have no idea if Zach is okay. He bolted from the bridge when I left to observe the interviews of the Martin brothers. He was supposed to be in our cabin at six this evening, but he wasn't there. I was late, but he should have waited. And he's not answering my texts."

Joe took out his phone. "I'll ask Jonah is he's seen Zach."

"I'm sure he's fine, Jenny," Elle said. "He probably just waited for you and left. We'll get the others to look for him." She watched Jenny attempting to hold back tears. "Is that all that's bothering you?"

"No." Jenny inhaled deeply. "I'm meeting with management tomorrow. I may receive sanctions for allowing Ronnie to go down that hole. They expected me to wait for the Coast Guard."

"Oh my," Elle uttered. "You made a brave decision. It probably saved Josh's life. They should be awarding you a medal, not punishing you."

"What can we do?" Joe asked. "I would be happy to write a letter."

"I'm afraid it's too late for that. But thank you for the offer. Please pray."

Elle subconsciously waved at an older couple walking by. "We will certainly be praying. What time is your meeting?"

"It's at nine. And thank you again." Jenny rushed off but stopped a few feet away and turned. "Joe? Does God ever speak to us out loud?"

"The Holy Spirit speaks to us in many ways," Joe answered as he reached for Elle's hand. "We just have to listen."

"Thanks!" Jenny disappeared in the direction of the medical facility.

Joe and Elle walked into the dining room. The tables were again set elegantly with crisp white tablecloths and flickering, battery-operated tea lights. A low hum of diners chatting filled the two-story space, as did the familiar smell of oregano.

A maître de led the couple to their table. Elle looked all around. "We don't do this enough."

"No, we don't. I am so thankful that Jenny arranged this trip." Joe chuckled. "We certainly can't afford mega-cruises on my pastor salary."

"Ha! We'll be just fine." Elle took her seat, then Joe. "Has Jonah written back?"

Joe looked at his phone. "He hasn't seen him. I'm sure Zach is fine. I can't imagine him getting into trouble two days after he was thrown into a cave."

Elle's face grimaced. "I sure hope not." The two inspected the oversized menus. Elle chose the halibut dinner, and Joe settled on beef Wellington.

He was concerned about Jenny but didn't bring it up to Elle. He was in "pastor mode" and wanted to respect their friend's privacy.

"Did you hear that Josh is feeling better?" Elle broke Joe's thoughts. "Bettina wrote me while I was napping. She said that his mind was a little muddled. Called it 'higgledy-piggledy.' But he was becoming sharper after lunch."

"That's great. Do you know if he will see a doctor when they get back home?"

"Yes," Elle said, dipping her focaccia bread in one of the flavored oils. "Marissa already has an appointment for him. And Gene will be driving them home. Bettina joked that he is probably already sitting at the port waiting for them now."

"I can't imagine how helpless he must have felt so far away. I should send him a message."

"He doesn't have a passport. That must have been frustrating. Oh, have you heard from your dad?"

Joe reached for another seeded roll. "Yes, he is keeping the prayers going until we get back home. I thanked him for covering us."

"He's doing so well. I can't believe your mom has been gone for five years. Time sure has zipped by. I really miss her. Do you remember the time a bird flew into the house on the Fourth of July? We were freaking out. The kids were freaking out. And your mom just kept stirring the barbecue sauce."

"And the bird landed on her elbow, and she kept stirring. Hilarious!"

"She named it Freedom and acted like that happened all the time."

Joe smiled. "I wish we had pictures of the big cross-country trip we took when I was eight. We only went to Tennessee, but it felt like we were traveling to the moon."

"The tornado?"

"Oh, yes." Joe sat back in his chair. "We were driving somewhere in Georgia, and we saw a tornado out the driver's side windows. My dad and all the other drivers were trying to outrun it, but my mom announced that it was noon and time for lunch."

"That is so Ria."

"My dad was racing down the highway, and Steve and I were begging him to speed up. Mom was ordering him to pull over so the ham sandwiches wouldn't spoil."

"She was such a force. I really do miss her."

"I do too." The food arrived, and Joe declared that his beef Wellington was too fancy to eat. "This needs a frame."

"Ha! Let's pray. I'm hungry."

"Man, this is getting serious." Ryan shook his head. "Dinner with her family?"

Josh finished towel-drying his hair. "It's not that big of a deal. Winnie just wants me to spend some time with her parents. They seem pretty cool."

"You probably shouldn't have eaten three burgers at lunch."

"Ha! You're probably right. I'm not even hungry." Josh finished dressing and promised to meet Ryan for *Charlie Tuna* at nine thirty. "Back left of the theater?"

"Yep. We'll be looking for you. Jonah is with Evie, so we're all gonna hang out at Oro for pizza and the game room till then. Have fun."

Josh rolled his eyes. "I'll try."

As he was leaving the cabin, Ryan offered one last suggestion. "Don't forget. Use the forks from the outside in."

"Thank you for the last-minute family science lesson. Ms. Ellis would be proud."

Josh stopped next door at his mom's cabin to say hi. She and Bettina did not answer, so he continued to the dining room. Standing in the elevator, his heart was beating faster than it should be. This was just dinner. But it felt like more. It felt serious.

Before Josh could get fully nervous, the doors opened on Deck Five, and Winnie and her parents turned to face him. "Hi," Josh squeaked awkwardly.

Winnie stood on her tiptoes. "Hey. That was good timing. You remember my parents, don't you?"

"Yes. Hi, Mrs. Yearling. Hi, Mr. Yearling."

"Call us Anna and Jude," Mrs. Yearling said as she adjusted Josh's collar. He hadn't realized one side was flipped up.

A server rushed them to a table near the center of the lower dining room. Pastor Joe and Elle walked past as they were arriving.

"Hey, Josh. Hey, Winnie," Joe said before they sat down. "And you are Winnie's parents. I remember you from the prayer walk."

"That would be us," Anna announced. "We are so glad that Josh is safe and sound. Yesterday was so scary."

"So are we!" Elle added cheerfully as she looked at Josh. "Have a nice dinner. The beef Wellington was almost too artfully plated for Joe to eat."

Jude pointed a finger in the air. "Duly noted."

When they were finally seated, Josh remembered to put his napkin on his lap right away. Anna seemed pleased. Talk around the table was easy. The Yearlings wanted to know every detail of Josh's ordeal. Reluctantly, he even shared his hallucinations about being Pooh stuck in Rabbit's doorway.

Winnie got a kick out of that part of the story. "Now we are both Winnies."

Josh quickly changed the subject after that comment. "Do you know what you will major in at college? You said something about being a missionary in Honduras."

Winnie set down her fork. "Yes. I'm majoring in early childhood education. I want to teach at the orphanage."

"And you've never been there?"

Anna spoke up. "Exactly. Winnie has made all these plans, but she hasn't even seen Honduras. I still don't like her even visiting."

"But," Jude added calmly, "we are trusting her to make the best decision for her future. Aren't we, hon?"

"Yes. But I still don't like it." The others laughed as Anna made a pouty face.

"Remember, our church is taking a team next summer," Winnie beamed. "You should think about going. If you start saving now, you can afford the installments. The biggest expense is the plane flight."

"That sounds cool," Josh replied. "But I've never done anything like that."

"Well, I think getting stuck like Pooh now qualifies you to help orphans in Honduras."

The table grew quiet. Winnie's plans weren't the whims of a teenager. She truly wanted to dedicate her life to serving children in a third-world country.

Josh broke the silence. "I'd like to go. Can you send me the information? I'll have to ask my parents."

Winnie took out her phone to send a link to Josh but remembered that he did not have a phone. "I'll give you my number. As soon as you get a phone, text me and I will send you a link to our church's website. Or you can look up First Baptist in Wonder. There's a link."

"I'll do that."

Jude clapped his hands. "Okay, let's talk about dessert."

After dinner, Anna and Jude took some fancy coffees to the walking track while Josh and Winnie went to Deck Eight to find the others. Ryan spotted his friends as they approached the game room. "Over here!" Jonah was approaching the high score on a Mario Bros. game, and the others were cheering him on.

Josh watched the excitement for a few minutes before settling at a nearby café table. Winnie, Macy, and Ryan joined him. Macy was unusually quiet, and she was drinking a Dagger drink. "How are you feeling, Josh?"

"I'm good," Josh said while arranging the salt and pepper shakers into a line. "My shoulders are sore when I move them. That's about all."

"Will you have to testify against those guys?" Macy asked.

"What do you mean?" Josh looked concerned.

"They arrested them for kidnapping. That's what Zach told us."

Josh looked up. "When did you see Zach? I haven't seen him since we left the medical facility last night."

"He and Laney got some pizza earlier."

Josh was confused and disappointed. He's still running around with Laney when Ms. Jenny told him to stay away from her. Had Zach gone back to his old ways? Did he not learn anything from their ordeal? "I don't know if I'll testify. My mom hasn't told me anything about that."

Winnie added her thoughts. "If they confessed to everything, you shouldn't have to be involved. At least, I hope not."

Josh hoped the entire matter would fade away. The "Pooh" incident was embarrassing. His dad would want to hear every detail—again. But that would be it. He did not want to revisit the past two days over and over.

After eating a slice of pepperoni pizza, Josh went to Deck Seven with the rest of his group. They wanted to watch the ice-skating show again. Winnie sat next to him, and her shoulder kept bumping into his. He did not mind at all.

After her evening shift on the bridge, Jenny made her way back to her cabin. A dozen families stopped her to take pictures with them. She normally enjoyed these interactions but was anxious to get back to her room tonight. She needed a detailed plan for the next few days.

Jenny collapsed on her bed. She still had not seen Zach, so she sent another message asking him to write back. He hadn't responded to any of her previous pleas. Jenny took a quick shower and dressed in a green-and-white striped pajama short set. For some reason, cute pajamas calmed her mind.

But tonight was different. Her mind was racing. So Jenny took out a pad of paper and a pen. She sat at her desk and wrote "Action Plan" at the top of the page. She then listed "Hearing," "Zach," "Brothers," and "Breach" with gaps in between. She would come up with her strategy to right all the chaos drowning her today. Just starting the task was overwhelming.

Jenny put her head in her hands. Where did she even start?

Be still.

There it was again. Where was that coming from? Jenny looked around her cabin but knew in her heart that God was speaking to her through the Holy Spirit. There was no one else in the room.

Jenny looked at her list. She badly wanted to make a plan to "fix" all her worries. But is that what God wanted her to do?

Jenny decided that it would not hurt to make a list of her thoughts and the moves she should make to right the ships in her life sailing out of control. First, the hearing. She should look up the policy, although she knew it thoroughly. It wouldn't hurt to review.

Be still.

That was clearly a message for her. Be still? How could she be still? She didn't even know where Zach was. Her career was on the line. What about the stowaways? Jenny's shoulders felt tight, and a headache was building. Was it possible to even be still? How would she begin? What would it look like?

Jenny sat at her desk and closed her eyes. As she sat in the quiet, she felt a wave of peace pass over her. "Okay, Lord. I will be still. It feels weird, but I will take my hands off the helm. Please take the wheel."

So, what should I do? It was too early to fall asleep. Jenny laughed to herself. Her life was spinning out of control, and she was just going to sit back and watch the destruction. She shook her head and decided to order some hot tea. She would read a light book until she got sleepy. The thought of relaxing was so appealing but foreign. After she ordered room service, Jenny began to write another message to Zach. But she stopped. She put her phone away. Tonight, she would simply trust God to calm her stormy seas.

CHAPTER NINETEEN

Friday, June 19

Treasure Island

"Yo, ho-ho, mateys! Passengers may now disembark at Treasure Island. All-aboard time is four o'clock. Have a 'Bountiful' day!"

"C'mon, you guys. We need to hurry." Evie began shoveling the rest of her cereal into her mouth.

Elle held up a palm. "Slow down. We have plenty of time. It's still very early."

"But we have to be the first ones down on the pitch." Evie began chugging her orange juice.

"It doesn't look like people are in a big hurry," Joe added as he looked around. "Let us finish our coffee. Then we will go straight to the soccer field. I still think that 'hands off' has to do with the big steering wheel that Ms. Jenny uses to drive the ship."

"The helm?" Evie giggled.

Joe smiled and rolled his eyes. "Yeah, the helm."

Elle added her thoughts. "I don't think the 'hands off' is a clue at all. That was just a sticker on the towel hut.

"I agree," Joe said. "But we will check out the soccer field to be sure. Will that make you happy, Evie?" Evie nodded happily.

"Stevie's mom said that they will be near the kiddie area today, so we can go there after the soccer field."

"Sounds good. Do we even know where the 'pitch' is?" Joe asked.

Elle took out her phone. "I found it on the app map. Looks like it is past the very center of the island. Past the big pool."

Joe looked at the map. "Should be easy to find. Let's get back to the cabins and get our stuff. Jonah is probably still sleeping. I'll let him know where we will be."

Elle stood to leave. "I think most of the boys are staying on the ship with Josh today. That sounds like a good idea to me. We don't want another incident at our last stop." The threesome left the dining room with Evie skipping all the way.

As they exited the ship, Evie pulled her father's hand. "Let's go. We're running behind."

Joe looked at Elle and smiled. "Okay. We will go full speed on this treasure hunt. But Mom and I get to chill and relax for the rest of the day."

"Ha!" Evie laughed. "Not agreeing to that. Stevie and I want to hunt for seashells, and the beach bonfire party is after supper." Joe sighed . . . twice.

At the early hour, only a few families were making their way to the island. When the Wallers stepped onto the island from the pier, they were the only ones walking straight ahead. Everyone else turned either left or right in search of the perfect lounging spot on the beach.

"This is a good sign," Joe whispered to Evie.

Pirate music filled the island, creating a festive mood. Soon the family walked past the island's main attraction, a massive salt-water pool. It boasted a tall waterfall and small planks for children, acting as pirates. Two-dozen kids were already splashing in the water.

Joe maneuvered around the hundreds of lounge chairs to exit the pool area. The girls followed closely behind. After passing the chairs, Evie stopped to admire the colorful rafts floating through the lazy river encircling the pool.

"C'mon," Joe urged. "I see it."

In front of the family was a half-sized soccer field surrounded by palm trees. It had bright green grass with white field lines drawn on top. A lone man was standing by the goal and setting up a tripod and video camera.

"That's it!" Evie squealed as she rushed to the field. "This is so cool!"

"Well, go look away, Miss Blackbeard. Find the treasure." Joe stood beside Elle as their daughter ran all over the field. She ran back and forth but did not seem to find anything interesting.

When she was convinced that the treasure was not anywhere near the soccer field, Evie skulked back to her parents. "It's not here."

"Are you sure?" Elle asked softly. "We may never be back to this island again. You better check everything."

Evie nodded. "I don't see anything but a normal soccer field cut in half."

Joe put his hand on Evie's shoulder. "It was a good idea. Let's take one lap around just to be sure. Do the markings look correct?" The group walked across the field toward the goal and the videographer.

"Hey, there!" Joe hollered. "We're just looking at the soccer field. Are you with the cruise line?"

"Oh, no," the man replied. "I'm Flying Fred. From YouTube. You may have heard of me. I had dinner with J-Lu on the first night."

Joe looked at Elle, who shook her head. "I don't believe we have heard of you."

"Well, I make travel videos and show the off-the-beaten-path venues so viewers get the full lowdown of the location. I've been recording all the men's bathrooms on the ship." Joe raised his eyebrows. "When they are empty, of course. My followers appreciate views of the paper towels and such. I'm also documenting all the carpeting. Did you know that the flooring on Deck Ten has little crabs sewn in? You have to look at it like this." Fred tipped sideways like a little teapot.

"We had no idea," Joe answered. "But I am going to check it out as soon as we are back on board."

"Great. And be sure to like and subscribe to my channel, Flying Fred's Fantastic Journeys."

Joe shook Fred's hand. "We will check it out. Are you always out here this early?"

"Sometimes," Fred said while he began packing up his equipment. "I like to get some footage without people. You know, the natural habitat before it's flooded with thousands of people. Fresh."

"Like a soccer field?"

"Exactly!"

Joe watched Fred finish arranging his camera and tripod in the case. "Why did you mark the penalty arc with an *X*?"

"I didn't mark it. That was there when I got here."

Joe's heart began to race. He couldn't look at the girls or he would give it away. "Oh, okay. Well, have a good day. And we'll be sure to check out your station."

"Channel," Fred blurted as he picked up his equipment.

"Oh, right. Channel." Joe watched Fred amble away before he spoke. "Do we have a shovel in the beach bag?"

Evie began jumping up and down. "I knew it! I knew it!"

"Shh!" Elle whispered. "We don't want to draw attention to ourselves. I'm going to get out the little shovel. Evie, you casually start digging with it on the X. Dad and I will run cover."

"Run what?" Evie asked as she snuck the shovel from her mother.

"Cover." Elle giggled. "It means we'll distract anyone who might be looking."

Evie began humming while she dug a small hole. She was making very little progress in removing any of the grass. Joe finally took over. "Give me the shovel," he murmured with a huge smile. Joe began moving large quantities of grass and dirt. The girls were cheering him on, and they were no longer in "stealth mode." Anyone nearby would know what they were doing.

"Keep digging, Daddy."

After digging an eight-inch hole, Joe looked at Elle. "Are we going nuts like I warn my students not to?"

"Yes," Elle snickered. "But keep digging."

On the next dig, Joe hit something hard. The three became quiet and looked at each other. No one said a word as Joe continued to dig. The sound of the tiny shovel hitting wood became louder and louder. Joe leaned over the growing hole and grinned. "Eureka! We've struck gold!"

"Are you serious?" Elle asked. "Don't joke right now."

"Very serious, Mrs. Waller. Our daughter is a treasure-hunting genius." Evie began jumping up and down. As Joe worked to get the wooden box out of the hole, Elle messaged Jonah, asking him to come to the island if he could. It was urgent. She then began snapping pictures of the find.

As soon as Joe lifted the treasure chest out of the ground, a loud boom sounded. Red and black confetti began falling from the sky. Two cameramen and a female crew member walked out from behind a group of palm trees. "Congratulations!!" the woman shouted. "You have found the treasure." Joe and Elle stood amazed as Evie continued to jump.

"Open it, Daddy!"

"I'm not sure that is a good idea."

"It's fine," one of the cameramen said. "That gold isn't real. You will receive a $50,000 check at a press conference when you leave the ship on Sunday. Congratulations again." The two men continued filming as bystanders began gathering on the soccer field. They were hoping to catch a glimpse of the elusive treasure chest. Flying Fred stopped and was frantically taking a camera out of his bag. A few more crew members approached and took pictures. One asked for the names and cabin numbers of the winning family.

"You must be with the captain's church group?" a woman with a nametag that read Charity asked.

"We are," Joe replied. "I'm the pastor leading the group."

"How wonderful!" Charity said. "We would like to take a few more pictures and ask a few more questions. Then we will escort you back to your cabins. You may leave the chest there until the press conference on Sunday. And you may return to the island today to enjoy our facilities."

Joe nodded and stood beside Elle for the photos. She had tears streaming down her face.

"Are you okay?" Joe asked his wife.

"I'm very okay," Elle answered. "How does He do it all?"

Jenny stared at the screen while she waited for management to join the virtual meeting. She sat at her desk quietly. In a matter of minutes, she would know her fate. She could be fired and asked to clear out of her cabin immediately. Or she would be reprimanded with unpaid leave. Any type of scandal would remain with her professionally for life.

Zach had not come back to the cabin again last night. And he hadn't returned any of her messages. She had lost control of the two most important aspects of her life. She was floating in rushing water without a rudder.

But somehow she felt at peace. Jenny had slept well and enjoyed a healthy room service breakfast. She was making a sincere effort to be still. To let go of the helm. The entire concept was new to her. Jenny's fast-paced career led to a fast-paced lifestyle. She planned every aspect of her life, and she felt guilty for not worrying and strategizing over every detail. But God told her personally to be still, so she would make the effort to obey.

While Jenny was staring at the choppy sea through the porthole window in her cabin, three windows popped opened on her screen. She recognized Gayle Parker, the chief operating officer for Jewel Cruise Line, and Leanne Lockhart, the chief human resources officer. The person in the third window must be from the legal department.

"Good morning, Jenny," Gayle piped.

"Good morning." Jenny had expected her voice to quiver, but it hadn't. She wasn't as nervous as she had expected to be.

"You remember Leanne. With us is Jeremy Stewart from Legal. He joined the line in January."

Jenny inhaled and smiled. "Good morning, everyone. I look forward to answering your questions."

Gayle paused. "Questions? We have no questions for you? We are happy to answer *your* questions?"

"I don't understand," Jenny said as she leaned forward and increased the volume of her computer.

Leanne smiled. "Jenny, we are calling to commend you for your actions. We believe that you saved two lives by thinking quickly and using the resources available to you."

"I'm afraid that I still don't understand."

"Have you received the briefing?" Gayle asked.

"No, I haven't."

"Then let me start from the beginning." Gayle shuffled some papers and began recapping. "We have reviewed the actions regarding the kidnapping of two of our passengers. You and your team followed all policies and handled the situation appropriately. Moreover, you went above and beyond by authorizing the civilians to assist in the rescue." Jenny could not believe what she was hearing. "You will find more details in the report. Jeremy, would you resend the report to Jenny? I'm not sure she received it. Jenny, we discovered that Todd at headquarters sent the incorrect paperwork to the Coast Guard, causing their delay. The line is immensely grateful for your quick thinking and creative approach. It is likely that you saved lives with your action."

Jenny was floored. "Thank you."

"You seem surprised by our report," Leanne noted. "Is there something that we are missing?"

"No, I don't believe so. I'm just surprised. I thought I might be censured for including the civilians."

"Well," Gayle began, "including passengers in a rescue mission is unconventional. But the entire situation was unconventional. The alternative would have been to wait and do nothing. We commend you on behalf of the line for taking quick action."

"Thank you," Jenny said again. She was too surprised to say anything else.

"PR has alerted the media, so we expect you to answer a few questions about the rescue at the treasure hunt press conference."

"Of course. No problem."

Jeremy interrupted. "Have you heard that someone from your church found the treasure this morning?"

Jenny's eyes widened. "No. I hadn't heard that the treasure had been found. How wonderful."

"The purser submitted the names. Let's see . . . Joe and Elle Waller and family."

A shiver ran up Jenny's spine. Pastor Joe's family had found the treasure! Another miracle from God.

"He's the youth pastor at my church. Will that cause any problem?"

Jeremy shook his head. "As long as you didn't know where the treasure was hidden, the hunt is legitimate."

"Jenny, we would like to meet with you and the security team immediately after the press conference," Gayle said. "I know that you have a quick turn-around before the next sailing, but we have questions regarding the stowaways. They have pled guilty, by the way."

Once again, Jenny was amazed at God's provision. "Of course. I am eager to hear more about their situation. Tyler thinks . . ." As she was speaking, her cabin door opened. Zach marched in and slammed the door.

"Momma mia," Zach said with slurred speech. "Whatcha doing?" Jenny tried to mute her computer's microphone but hit the wrong button and increased the volume. Meanwhile, Josh leaned into the camera's viewing area. "Hey, Auntie Gayle. Hey, other people."

Gayle answered awkwardly. "Hi, Zach. I'm happy to hear that you are doing well."

"I'm fine. But you owe me a pair of flip-flops." Zach giggled, then burped loudly.

"Zach!" Jenny screeched. "That was rude. Gayle, I apologize for Zach's behavior."

"No worries, Jenny. We will let you go. I will be at the press conference. See you then."

"Thank you, everyone." Jenny exited the meeting quickly and turned toward her son. "What is wrong with you?"

Zach plopped onto his bed. "Don't get heavy on me, Captain Lu. I've had a long night." He kicked off his tennis shoes and moved closer to the head of the bed. Jenny watched in amazement as Zach fell asleep without another word.

What do I do, Lord? You righted every ship. I see Your hand in everything. But Zach is still out of control. Please help. Jenny waited to hear the "Be still" message again but heard nothing. Does that mean she should take action? Or should she walk away and leave Zach for God to handle?

The choice was made for her because Jenny was needed at the bridge. And Zach was sound asleep. She made the decision to leave him to sleep. Hopefully, he would still be in the cabin at her lunch break. But what would she say to him if he were? He was clearly disobeying her conditions. But he was eighteen years old. He was an adult. She knew that her control was over, leaving only her influence. Mothering a teenager was not for the weary.

Jenny freshened up and rushed to the door. Before she left, she looked at her son. He was sleeping soundly. But he was wearing the same clothes as he wore yesterday. And his sling was tied around his waist.

Be still, Zach. I will be back soon.

Marissa was on the balcony of her cabin reading a book. She hoped to finish a few chapters before she took a nap. The morning had been a little "peopley," so she was treating herself to a little alone time while the other women baked in the sun on Treasure Island. Just as the book's heroine was about to discover the identity of her mystery admirer and the person leaving her homemade chocolate clues, Bettina rushed into their room.

"Marissa! Marissa! Are you in here?"

Marissa walked into the room from the balcony. "I'm here. Are you okay?"

"No . . . yes. Confetti! Gold! Reporters!" Bettina was breathing rapidly. "I lost a sandal. Where's my other shoe?"

"Sit down." Marissa patted Bettina's bed. "What happened?"

"Can't talk. Gabby game." Bettina was pacing from her bed to the door and back.

"What?"

"Gabby game. Like, Love, Leave.

"Just calm down. You are safe. Please sit."

Bettina sat on her bed. "Croissants. French toast. Cinnamon rolls."

"What in the world are you talking about?"

"Like, Love, Leave. Pick one you like, one you love, and one you would leave."

"Good grief, Bettina!" But her friend was staring back with pleading eyes. "Okay." Marissa sat in the chair by the desk. "I like cinnamon rolls. I love French toast. And I could leave croissants. Is that enough?"

Bettina tilted her head. "Really? That's strange. Leave croissants. Your turn."

Marissa was amazed to see the woman calm down so quickly. She was intently focused on the game. "Mmm . . . How about earrings, bracelets, and necklaces?"

"Talk about *good grief*. You had to start with a hard one." Bettina crossed her legs and began to giggle. "I like earrings. Love necklaces. And can leave bracelets. Don't think I'm weird."

Marissa internally rolled her eyes. "Are you okay now?"

"One more. Snails. Cats. Fireflies."

"I like cats. Love fireflies. And can leave snails."

"That's what I figured. I gave you an easy one. Joe found the treasure."

"What?!"

"That's what I was trying to tell you. Joe and Elle found the fifty thousand dollars in gold on the island. I think Evie was the one to find it." She dropped her legs back over the side of the bed. "When they dug the treasure chest up, confetti went flying. I don't know how they will clean it up. A broom won't work. And I don't think they have beach vacuums—"

"Bettina! What else?" Marissa had grown to appreciate Bettina's wandering mind, but she wanted to hear the rest of the details.

"Let's see . . . I don't know anything else. There were reporters and photographers everywhere. Pam and I saw a crowd walking past the big pool, so we went to check it out. Joe, Elle, and Evie were in the middle of the group. Joe was holding the treasure chest."

"That's amazing!"

"I know." Bettina began kicking her legs slowly. "We hung around for a while and then ate lunch. Pam and Toni went back to the beach. I had to come tell you the good news. And I passed Jonah and Ryan on the pier. They were rushing to the island. I guess Josh is still on the ship."

"Thank you for coming to tell me. That was sweet."

Bettina looked toward the balcony. "No problem. What were you doing out there?"

"Oh, I was just reading. I can see part of the island from there, so I was doing a little people watching too. I was about to take a nap."

"Would you want to go to the pool with me?"

Marissa felt slightly guilty, but she had eaten breakfast and walked on the track with the women already today. She really wanted to be alone. "I'd like to take a nap, if you don't mind."

"Sure. No problem." Bettina sighed. "But you are coming to the bonfire, aren't you?"

Marissa had forgotten about the late-night beach party. She'd probably never get another chance like this. Although, she was beginning to think that Gene would love to spend a week at sea. Marissa planned to ask him about the possibility of taking the family on an adventure cruise next year. They could save a little each month and get the cheapest cabin. This week had been fun, even with Josh's incident. "Oh, all right. I'll go to the bonfire. What time should I be ready?"

"Woo-hoo!" Bettina bellowed as she pumped a fist in the air. "It starts at eight. Wanna plan to leave around seven-thirty? We can eat dinner on the beach."

"Sounds fun," Marissa said as she retrieved her book from the desk. A beach party at night did sound fun.

"Wear the beachiest thing you own. I'll fix our hair. We are gonna paint the town red. Well, uh . . . paint the beach beige." Bettina giggled at her own joke as she repacked her beach bag. "I'll be on the pool deck if you change your mind. And we saw our dinner twins at lunch. They want to join us at the bonfire."

"Okay. Have fun. And tell Josh hi if you see him."

"Will do, bestie."

CHAPTER TWENTY

Josh had a great day, even though he stayed on the ship and chose to not go to Treasure Island. Winnie's parents let her stay on the ship while they explored the island. She hung out with Josh and his friends, even eating lunch with them at the fancy dining room. Ryan and Jonah left earlier and hadn't returned. Makenzi from the first-night dinner joined them for a little while at the pool.

Before Josh returned to his room at the end of the afternoon, Winnie convinced him to go to the bonfire party on the island. "You can't miss a bonfire beach party. You just can't." They decided that they would meet at the end of the pier at eight o'clock. Josh wasn't crazy about getting off the ship but figured that he would be safe with thousands of others on the beach. And he hadn't seen Zach all day. What could go wrong?

As he was drying off in the shower, Josh heard Ryan return to the room. "You in there?"

"Yeah!" Josh yelled. "I'll be out in a sec." Josh threw on his shirt and shorts.

"You won't believe what happened."

Josh opened the bathroom door while combing his hair. "What?"

"Evie found the treasure!"

"Are you serious? She figured out the towel hut clue?"

"Yep." Ryan shared the details of Evie spotting the "hands off" sticker and immediately concluding it referred a soccer field. He described the mob of people surrounding the family when he and Jonah rushed up. They had no idea that Jonah's family would be in the center of the crowd. Jonah joined them for pictures, and Ryan watched the celebration. The rest of the day involved beach burgers and frisbee with Jandro and Hunter. "Are you going to the bonfire?"

"Yeah. Winnie talked me into it. You?"

"I am. We can all go down together. Do you think Zach will be there?"

"I don't know. And I don't care."

"Oh, everyone is wearing Hawaiian shirts to the bonfire."

Josh rushed to the closet to change out of his T-shirt. "On it."

Josh spotted Winnie at the end of the pier. She was wearing a pale-blue sundress with white flip-flops. Her parents were beside her, and her mom was holding a huge pile of towels.

"I wasn't sure if they'd be handing out towels tonight," Anna said. "So I brought a bunch from the ship. We can spread them out on the beach. I figured the chairs would be taken." The group, including Josh, Ryan, Jandro, Macy and Lena, agreed and followed the Yearlings to a small clearing near the water. The beach was already filling with excited passengers ready to enjoy an evening escape.

"Where is the bonfire?" Macy asked.

"I'm not sure," Winnie answered. "Let's go look." The teens took off while the parents spread out the towels.

"I think it will be farther down this way." Jandro pointed away from the ship. After a few minutes he and the others spotted a towering pile of wood and logs arranged in a teepee shape. Crew members were guarding the perimeter to ensure that it wasn't toppled by careless guests. Festive beach music was playing in the background, and the smell of grilled fish mixed with fresh fruit filled the humid air.

"When will they light it?" Lena asked.

Ryan looked around. "I don't know. It's a little after eight now."

As soon as Ryan finished speaking, jaunty parade music began playing over the island's sound system. The crowd quieted, and the much-anticipated announcement was made: "Ahoy, landlubbers. All hands on deck for the world's largest bonfire beach party. Kick off your shoes and dance to the sea shanties. Enjoy the pirate feast. And try your hand at Captain Hook's bag toss. Be sure to return to the ship by the middle watch or midnight. You don't want to be marooned. Har-har!"

Josh winced at the "marooned" comment. He had been marooned by this very ship only three days ago. It was still difficult to believe. And he still hadn't seen Zach today. Ms. Jenny must be keeping him very close by her side.

With a countdown from ten, three crew members lit the dry timber, and the bonfire filled the sky with an amber glow. Instantly, the mood on the beach changed to a celebration. This is how Josh envisioned summer should be. He lived near the coast but had never experienced a true beach party, complete with great friends and a roaring bonfire, until tonight. He was grateful that Winnie had talked him into coming.

"Let's go back to the towels," Winnie suggested. "I think we will be able to see the festivities from there." The group agreed and retraced their steps back to Winnie's parents.

When they spotted Anna and Jude, Josh noticed his mother. She was standing with a group of women about twenty feet away.

Some were parents from their group. But the woman she was speaking with was new and she looked like his mom's twin. In fact, each of the moms had a twin. Weird!

"I'm gonna say hi to my mom!" Josh yelled to his friends as he jogged toward the women.

"Josh!" Marissa squealed. "Give me a hug." Josh obliged and was introduced to his mother's look-alike, Marley. "I'm so happy that you came to the party."

"Same to you, Mom. I'm glad to see you are having fun."

"You know," Marissa said softly, "I think your dad would really like this. Maybe we can work out a family cruise next summer."

"That would be great! I'll try not to get pushed into a hole next time."

"Thanks." Marissa laughed. "Go have fun with your friends. Maybe we can have breakfast together tomorrow."

"Sounds good." Josh took a few steps. "I'll be right over here with Winnie's parents. Come hang out if you want." His mom smiled, and Josh jogged back to the group. Lauren and Kinsley had joined while he was gone.

The entire night was a blast. Josh and the group hung out on the towels and later ate at picnic tables near the outdoor buffet. A few of the boys tossed a football at the water's edge.

The highlight of the evening was dancing by the bonfire. Hundreds of sunburnt passengers Twisted and Cupid Shuffled and Wobbled in the sand to the piped-in music. Josh did not dance much back home, and he was self-conscious of his lack of rhythm, but hopping and turning under the stars with Winnie and his friends was one of the highlights of the summer.

At one point, Josh spotted Zach dancing with Laney near the beach. He was swinging his arms around wildly, without his sling, and bumping into nearby kids. And he never noticed his friends. Eventually, he rushed away from the festivities with Laney.

Josh also noticed his mother dancing in the sand. She was joined by Ryan's mother, her new twin, and the other women. He didn't remember his mom ever letting loose like she was tonight. She was barefooted and giggling like a teenager. Back home, his mom was a full-time positive and happy person, but she always remained reserved in her behavior. Josh felt slightly guilty for not helping her more with cooking and chores so she could have more fun like this. He made a mental note to give her some time to relax in the future.

Winnie broke Josh from his thoughts. "I'm getting sweaty. Wanna get some punch?"

"Sure." Josh made eye contact with Ryan and pointed to the food station. Ryan saluted.

"This has been so much fun," Winnie said. "I'm cracking up at my mom. She is spending more time straightening the towels on the sand than dancing."

"I saw your parents dancing for a little while."

"Yeah. They did. But it's hard for my mom to let go."

Josh raised his eyebrows. "My mom too. Did you see her dancing with her friends? I've never seen her like that."

"I did. She's having a good time. So, what do you think about Honduras next year?"

"I've been thinking about it," Josh said as he dispensed two cups of mango punch. "I think I'll be able to get time off from the store. And I can start saving money right away."

"Yay!" Winnie clapped her hands before she accepted one of the cups of punch.

"When do I have to sign up again?"

"I think the deadline is in October, but our pastor said that is flexible because people cancel all the time and open up spots."

Josh drank his entire cup of punch at once. "That works. I just need to talk with my parents and come up with a savings plan. I'm hoping to get my own apartment in a year or two. And a dog."

"And a phone. You need a phone so we can text when we get back home."

"Definitely. As soon as I get my first paycheck." The couple started back to the group now sitting on the beach. They were waiting for the fireworks display to begin. "So, when do you leave for college?"

Before Winnie could answer, Zach and Laney walked up. Both were holding their flip-flops in their hands. "Hey, Josh. Help me avoid my mom. She came down on me hard at lunch. She's threatening to not pay for my apartment in Gainesville."

"What do you want me to do?" Josh stammered.

"Tell her that the cave incident wasn't my fault. And don't tell her that you saw me with Laney. I'm supposed to stay away from her the rest of the cruise."

"Um, I can't lie to Ms. Jenny," Josh said. Zach made a soft growling sound. "But she's not out here right now. So I don't think I will have a chance to talk with her anyways."

Zach grabbed Laney's hand and began walking away. "I thought we were friends. Thanks for nothing!"

Josh didn't respond.

"Don't listen to him," Winnie said as they continued walking. "'The fear of the Lord is the key to this treasure.'"

"Thank you."

During the fireworks, Josh sat beside Winnie. Their elbows were touching. Something about her just felt right. Like she understood him. During the flashy finale, Josh took Winnie's hand and held it. She squeezed back, and his heart fluttered. He didn't even notice the colorful show—just the feel of Winnie's small hand.

The group joined the thousands of weary passengers on their way back to the ship. Talk turned to plans for the last day at sea. Josh told the others that he would be eating breakfast with his mother in the dining room but would look for them on the pool deck afterward. Winnie smiled at him. Today was a very good day.

Joe convinced Elle to wait for the crowd to thin down before they went back to the ship. "The elevators will be jam-packed." Evie agreed, because she got extra time to play with Stevie and her sisters.

"What a day!" Elle remarked. "I feel like a celebrity anywhere we go. Somehow, the entire ship knows that we found the treasure."

"It's weird, isn't it? And we get to speak at a press conference. Never in my life . . ."

"No kidding."

"Jehovah Jireh. The Lord provided."

Elle smiled. "He did indeed. I've already started praying about how God wants to use this money."

"Me too. A new truck would be nice, but we must make sure that is His will. There are so many needs in our church and our community."

"I love you so much, Pastor Joe."

"Back at ya, Ellie Bean."

Joe finally declared the evening closed, and the family began gathering their things. Evie was yawning as she put her sandals back on her feet. While they were walking along the water toward the pier, Zach and Laney ran by.

"Hey, Pastor Jojo! How are you doing?" Zach yelled.

Joe stopped. "Zach? Got a minute?"

"We'll be fine," Elle whispered as she and Evie continued to the ship. Joe nodded.

"We were about to hang out by the fire," Zach answered with a winded voice.

"This is important," Joe answered. "Can Laney go on without you?"

Zach shrugged his shoulders. "Sure." The girl continued on, shoes in hand. "Whatcha need?"

"Sit down, son. I'd like to ask you a few questions. That's all."

"Shoot." Zach and Joe sat at the ends of two beach chairs.

"First, does your mom know where you are?"

Zach sighed louder than necessary. "She's working right now. It doesn't matter."

"I don't think that's true. It does matter. Why don't you text her and let her know that you are on the island?" Zach looked up. He had no plans to text his mother. "I'll wait."

Zach took out his phone and typed "on the island." "Happy?"

"No," Joe replied. "I'm not happy right now. What's with this attitude? You are acting very rude to your mother and to me right now."

"Why is everyone so heavy on me? I'm a grown adult, and I can take care of myself."

Joe chuckled. "I'm not so sure about that after this week. Is your mom paying for that phone? Do you pay rent for your room at her house? What about your food and your clothes? And I didn't hear that you got yourself out of that hole." Zach sat speechless. "And are you paying for college next year in Florida? Besides the small scholarship you got?"

"No, but she's required by law to pay for those things?"

"Not once you turned eighteen. Everything from here on out is voluntary from your mother's love and kindness." The two sat quietly. "I'm concerned about your attitude, because a bad attitude can squelch the Holy Spirit. That can lead to sin, anxiety, and bad decisions. I don't want that for you, Zach. You know Jesus doesn't want that. He wants you to have an abundant life." Zach was listening. "You see, the Holy Spirit is a hedge of protection from Satan's attacks. You lower that protection with things like drugs, pornography, and other sins. You get into trouble when the devil breaches your hedge."

"I'm just having a little fun. When I get a job and a family, I'll do the boring thing. I promise."

"Listen," Joe said, shaking his head, "you will never regret doing the *boring* thing. Jesus called it the narrow path. And don't think of it like this small area without fun. That's not the truth. The narrow path is the smoothest and easiest way to get to your goals. To God's perfect will for your life."

"What do you mean?"

"Do you still want to be a sports lawyer?" Zach nodded. "Well, the smoothest way to get there is by following the narrow path. Obey God's laws. Love people. Respect your mother. Check your attitude.

You nearly lost your life this week by getting involved with the wrong people."

"I just got pushed into a hole," Josh snarled. "Joseph's brothers pushed him into a hole, and he became king of Egypt."

Joe chuckled. "That's not exactly true. But yes, God did turn around what Joseph's brothers meant for evil. Bad things happen in this life. To everyone. Some are caused by other people. Some are caused by Satan. But the majority are caused by us. We do it to ourselves. Don't do that to yourself. You know the lessons of the Bible. You know how God expects you to behave. Make the right choices. You will never regret it."

"That sounds like preacher talk. You don't know what it's like."

"Look. In life, you are either running away from God, to God, or with God. I promise you that the best choice is running with Him. Every day. Trust me on that."

"You don't know. You've never made a bad decision in your life."

"Let me tell you one story. Then I will let you go on your way." Zach nodded reluctantly. "There was this guy in my high school who grew up in church but avoided going whenever he could. He ignored God's teachings for a prosperous life journey. He didn't participate in the youth group. And he had a bad attitude."

"Like Ronnie?"

"Ronnie saved Josh's life. He made the right decision, and I have a feeling that God is going to reward him for his bravery." Zach rolled his eyes.

"Anyways, this guy was hanging with some punks. That's the best way to describe it. His parents warned him about getting involved with those guys, but he didn't care. One night they were hanging out in a parking lot, and one of the guys, Tony Weaver, started throwing rocks at the parked cars. He broke a dozen windows. The rest of the guys were telling him to stop, but a police car showed up in an instant. All five of the boys were arrested and taken in for criminal mischief and a weapons charge. The one guy I'm talking about had turned eighteen. He was the only one, and he was charged as an adult. It is still on his permanent record, and he didn't throw one rock." Zach dragged one of his toes through the sand. "Even worse, he lost a scholarship to play baseball at a community college."

"That stinks." Zach was now drawing circles in the sand with one of his feet.

"And he had to spend four weekends in jail during the spring of his senior year." Zach looked up. "Yep. I had a lot of time to think while I was sitting in jail. It was horrible. But God got my attention. I have made it my life's mission to take the narrow path, and I don't regret following God's plan. Never. I'm not perfect, but I'm trying to be."

"You were in jail?" Zach asked.

"Oh yeah. I was very much like you. Same attitude. So I get where you are coming from. But I also get where you are going. And skirting on the edge of sin will only lead to disaster. Trust me on that."

"I hear you. Why haven't we heard that story before?"

"I haven't had a prodigal to share it with yet."

"Ouch."

"You would do well to take captivity of your thoughts."

Zach rolled his eyes. "What?"

"Second Corinthians chapter ten verse five says that 'we demolish arguments and every pretension that sets itself up against the knowledge of God, and we take captive every thought to make it obedient to Christ.'"

"Uh, sure."

"Listen, Zach. It's simple." Joe became serious. "You should be doing three things: Put out the imaginations in your mind that the Holy Spirit shows you that do not line up with the Bible, replace them with things of God, and right any wrongs you have done toward Jesus and others."

Zach was listening.

"I'm giving you a choice," Joe said. "You can go back to the ship with me, and we'll find your mom on the bridge. You can apologize to her. Then we'll go get some late-night pizza together. Or you can go find Laney and continue on a rocky path that will derail your plans and dreams."

Zach sat in silence before he stood and turned toward the bonfire. "I'll be right back. I want to tell Laney that I'm going back with you."

Joe's heart soared, but he played it cool. "Dibs on the pepperoni!"

CHAPTER TWENTY-ONE

Sunday, June 21
Disembarkation

Marissa still did not see Gene. She was standing with the church group as they were loading the vans, which would take them back to the church. Gene had insisted on meeting her at the port. He was probably having trouble finding a parking spot.

The entire youth group and their chaperones were able to attend the press conference thirty minutes earlier. Reporters asked the Wallers about the treasure hunt, and Evie was very eloquent explaining her interpretation of the clues.

Questions were then directed at Jenny. She handled them expertly as she explained the missing passenger situation and the decisions that were made to rescue them. She praised the veterans and Ronnie for selflessly offering their expertise and strength to the crisis. She updated the media with a report that her son and his friend were in good health. And she shared that the stowaways had been charged with kidnapping and a few other charges. Before Jenny's final remarks, YouTube reporter Flying Fred asked her to marry him. She politely declined and promised to like and subscribe to his channel.

Finally, Jenny shared that she knew God had His hand in the entire week. He reminded her to take her hands off the helm and let Him steer. A few reporters chuckled at the thought of the ship sailing without Jenny's control.

"God told me to 'be still' when I wanted to react the most," Jenny shared. "Much like the hands-off clue that Evie Waller deciphered, God's plan for our lives is often hands-off. I encourage you to seek God's will before you act. Listen for His promptings before you jump. That will remove a lot of anxiety and stress."

Jenny and the Waller family posed for pictures before they left. Jenny had to get ready for the next sailing. *Buccaneer Bounty* would be leaving again in seven hours. Joe had to lead his group off the ship. Wearing his pirate's hat, he commanded the team to "Land, ho!"

"Here you go, Mrs. March." Zach rolled Marissa's suitcase beside her. He was smiling and being quite helpful in dispersing luggage to their group. Josh told her that Zach would be sailing again this week with his mother. He wanted to spend more time with her before he left for college in a few weeks.

Bettina walked up with Pam and Toni. "Bestie! We are going to meet for lunch on Saturday. Do you think you could make it?"

Marissa thought about her usual Saturday chores and her beloved Saturday nap. "I'd love to." The week had been fun, and Marissa wanted to continue with her new friendships. "Just tell me when and where."

"Great!" Bettina squawked. "I didn't want to have to bring my imaginary friend, Polly, instead." The women laughed.

"And I have something I'd like to talk about with the group," Pam said softly. Marissa imagined that Pam would share about the separation with her husband.

Godly friends were important in times of uncertainty, Marissa thought.

"Have a great week, everyone," Bettina declared. "And I will see you on Saturday. Anything but pizza." The women giggled as they left Marissa waiting in the pick-up area.

Josh was saying goodbye to Winnie. Marissa tried not to spy on him, but she couldn't help herself. He and Winnie were talking rapidly and ignoring the crowd around them.

"Maisy!" Gene came rushing to Marissa and enveloped her in a bear hug. "I've missed you."

"Oh! I've missed you too. Happy Father's Day! Has that shirt always been pink like that?"

"Ha! No, it hasn't. I had a little laundry mishap and thought you would like to see my handiwork. Where's Josh?" Marissa looked in the direction of their son. "Ahh, is that the girl?"

"Yep, that's Winnie. She's sweet. And very sharp."

"Is this serious?"

"I have no idea, but Josh looks like a puppy dog in love."

"He sure does. I remember that look." Marissa smiled as Gene put his arm around her. "Let's go interrupt their conversation."

"Sounds good."

Gene took Marissa's backpack and pulled her suitcase. "I have missed you, Maisy. And I was freaking out when Josh was missing. Really freaking out."

"Next time, try High, Low, Buffalo."

"What?"

"It's a long story. You'll get a kick out of it."

Epilogue

September 2031

La Ceiba, Honduras

"Winter Grace Yearling, will you marry me?" Josh was poised on one knee with an open ring box in his hand. The children from the younger school behind him erupted into cheers.

"What?"

"Will you marry me?"

"I'm in the middle of a lesson."

"Yes, I know that. You are at your best teaching these children. That is why I chose the classroom as the place to ask you. Your mother wasn't crazy about the classroom but accepted it."

"My mother? You talked with my parents?"

"Yes, your whole family knows. And they gave me their blessing. Now, will you marry me?"

"Of course, I will marry you, Joshua Lee March. I will marry you a million times." Josh placed the ring on Winnie's finger and scooped her up. He twirled her in the air, and the children rushed from their seats to surround the happy couple.

Josh lowered his fiancé to the ground. "My two weeks here are almost up, but you return to the States in two months for your respite. Do you think we can plan a simple wedding in that time?"

"This is all so fast," Winnie replied as she admired the diamond ring on her finger. "But I've been hoping. What did my mom say?"

"She's already reserved the church for Thanksgiving weekend and is making a slideshow of possible wedding colors to send you."

Winnie laughed. "That's my mom, all right."

"Maya and Whit can stay at your parents' house. And my parents can stay at your grandparents. They've already taken the entire week off work. Ronnie can take time off from the Coast Guard and drive up from Jacksonville. I would like to ask Ryan to be my best man. Ronnie and Jan can be groomsmen."

"So, everybody knew but me?"

"Pretty much."

"Should we ask Pastor Joe to marry us? Or your parents' new preacher? Or even Ms. Jenny?"

"I don't know. This is all happening so fast. I knew you would ask me someday. But not today."

Winnie ushered the children out to the playground for an impromptu recess break. She and Josh stood by the building, watching the young ones playing. Winnie was admiring the simple diamond ring that was absolutely perfect. "Why did you wait a week to ask me? You've been here since last Saturday."

"Well, we met on the fourteenth and will probably get married on the twenty-eighth, so I thought we could get engaged on the twenty-first. Multiples of seven."

"I love that. You never cease to amaze me, Josh."

"Don't get your hopes too high," he added with a snicker.

Winnie got quiet. "Where will we live?"

"That's my other surprise." Winnie looked confused. "I've been talking with Pastor Marco. He has a position for me at the bakery. They will need a manager soon. If you will have me, I will move to Honduras permanently with you. Married."

"Oh, Josh! I've been praying for that, but I didn't see how it would work."

"God is making it all fall into place. Zach is already working on my residency permit and sponsor application. My mom's friend Ms. Marley is putting together some honeymoon ideas. And Aunt Dinah wants to pay for the trip since I am the only child she and my mom have."

"Wow!"

"And Jan's new girlfriend. What is her name?"

"Michele with one *L*."

"She wants to make your dress. She can do it quickly if you are okay with something simple."

"You know I would only be okay with something simple."

"That's what I told her."

Winnie and Josh walked to the swings where two girls were waiting for pushes. Winnie looked up. "We are the ones who found the real treasure on that cruise. I love you!"

"I love you, too, Silly Old Bear."

"The best course to prevent falling into the pit is to keep at the greatest distance from it; he who will be so bold as to attempt to dance upon the brink of the pit, may find by woeful experience that it is a righteous thing with God that he should fall into the pit."

— **Thomas Brooks,**
Precious Remedies Against Satan's Devices

"Veteran's Voices: Tunnel Rat, a Soldier Searching for the
Viet Cong Underground," *DCNewsNow.com.*

About the Author

Christine R. Whitlock is a wife, mother, Sunday school teacher, and chemist. She and her husband, Robert, have been married for thirty-six years and have one incredible son. They have also cared for twenty-four foster children. In their spare time, they enjoy traveling, especially to the Caribbean. Christine has a bachelor's degree from Huntingdon College and a doctoral degree from The University of Alabama. Her entire professional career has been as a chemistry professor at Georgia Southern University. Outside of the lab, she enjoys jogging, pizza, and jigsaw puzzles.

Visit her online at ChristineRWhitlock.com.